SALVAGE RITES
and Other Stories

SALVAGE RITES

and Other Stories

by

IAN WATSON

LONDON
VICTOR GOLLANCZ LTD
1989

First published in Great Britain 1989
by Victor Gollancz Ltd,
14 Henrietta Street, London WC2E 8QJ

ACKNOWLEDGEMENTS

"Salvage Rites" first appeared in *The Magazine of Fantasy and Science Fiction*, 1987; "The Moon and Michelangelo" first appeared in *Isaac Asimov's Science Fiction Magazine*, 1987; "Jewels in an Angel's Wing" first appeared in *Synergy* (volume one) edited by George Zebrowski, 1987; "The Legend of the Seven Who Found the True Egg of Lightning" first appeared in *Universe 16* edited by Terry Carr, 1986; "Hyperzoo" first appeared in *Isaac Asimov's Science Fiction Magazine*, 1987; "Letters from the Monkey Alphabet" first appeared in *Last Wave*, 1984; "Day of the Wolf" first appeared in *Changes* edited by Michael Bishop and Ian Watson, 1983; "The Mole Field" first appeared in *The Magazine of Fantasy and Science Fiction*, 1988; "The Emir's Clock" first appeared in *Other Edens* edited by Christopher Evans and Robert Holdstock, 1987; "Lost Bodies" first appeared in *Interzone*, 1988; "Samathiel's Summons" first appeared in *Fantasy Book*, 1984; "Aid From a Vampire" first appeared in *Science Fiction Eye*, 1988; "When Jesus Comes Down the Chimney" first appeared in *Interzone*, 1986; "The Resurrection Man" first appeared in *Other Edens 2* edited by Christopher Evans and Robert Holdstock, 1988; "Joan's World" first appeared in *Isaac Asimov's Science Fiction Magazine*, 1988.

British Library Cataloguing in Publication Data
Watson, Ian *1943–*
  Salvage rites
  I. Title
  823'.914[F]

ISBN 0-575-04447-0

Photoset in Great Britain by
Rowland Phototypesetting Ltd, Bury St Edmunds, Suffolk
and printed by St Edmundsbury Press Ltd,
Bury St Edmunds, Suffolk

CONTENTS

	page
Salvage Rites	7
The Moon and Michelangelo	21
Jewels in an Angel's Wing	52
The Legend of the Seven Who Found the True Egg of Lightning	69
Hyperzoo	79
Letters from the Monkey Alphabet	91
Day of the Wolf	102
The Mole Field	113
The Emir's Clock	125
Lost Bodies	144
Samathiel's Summons	158
Aid From a Vampire	170
When Jesus Comes Down the Chimney	184
The Resurrection Man	189
Joan's World	205

SALVAGE RITES

Tim and Rosy had cleared out their spare room ruthlessly. They had almost emptied it of the various categories of things that haunt spare rooms: surplus things, fatigued things, souvenir things, exiled things, scraps of things, things that might conceivably be repaired or cannibalized, things that might one day come in handy – all the time vault of twenty years.

"Trouble with being poor," Rosy said while they were loading the car, "is the way you store rubbish like treasure." As if she blamed him for the accumulation.

"We aren't exactly poor," Tim said awkwardly. "Compared with, say, someone in Africa, we're well-off. We get by."

Yes, they got by, on the income from the grocery shop. They were able to pay the interest on their debts, which lodged with them like a greedy, infirm uncle; like a senile, crippled mother who stopped them from ever going on holiday. Tim's poetry earned a bit of extra money. His short, fierce lyrics could be roughed out during slack half-hours – jotted down like customers' grocery lists – then polished before bed. Two small collections had been published and well-received. And of course he was working on his sustained mock-epic set in an imaginary Central European country, forever adding ten lines, crossing out five. The country in question needed to be imaginary since he and Rosy couldn't afford to travel abroad.

"Modern life is rubbish," said Rosy. "I saw that sprayed on the front of the cinema. It's perfectly true."

"It's the fault of the recession," he replied.

7

"It always costs more to be poor, doesn't it? We buy the cheapest, so it's trash. We wear clothes from charity shops, so we look like paupers and people try to swindle us. The poor always rob the poor. This car's a heap of junk; it costs more to keep on the road than a Rolls."

Their car was over ten years old, and rust was eating the bottoms of the doors. The hydraulics of the hatchback had failed; thus the hatch had to be propped up with a broom handle when open. The erratic engine guzzled oil.

When the car, with its rear seats lowered, had been crammed with off-cuts of carpet, underfelt, old curtains and coats, bags of lank sweaters and sad shoes, tatty toys, a sick television set, and such, Tim felt oddly refreshed and clean. Whenever he scraped out the last smears of marmalade or pickle from a jar, whenever he emptied out a cereal box, he would feel a similar minor surge of satisfaction, as though now something new and different might happen. Freud might explain this as a babyish pleasure in the expulsion of faeces. True, Freud also spoke about anal retention. Next to nothing had been retained in the spare room.

The clear-out coincided with daughter Emma's departure to college. Her choice of Geography to study wasn't so much a poignant comment on her parents' immobility as due to geography being regarded academically as an easy option. Emma would probably become an underpaid teacher in a mediocre school; she might marry another teacher. Emma didn't know this yet. Kids were as bouncy as bunnies, before the fox ate them or the winter froze them. Nature pumped the hormone of optimism into each generation. In recent years, Tim had reconciled himself at last to dwelling in the geography of the imagination.

So the house above the shop was doubly empty. It was empty of accumulated clutter; and empty of Emma. Sadly, yet somehow refreshingly empty, like the late-autumn Sunday itself. The sun shone brightly on the empty street. People were still in bed, sleeping in. But the public dump five miles away would be open. Dawn till dusk.

"Junk," repeated Rosy. Tim hoped she wasn't going to turn bitter when it came time to throw their past away.

He removed the broom handle, let the hatchback slam itself, and patted it reassuringly. "Don't discourage the old thing."

Rosy plucked at a loop in her saggy sweater and eyed a box of Emma's childhood toys inside.

"Well, we've got rid of her at last," she said, apparently changing the subject. "Now we can start living, I suppose. If we still know how. Before we're too old."

Automatically, Tim smoothed his hair around the tonsure of his bald patch. They climbed into the car, which started without too much fuss.

As they drove off, Rosy said, "If we won a fortune, I shouldn't be able to spend it, you know. I could never bring myself to buy a coat at *new* prices. Or a meal in a restaurant. Or a proper hairdo. It would seem obscene. I've been trained."

"Me too. I wonder how we'd win a fortune." He spoke flatly, not asking. Most houses and gardens they passed were blank and lifeless, but one man was out washing a car with last year's registration. Tim hardly knew what model it was. He failed to imagine himself driving it. He and Rosy had originally started the shop with help from parents, back in the days when he had dreamed of becoming an internationally regarded poet who travelled places. Parents were now all dead. Legacies had gone to assuage the upward-creeping debts.

"Beautiful day."

Rosy said nothing in reply. She pulled down the sun visor briefly and sought wrinkles in the mirror on the back.

"My hair needs cutting," she said presently.

"*Go* to a hairdresser's," he murmured.

"I'll do it myself. As usual."

Tim thought he needed a haircut, too. When you wore cheap old clothes, short hair was best.

"The roots are showing," she said.

"That's fashionable nowadays. Look, you said we ought to start living. If you couldn't ever splash out in a restaurant, how can we start living? A bit of a contradiction, isn't it?"

"An economic contradiction. Why should we have to own a shop? The state should own everything. There shouldn't be private cars, either. There should be enough good buses and railways."

"True. But there aren't. The services have been castrated."

A poem occurred to him: about eunuchs in Arabian robes driving harems of passengers who peered not through windows but through intricate lattices.

The dump would be open today because the dump was a market, too. A bazaar, of sorts. Just as charity shops sprouted like fungi in any temporarily empty commercial premises in town, selling the rags of richer people to poorer people to send aid to the totally poor in the Third World, so, with the deliberate decline of the economy, rubbish dumps had changed their nature. Concessionnaires bid for the salvage rights. Anything reusable was sold back to the public. Ecological recycling? Logic of poverty? One or the other.

Tim and Rosy had visited the dump outside town a year before and bought a washing machine for a song. The machine worked for three months before breaking down. Cheaper than renting with an option to buy. Now the carcass, with holes cut in, acted as a compost bin in their patch of back garden. According to gossips visiting the shop, the dump had since undergone a further metamorphosis. A hot-drink vending machine had been installed so that browsers could refresh themselves with a plastic cup of coffee. That summer an ice-cream van had visited the dump most weekends.

"Next thing," he said, "people will be having picnics at the dump. There'll be a play area for kids. Tours of the infill. Bulldozer rides. *Déjeuner sur le dump.*"

"What?"

"The Manet painting. Imagine that fellow and his naked

10

mistress sitting on the dump drinking champagne. I presume she'd have to wear a bikini."

A poem? "Manet at the Dump." Maybe. What word rhymed with "rubbish"?

Driving along the two-lane road between the first ploughed empty fields of the countryside, Tim spotted a cloud of gulls milling in the sky over the sprawling infill acres of the dump, like so many scraps of white paper. Rusty corrugated-iron sheets walled off the visitors' zone.

Which they entered, in low gear, the suspension creaking ominously as the car humped itself over the sleeping-policeman ramp.

A large concrete yard was lined with bulky rubbish bins into which their car could probably have fitted. Down one side the high bins were already loaded with rubble. Those along the opposite side were empty; however, most were roped off with a notice prohibiting use. An arrow pointed to the far end, where several bins stood behind notice-boards indicating "glass", "garden refuse", "metal". Those bins were already full; sunlight glared from a pile of windows.

A battered bulk-shipping container the size of a railway carriage blocked the view beyond, though another mounted wooden arrow pointed behind it.

Nearer to hand stood a black oil sump, and a bottle-bank painted camouflage green that resembled an armoured car, with slots for clear and coloured bottles reminiscent of muzzles from which howitzer shells could be fired. A score of ripped-off doors were stacked against one end.

Tim stopped the car by a truck trailer that was packed with a mound of old clothes and rags. Shirt sleeves hung down as if they had tried to climb out and failed, all the breath crushed out of them.

Beside this trailer, another huge shipping container, open at one end, was labelled "shop." Within, Tim saw clothes on racks,

11

shelves of paperback books, electrical goods. A fat, vacant-faced woman of indeterminate middle age, wearing a pink parka, occupied a deckchair outside. The shop forecourt displayed collections of tools, lamp bases and shades, mirrors, ambiguous metal paraphernalia, a cocktail cabinet with the veneer peeling.

Inside a makeshift pen, cobbled together from car roof-racks, an Alsatian guard bitch woke to life when Tim opened his door. The powerful animal reared, barking, raving.

"Jilly!" screamed the fat woman. She ignored Tim. The Alsatian slumped, and whined.

Apart from their own car, the yard was deserted. Too early in the day, perhaps. By this afternoon the bazaar of rubbish might be buzzing; then the beast wouldn't be on edge. Tim stepped nervously round to the hatchback, raised it, and inserted the broom handle. He carried the first plastic bag of clothes to the open trailer, and swung. The bag landed high up the hill of garments, jamming against the roof. He noticed a movement in the inner gloom. Some rags shifting, knocked off balance?

Rosy wound her window down. "Why can't you save the bags?"

"Oh," he said stupidly, measuring the height of the trailer floor, the incline of the clothes hill. Should he climb up and empty the bag? "There's no space left at the front. Our stuff would fall out."

Supposing you tried to repossess a coat you'd thrown away – having changed your mind about discarding it – would the Alsatian be within its rights to rip your throat out? Because you no longer owned that coat? A sign fixed to the dog-pen forbade visitors from taking anything, except by way of the shop. Salvage rights had been granted. To a firm called Griffiths Scavenging. Associates of the fat woman in the deckchair.

"Tim, come back here!"

He hurried to the car window.

"Someone inside there," Rosy whispered.

In the dim interior of the trailer, almost hidden by the summit of fabrics, Tim spotted a skinny girl with ratty hair. As he watched, she ripped open the bag he had thrown, and tossed the contents this way and that, examining, sorting.

"It's obscene," said Rosy, "having your socks and knickers picked over before your very eyes."

"Maybe we should have washed all our old clothes before we threw them away?"

"That isn't funny. Find somewhere else, will you? Down there by those signs."

Leaving the hatchback propped, Tim got in and started the engine. He drove down toward the other freight container and followed the arrow round behind it.

Another arrow pointed the way down a long lane lined by bins. As Tim and Rosy entered the lane, shadow fell upon them from the high metal sides and suddenly the day was cold. The occasional freestanding notice announced "plastic," "rubber & tyres." As well as being inconveniently tall, the bins were mostly full.

Heeding a further arrow, he turned the car along a side-lane similarly walled with bins and intermittent notices.

"Carpeting," he read. "Here we are. Get rid of *that*, at any rate."

On his second attempt, he managed to raise their rolled threadbare carpet to head-height and tumble it over the metal lip. It fell dully within. From the car, he hauled the first bundle of heavy underfelt, which they had stored for years on the off-chance.

"That isn't exactly *carpet*," called Rosy.

"Undercarpet. Same thing. What do they expect? We should sort out everything for them? Bother that. I'll toss the lot in here, clothes and all. Who cares?"

Another plump, empty-faced woman, in raggy woollens and baggy trousers – an obvious sister of the deckchair occupant – squeezed her way from between two bins and stood watching. A boy of five or six in shorts and black zipper jacket followed her, clutching a torn picture book.

Tim walked over to the woman. "Is it all right if I throw underfelt in that one?" Her skin oozed grease.

"Wha'?" she said after a while.

He repeated himself.

"Uh," she said, which might have meant anything. He realized that the woman was stupid, moronic. Maybe she had no connection with Griffiths Scavenging, after all. She might just be wandering around.

"Well, I will, then." So Tim disposed of all the underfelt, awkwardly heaving and hurling aloft while the woman stared silently at him.

He got back into the car. "There'll be bins for clothes and stuff further on."

True enough. The next arrow directed them into another long, narrow roadway of bins, all brimful of different categories of clothing. Signs were hardly necessary. Suits. Shirts. Skirts. Underwear. Boots and shoes. Buttons; there was even a bin full of buttons, a mountain height of multi-coloured shingle.

He cruised at walking pace. "Must be their storeroom, hmm? Maybe they export to poor countries. Or places hit by disaster. Cyclones, earthquakes. We oughtn't to have come so far. We should have dumped the lot back in the yard."

A pair of acne-scarred youths in jeans, heavy steel-tipped boots, and bomber jackets emerged. One slapped a hand on the front of the car, forcing Tim to brake. The other strolled grinning round to the open boot.

"Help yer, mate?" The youth tore a bag open and pulled out an old skirt of Rosy's. He ran and tossed this up into a bin of skirts, returned and burrowed, while his companion joined him.

"Hey," objected Tim. "Get out of our car. Now."

As though instinctively alert to the contents, the youths grabbed the other clothes bags out of the back and ripped them open to sort on the ground. Tim immediately drove on and soon

14

rounded another corner. Yet another lane of bins – all apparently empty – stretched ahead, with an arrow indicating a turning halfway along.

"Stop and reverse," said Rosy. "Go back the way we came."

"We still have the TV to dump, and the –"

"Stop! Back up and turn. Unload the rest in the yard. Anywhere! Drive away. Home."

Home. That house above a shop that fed them and imprisoned them. The house with an empty daughter's room. And now with an empty spare room. Tim experienced an odd feeling of certainty that before leaving that morning they had emptied the entire house – of furniture, stove, refrigerator, everything – and that there was nothing left any longer to connect them to the place. As if they had cleared all the shelves in the shop, too, leaving bare boards. They were free; they had escaped – hadn't they? Something new could begin.

Vacant shop, vacant house, vacant debts. As vacant as this street of empty bins; as vacant as the rear of the car was fast becoming. He wished he had closed the hatchback down. Otherwise something more precious than junk might escape, might be snatched or simply drift away into the chilly air here between these looming steel boxes that mockingly imitated a decrepit city street – from the future, perhaps, after a war.

He halted the car and shook his head to clear a cold fog of apprehension from his brains. Before he could engage reverse gear, he saw in the driving-mirror the high front of a truck loom around the corner behind. Piston arms, at attention, dangled chains embracing the steel bin on its flatbed back. Somehow the bin-truck negotiated the turn. He wondered how it could ever manoeuvre to pick up or deposit any of the bins ranged on either side. Maybe there was a turntable built into the chassis. Standing in the bin as though navigating the vehicle was the moronic woman. Suddenly the sight of her terrified him. The truck slowly approached, and honked.

"It must be one-way-only, Rosy." Tim drove forward to the

15

next intersection and swung down a lane of close-packed bins containing scrap metal. By the time they reached another arrow, and another turn, the bin-truck had already entered the scrap metal street.

Tim took another turn, then another, losing the truck way behind. *If* it had been deliberately following, to begin with.

Arrow followed arrow. Turn followed turn. Lane of bins succeeded lane of bins. Once they turned into the street of clothing bins, yet this led to a street of scrap metal bins, not a street where the bins were empty. Unless his memory was deceiving him. No, it wasn't. The clothes bins must have been different ones. They were lost in a maze.

"This is ridiculous," he told Rosy. "There isn't space for all these lanes."

"We've entered the world of rubbish," Rosy whispered back. "Where we've been heading for the past twenty years."

The engine coughed and missed a couple of times. Tim pulled the choke half out, racing the engine, though of necessity still driving slowly.

"It's all this damn crawling in first gear. The plugs soot up."

The very next lane opened into a long concrete yard walled in by bins. It wasn't the yard that housed the shop. Slamming the choke back in, Tim gunned the car toward the arrow marking the exit at the far end, hoping to burn the plugs clean. He braked violently in time to enter the next narrow alley.

Six lanes later the engine quit. Tim couldn't restart the car.

"What do we do now?" asked Rosy.

"Walk. I'll leave the keys in the ignition."

The bins on either side stood shoulder to shoulder. They seemed twice as large as previously. You couldn't even squeeze sideways between bins, though you might just manage to crawl on your belly. The only route was the concrete road.

"I wonder if this was once an old airfield?"

Then Tim remembered the gulls flocking about the infill. But no gulls flapped in the sky now.

"What's in the bins, Tim?"

Not since that second yard had they passed a single sign announcing the contents. He peered up. Suddenly he understood the assorted shapes peering over the lips of the containers.

Car doors.

Further along . . . a forest of exhaust pipes like several church organs jumbled by a bomb blast.

"Bits of cars," he said, opening his door.

Two lanes later they heard from somewhere behind them the whine of a power tool, then the clanging of metal. He felt sure that their stalled car was being broken up into parts. Taking Rosy's hand, he hurried her onward and along another lane. Faintly, he heard a thump of boots and a silly, idiotic giggling.

Clothes bins again! Jackets, shirts, sandals, nightdresses looked over bin tops. Before they could reach the next corner, the moronic woman waddled out from it ahead of them. She was accompanied by a big, bony, overall-clad man in his mid-forties, his thick black hair slicked back in waves, his nose an absurdly small squashed blob in a large, battered face.

"Yer need a hand, squire?"

Tim jerked around. One of the youths sat perched on the edge of a shirt bin behind them. The youth dropped to the ground just as his partner came wading over the bin of summer dresses opposite. He leapt down, too.

"Show us the way out of here!" cried Rosy. "No, go away! Leave us alone!"

The two youths rushed and clamped Rosy by the arms. At the same moment the man seized Tim, who struggled uselessly; the grip was like granite.

"Yer need a hand," the youth repeated.

The plump woman ambled forward. While the man manipulated Tim like a toy or a life-size doll, the woman undressed him, taking her time about it, tossing his clothes up into various bins. Soon Tim shivered nakedly, still held tight.

17

Then it was Rosy's turn.

Their captors led Tim and Rosy, both stripped naked, to the turn and released them, thrusting them into the next steel and concrete lane.

"Ge' on, now, squire!"

The woman and her three companions remained at the intersection, blocking any return to the bins where Tim's and Rosy's clothes and shoes had been discarded. Shaking with cold and shock, Tim and Rosy ran along numbly to the next turn, as much to hide their nakedness from the blankly watchful eyes and chilly breeze as to escape.

Tim's teeth chattered. "We'll f-find something to wear. F-further on. Any old rags. Or c-curtains."

The bins in this new lane were loaded with sheets of cardboard, rolls of wallpaper, bundles of old magazines. Tim wondered whether he could scale the side of a bin with bare feet. He would have to!

Rosy wailed, "I thought they were going to rape –!" Her breasts bounced. "They did! They did. It was the same."

"Listen, this is all a vicious joke. Next we'll come across some rags to put on. Then we'll reach the yard where the shop is, looking like scarecrows. And we'll find our car waiting for us – with our clothes folded on the seats. Nobody will believe us, but. . . ." He had to believe it. "They could have hurt us. They didn't."

"You think they didn't hurt us? I'm hurt forever."

The bins in the next lane all looked empty; nothing peeped over the tops. Tim rapped his knuckles against several; all rang hollowly. He didn't feel inclined to try to climb, to check.

They walked in cold shade. Whichever direction a lane led, sunlight seemed excluded. At last an arrow pointed the way down between rows of bins full of broken furniture, to a concrete-surfaced yard.

"It's the way out," he said. "We've arrived."

However, the yard, lined with more giant bins, was only as

large as a tennis court, and no arrow pointed to an exit. There was only an entrance. Half of the yard was bathed in sunshine, where Rosy ran to warm herself. Her bare flesh quivering, the breeze still nipped her. Whatever these bins contained couldn't be seen from ground level. A car roof-rack rested against one. Side-on, its metal bars were steps.

"I'll see the way out!" Wincing, then planting her feet sideways so as to spread her weight along the thin steel bars, Rosy ascended.

Shading her eyes, she stared around helplessly.

She looked down inside the bin itself. And screamed. And screamed.

Tim scaled the bars; there was room alongside. Clutching her cold shoulders with a chilly arm, he, too, gazed down.

For a few seconds he hardly understood what he saw. A layer of slime-coated ping-pong balls? Hundreds of hard-boiled eggs?

No. Eyes. The optic cords sprouted like tiny lengths of electric cord torn out of plugs.

Sheep's eyes? No, he didn't think so. Not the eyes of sheep, or any other animal. Rosy had stopped screaming, out of breath. She shook convulsively, clutching the top of the bin, screwing her own eyes tight shut as if to hide them.

He could see into the neighbouring bin as well. A heap of french fries? Baby parsnips? No.

Fingers. Chopped-off human fingers.

He stared wildly around the yard. What did all the other bins hide in their depths? Toes, tongues, lungs? Arms and loins and brains? The parts of the body, sorted out. . . . Yes! He knew this was so, even before the grind of an engine dragged his gaze to the entrance of the little yard.

The bin-truck heaved into view and halted in the entrance, completing the circuit of metal walls. The front jutted sufficiently into the yard that the truck doors would be free to open. Crowded side by side in the cab were the man, at the wheel; the two youths; the moronic woman with her boy on her knee; the

19

blank-faced fat woman in the pink parka; and the skinny, ratty girl. All of the passengers, even the little boy, were clutching assorted tools. Saw. Pincers. A gouge. A small axe.

The truck engine died.

"For God's sake, climb on top, Rosy! Walk along the side to the bin beyond. We must get out of here."

Beyond the yard for as far as he could see in all directions were endless rows of bins.

Desperately, bruising his naked body, almost crippling a toe, Tim scrambled on top, struggling to balance, half-helping, half-dragging Rosy with him. The top edge was far too narrow ever to walk along with bare feet, tightrope-style. Nude, he knew they couldn't even slide along, astride. That would be like riding a blunt steel blade. After a while it would cut up through them, between their legs. Instead he slid down inside, pulling Rosy howling with him.

"We'll climb out the back way into the next one! And the next!"

Jelly lumps squelched underfoot. He skidded in the six-inch-deep pool of eyes and fell, nauseated. Scrambling up, he waded, then leapt at the high rear edge of the bin. He did catch hold, with outstretched fingers, his front smashing against the metal, but he couldn't pull himself up. He hadn't enough of a grip. There was no purchase. His feet were slipping on soft marbles.

"Yer need a hand?"

A crowd of heads popped up behind. Vacant faces smiled vaguely. The man, the women, the youths, the ratty girl, even the little boy.

Hands rose into view, displaying a gouge, an axe, pincers, saws.

THE MOON AND MICHELANGELO

Peter Catlow woke from a dream of a wide straight road stretching invitingly through cow pastures and willow trees upon a sunset evening towards, yes, some village with a pub where the real ale would be strong and malty just the way he liked it.

He lay trying to keep hold of the dream, since it was years since such rural scenes had existed in such an unprotected form. As an earlier image clarified he realized that the dream had only been a half-happy one, for the road of his dream had set out from one of the gateways of the alien city. His right arm had been trapped in the mouth of one of the stone Herms; he'd been struggling to pull free.

Pins and needles stung Peter's hand as paralysed flesh thawed. He'd been sleeping on his arm, squeezing the blood-flow.

Though he was sure that it must still be the middle of the alien night, as soon as he turned over to catch more shut-eye his alarm began to bleep. Disbelievingly he slapped the alarm off, slapped on the light (and his wake-up tape of Vaughan Williams' *Variations on a Theme of Thomas Tallis*), and swung out of bed before he could relapse. A button unshuttered the window upon another streaky-bacon dawn on Rock.

Not that the landscape was barren; the brightening light of swiftly-rising Tau Ceti was disclosing lush herbage, the vegetable fields checkered purple and emerald, a sinuous fish-rich river, and a forest of giant ferns and bottle-trees. But whereas Earth people had named their world after the flesh of the planet, the soft fruitful soil, the lemur-like natives of Tau Ceti II apparently

21

preferred to call theirs after the bones of the planet, the hard skeleton. Apparently.

From the edge of the window of his little cubicle Peter could see a kilometre away the southeastern flank of the city writhing with its gargoyles and grotesques.

Mary Everdon had said to him: "Perhaps for the natives the hardness of rock, and the manipulation of rock into shapes dense with meaning, equates with their emergence from biology, from organic nature, into culture and permanence and history? Carved rock and sculpted stone equals thought solidified and redeemed from timelessness into the new stream of sapient time."

Each time that she voiced her embryonic theory, it seemed to put on more weight, to become ever more viable. But Peter thought of it as her intellectual phantom pregnancy – which could become ever more convincing until one embarrassing day she might need to face the fact that there was nothing in it, after all. Of course, that was Mary's merit too, in an extraterrestrial context: the ability to make speculative leaps.

Mary pointed out that this city near which the expedition had set down was only one of many such carved wonderlands (or horror-villes) scattered about the two habitable continents which shared the same side of the world, nestling together like a pair of cashew nuts. The closest distance between any two cities was a couple of hundred kilometres. Forest or swamp, desert or mountain intervened. No road network existed. So the architecture must display the psychic bedrock of the inhabitants, must be a way of perceiving and celebrating their own triumphant separation from unthinking nature.

As Peter let the pastoral swell of Vaughan Williams tone up his nervous system (while he washed quickly, while he shaved) he contemplated another day which wouldn't last long enough to tire a fellow without taking a pill, to be followed by another night not long enough to rest oneself adequately.

*

22

"This planet makes me feel prematurely old," he'd confided to Mary in the refectory the evening before, while they hastily spooned up their dinner of chili con carne before the nightly info-swap began, prelude to bedtime.

The forty-strong complement of the shuttle base munched their spiced beans and chattered science at twenty little tables. (Prevent cliques; prevent isolation. Nevertheless, there were cliques. Nevertheless there was. . . .) Cheery yellow plastic walls; several doors open to the corridor; Commander's podium; large video screen showing a Californian beach-scape that particular evening. Overhead the large bubble skylight framed one of the two bright moons chasing its partner in vain, or being chased. Periodically (not now) you saw the glint of the orbiting voidship, *Michelangelo* – named a touch arrogantly after Earth's supreme sculptor – with the non-landing crew on board. They would soon get their treat: a trip out to orbit the third, fourth, and fifth planets which were two modest airless deserts plus an awesome gas-giant with a family of moons; before returning for pick-up.

Since Mary usually generated a theory she asked, "Does your specialty make you feel you're a sort of medieval person, who's ancient compared with all this?" She smiled with sympathetic bonhomie.

He shook his head. "No, it's because when you're young the days seem to stretch out endlessly, yet they shrink as you grow older. Here, the days have all suddenly grown very short, as though I've aged twenty or thirty years."

"How old are you? I've forgotten. Is it forty-eight?"

"That's right." She hadn't forgotten.

They had all had access to each other's bios, and according to the bare bones of hers Mary Everdon was thirty-nine years old, doctorate in cultural anthropology from . . . Peter couldn't care less where. Mary was unattached, plumpish, red-haired. She reminded him of . . . (Had she taken lovers? What were her erotic preferences? If any.)

23

Peter nodded in the direction of Carl Lipmann, the scrawny blond linguist.

"It's a pity we can't ask the natives how they feel, and understand the answers." It was a pity he couldn't bring himself to ask Mary outright how she felt about him.

"Not yet. We're making progress, aren't we?"

Was *he*?

"They twitter and warble like birds."

"Ah, but in a flexibly structured way. And we have quite a few sound-groups provisionally pegged with meanings. So it's a true language." She raised her voice. "They're far from being some sort of mammalian *termite*, as Fremantle had the nerve to suggest."

Barney Fremantle, bald and natty, sat two tables away with Sandra Ramirez the ecologist (black waterfall of curls). The biologist cocked an ear and shrugged. He had a sample bag beside him, which he patted like an obedient dog. Fremantle had suggested that the building of the city and the intricate carving of the natives might simply be wired-in, instinctual behavior – akin to the artistic forecourts of bower birds – and that they weren't genuinely sapient. This, despite their wooden agricultural implements and their sledge-carts, and their cooking bowls and their use of fire; despite the presumption that they must possess *metal* tools so as to have sculpted their ornate city.

Peter wasn't here in quite the same capacity as the other experts from sciences hard and soft. After the drone-probe had hyperpulsed its highly detailed aerial pictures of the cities of Rock back to Earth, it had been decided imaginatively to include a stonemason in the exploration team. A stonemason should have practical, existential knowledge of what seemed to be the main manifestation of the native culture.

When the invitation had come – when some computer had picked up his name as a master stonemason without family ties – Peter had been in charge of renovating the abacus of ancient statues on the front of acid-eaten Lichfield Cathedral, now that the town was safely protected by a Fuller dome. Perhaps it was nostalgia, rather than the promise of interstellar adventure, which prompted his acceptance. To be able to stroll through a city of uneroded carvings under an open sky, a city neither rotted by pollution nor air-conditioned like a museum piece.

As Peter scraped up his last spoonful, Commander Ash strode to the podium, short, stocky, crew-cut, her oval face nevertheless (or perhaps on account of the crew-cut) that of a delicate china doll. She blanked the screen.

"Need for brevity," she reminded. "I'll guillotine garrulity."

Oh yes she would; and during the info-swap they would all talk in the same clipped telegraphic way. How to cram a pint into a half-pint pot. Likewise activity by day and sleep by night. Likewise the Commander's own physique: a pint of power in a half-pint frame, with irrelevant coiffure shorn off. No time to bother with your hair on Rock. Emulate the name of the world; have head like a boulder. Made of china. Peter felt his brain gearing up to match the pace of the info-swap.

Yet Mary's hair was very long, a flood of generous fire. . . . Did Mary realize that this might subtly irritate Ash, and merit an impatient hearing?

"Change to double-day cycle?" the geologist (and temporary Rockologist) Stevens requested. "Field-work one day plus whole night's data analysis; sleep through whole next day and night?"

"Waste too much time sleeping then," judged Ash. "Be soldiers of science; learn to cat-nap. Next?"

It wasn't long before Fremantle rose, darting a look of amused triumph towards Mary.

"Reporting trip into forest. Bottle-trees come in dozen main shapes; all are hollow shells supporting fronds."

"Known," said Ash.

"Shells show fracture lines, large-piece jigsaw patterns. Stone smashes shells into constituent fragments." Reaching into his bag, he exhibited one of the native wooden spades with short curved handle, the specimen wrapped in film. "This." Now he

25

placed a native wok on the table. "Or this." He flourished a film-clad wooden knife. "Plus sharp shards. All known native artifacts readily available from nature."

Mary sat wounded, momentarily confused. All data would be put on the infonet for access and review by anyone else. Meanwhile, Fremantle seemed to have scored a coup.

"Bio-technology?" asked Peter helpfully. He knew the concept. "Trees bred for tools?"

Fremantle laughed brusquely but it was agronomist Vasilki Patel who supplied the answer.

"Bio-tech requires microscopes, laser scalpels. Farm crops indicate only simple improvement over wild strains."

"Amazing," said Stevens, with a note of sarcasm, "those trees falling apart so conveniently into identifiable tools; quite naturally too." He also was trying to be helpful: Rockologist in league with stonemason.

Sandra Ramirez spoke up from beside Fremantle. "Hypothesis: wrecking a tree has connection with reproductive cycle. Lemurs wreck trees which produce useful shapes. Thus evolutionary selection favours trees which split up usefully; against those which didn't."

Stevens looked towards Peter. "Bottle-wood tools sufficient for sculpture? If tempered by fire?"

Peter thought of his own power-tools and chisels back home. Power-tools to rough out a block of stone – in the old days apprentices would rough out a block more laboriously by hand – and chisels, strong sharp chisels. Their abrasive action, the sparks that flew, produced a protective surface on a stone which would let it weather out its first few years until the regular hardening could set in. How could the natives produce such strong, such detailed surfaces by banging away with wood, however hard?

No one had seen a single identifiable mason at work. One item Peter had to correct his colleagues about on arrival was the notion that masons carved anything in position by preference.

Stone was unpredictable; even the best master mason could spoil a piece through no fault of his own. The sensible way to work was down on the ground. Each figure should jut from a supporting block which was subsequently winched into position in a pre-planned gap. So you wouldn't expect to see lemur masons clinging to walls and chipping away. But even so.

Nor had anyone seen evidence of loose, unused blocks of stone lying around or in transit.

Maybe they simply hadn't yet stumbled upon a masons' yard in the maze of the city. Maybe secret ritual surrounded the art of masonry? Maybe the lemur masons had hidden their metal tools away when the expedition arrived, just as a sensible tribe might hide its treasures from potential conquerors?

Maybe the work had all been completed ages ago? But surely it hadn't been. And surely there should be some evidence of ongoing building work?

"Comment," said Ash sharply.

Peter shook his head.

"Maybe *you* should try," suggested the Ismaili agronomist. "Carve blank jut of wall using bottle-wood?"

"Carve *Michelangelo was here*," said Fremantle. "Might activate natives. Provide cultural insights for Everdon. Valiant effort at artistic communication using native mode, eh? If no response, native behaviour is hard-wired."

"How would you like it," asked Peter, "if aliens landed in Paris and started carving graffiti over the front of Notre Dame?"

"Improve it, probably."

In fact Peter had once carved a graffito of a kind upon an Oxford college: a playful caricature of his own head gazing out from the top of a tower. Wearing a veritable dunce's or wizard's hat parodying the mason's neatly folded daily paper hat which kept the dust from one's curls. His large ears exaggerated into jug-ears, his prominent nose sticking out like Pinocchio's, jaw dimpled as if by a pickaxe, eyes wrinkled up to a vanishing point (to avoid splinters).

The nose had been a mistake. Back then, Fuller domes were new and exhibited quirks of micro-climate. Little clouds could form. Condensation drops gathered on the end of such a nose and dripped as if he had a runny cold. Maybe that feature was considered a witticism by subsequent generations of students: the wizard with the drippy nose. Since no real rain fell inside Fuller domes and genuine gargoyles were forever dry, perhaps his nose was in a very minor sense the only working gargoyle left.

"You haven't proved they use wood tools!" blustered Peter.

"Take metal chisel, hammer, demonstrate human mason's art," suggested Vasilki Patel.

"Cultural interference," objected Mary. "Analysing categories of carvings more important, this stage. Catlow's viewpoint more valuable here. Establish lexicon of stone images."

"Report when complete," said Ash. "Enough on topic. Base security?"

"Sweet and simple," reported Leo Allen. The black man co-ordinated all outside surveillance and image-gathering as well as supervising the infonet.

"Medical?"

Doctor Chang said, "Clean slate. Still no interaction our micro-orgs, Rock's micro-orgs. Probably unnecessary even wear masks. Recommend continue, though, be double safe. Besides, the odours –"

The atmosphere of Rock was an acceptable oxy-nitrogen mix. Native proteins were based on D-amino acids that were right-handed, as were the sugars in the local nucleic acids – unlike the left-handed counterparts on Earth. Chang had declared that humans could eat the local veg and fish without any effect whatever; they would excrete everything unused. Nothing gut-wrenching, nothing nutritious. Protein incompatibility. So you had to bring a packed lunch to Rock, unless, as Vasilki said, you intended to set up in competition with the local veg by planting Earth seeds and letting the rivals crowd the native veg for available minerals. Charmed against any local bugs or viruses by their left-handedness, Earth crops ought to win hands down.

Ash said, "Am authorizing *Michelangelo* depart on grand tour two nights hence, sixteenth hour local. Returning after forty days, local, for flight Solward. Hope for full local info by then."

"We see *M* go?" asked a woman chemist, Liz Martel.

"Yes. Fusion fireworks overhead, fine show."

"Observe effect on natives?" asked Lipmann. "Night duty?"

"Indeed," said Ash. "That night."

Mary stood up, red hair swinging. "Depart farside world instead? Avoid cultural impact?"

Ash shook her head. "Best orbital departure."

"But *M* orbits whole world constantly! Well, depart daytime instead? Minimize shock from sudden light in sky?"

"Spoilsport!" burst from Liz Martel.

"Timing already computed."

"Change it! Cultural impact."

"May be fruitful." Ash smiled slightly towards Fremantle. "If true culture exists."

It was obvious to Peter that the matter was already fixed, in Mary's disfavour.

To protest further, or shut up? Possible black mark on bio. Insubordinate. Mary nodded and sat down.

"End of info-swap," said Ash.

Since you couldn't take your filter-mask off outside to feed, breakfast the next morning was a hefty, though hurried, affair of pawpaw, reconstituted omelet over huge slices of ham, waffles, and syrup, muffins and honey, pints of coffee. Afterwards Peter set out with Mary and Carl Lipmann for the city. Already lemur farmers were out in their veg fields, hoeing or harvesting. Fisherfolk were heading for the river. The humans joined one of the sledge paths.

"Bit swinish, that bottle-wood business," remarked Carl. Of course, reflected Peter, Fremantle's discovery was a slap in the face to the linguist too. If the natives were only highly programmed animals using tools that nature provided, their "language" might be an illusion too. A parrot could mimic speech with every appearance of beady-eyed intelligence, as well as screeching its own fixed repertoire. A chimp could chatter a sort of limited conversation, a dolphin could click and whistle. You'd still be barking up a gum tree if you hoped for full flexible communication.

"It would be enormously useful," said Mary, "to find some metal tools which had demonstrably been *made* – for sculpting, eh Peter?"

"You know how carefully I've examined their work," he said, "and I still can't swear to what tools were used. A fine bit of work isn't covered in chisel chips. Art lies in the concealment of art. Maybe . . . maybe they just rubbed away at the rock for years on end till they wore out the figures they wanted."

"Like the Skull of Doom?" she asked.

"What's that?"

"A perfect human skull in rock crystal. It's in a Mexican museum. The Mayans made it by rubbing away at a solid block of rock crystal. Must have taken years. I can't imagine the decoration of entire cities being rubbed into shape the same way!"

"Maybe," said Carl, "each figure occupies the whole of one lemur's lifetime, off and on. Maybe it's his or her ritual life-image."

"In that case you'd find half-finished work," Mary pointed out.

"Maybe they stopped making images fifty years ago, five hundred years ago? Funny self-image they must have of themselves, though!" For now they were nearing the south-east entry gate guarded by its grotesque Herms or termains, whichever term one preferred to name boundary or entrance markers. Peter had supplied both names. Herms, from the Greek god of doorways, Hermes. Termains, from the Latin word terminus. On either side of the Herms stretched the frozenly writhing, leering wall, massed gargoyles jutting as if vomiting.

"Exactly," said Mary. "These are the keys to their psyche."

And by now half a dozen lemurs were tagging alongside, wittering interestedly. None of the adults stood more than four feet high. The swirls and hues of their tight, close fur varied endlessly from individual to individual, fingerprinting each in auburn, russet, orange, brown which might be solid-hued or dappled or with hints of stripes. Lemurs wore no clothes or ornaments of any sort. Indeed, to hide the body might be to hide the self since their faces were all much the same: dun coloured, with the same large black melancholy eyes, pert twitchy noses, erect rounded ears, lugubrious mouths. The slight breasts and genital slits of the females and the retracted penises of the males were veiled by fur. Lemur arms were long and dangly; the hands had three thin fingers and a thumb.

A female plucked at Carl's tunic and warbled. Twitching his own nose behind the transparent mask with friendly humour, he adjusted the sound-bud in his left ear, fiddled with the minicomp and corder clipped to his belt, and twittered in response. Perhaps in response.

He explained: "I'm trying to say: want / see / tools / cut / rock. But maybe I just said, 'I want you to watch me dig the world'! Peter, would you please mime the mason's art? Oh yes, and rubbing too?"

Nowhere had they found any simple carved representations of lemurs. The Herms were soaring, elongated heads with eyes the size of dinner plates above gaping, sharp-toothed mouths. Stone beards burst from the sucked-in cheeks, straggling down like horsehair eviscerated from an old upholstered chair, knotting and massing to almost hide a stubby, squat, dwarf body. All in perfect stone, except that these Herms looked newly sloshed with night-soil liquified in urine.

The arch of the gate curving between the two Herms was a quartet of capering, interlacing babewyns, a popular motif. These were baboon-like beings, stretched out as though their bones had melted. Again, Peter had supplied the appropriate medieval name for such carved lusty baboon-buffoons.

31

While Carl twittered again, Peter stepped over to the nearest Herm, grateful for his mask. The lemurs collected their own night-soil assiduously, brown soup of excrement and pee. Instead of carting this out to fertilize the fields they hurled the contents of the bottle-wood buckets at their sculpted walls or poured the mixture with gay abandon over monstrosities and gargoyles

(At an earlier info-swap: "Ritual insult," Mary had theorized, "Thus to domesticate the fearful images."

Fremantle had retorted, "Maybe lemurs inherited cities from genuine intelligences that died out?"

Mary had returned to the fray: "Perhaps act of respect, reverence. Excrement not taboo – but gift of self. Stuff of one's own creation."

While Peter had said, "Maybe do that to protect, strengthen surfaces?"

That chemist woman, Martel, had hooted.

Since then, he'd also seen lemur cooks chucking over the stone art the water in which they'd boiled veg or fish.)

The lemur female watched with curiosity while Peter went through the motions of tapping away with a mallet and chisel and then – though he had to guess what these other motions might be – of patiently rubbing at stone.

True curiosity? Big glossy lemur eyes wore a perpetual expression of surprise and fascination, of alert astonishment.

However, this lemur then beckoned – surely she beckoned – and darted inside the gateway, to wait and beckon again.

"I do believe we're getting somewhere," Carl said in pleased surprise. "Well done."

As soon as they passed beneath the arching babewyns, their lemur set off along the northerly of three possible lanes; they followed.

Periodically Mary blazoned that day's personal code in invisible ultraviolet on protruding stonework. On the way out her bleeper would respond to those UV marks, and no others. Despite an annotated aerial survey map composited by computer

32

from *Michelangelo*'s high-resolution photos and their own over-flight before landing, it was no easy matter, otherwise, to trace one's progress with any confidence through the labyrinth of walls, pillars, lanes, yards, courts, archways, doorways, almost all of which were dense with statuary. Pathways branched frequently, almost arbitrarily, sometimes leading to dead ends. Lapids might block the way – figures emerging from or stepping into solid walls like spirits who could walk through stone. Gargoyles might sprout out overhead to join into ribbed vaulting so that what had been a lane became a hallway. A lane could enter a room through a narrow door, to resume as a broad lane beyond the far wall. Grotesques formed steps leading to tangled gargoyle bridges. Gaping stone mouths were entrances to what seemed to be cellars but which might open into airy corridors.

Their guide trotted ahead, warbling, glancing back, occasionally flapping an arm, though she may only have been slapping at the equivalent of a flea in her fur.

Peter noted a huge scaly devil-creature with ribbed, bar-like wings. This jutted from the top of a short free-standing wall which seemed to have no other rationale than to support that devil. The blocks of the walls, perhaps forty in number, were condensed, squashed stone bodies as though creatures had been crushed inside suitcase-sized moulds, there to harden.

"That chap's definitely new," said Peter, and took a holo.

"New?" queried Carl.

"New to me. I've never seen the like before."

"Oh."

"I've never been in this part of town."

Still wondering at the devil, Peter fell back a few paces so that now he brought up the rear. From that vantage point he could admire Mary's hips and the hang of her red hair as she bustled onward. No denying it, she did remind him of a certain buxom rural barmaid he'd known once. However, that bouncy barmaid had been keener on a recently widowed farmer who turned to her for sympathy, and more.

Peter had always been a bachelor, more by accident than design. Wedded to stone, he was. Somehow his work with stone had seemed to express – yet also to limit – the sensuality which he felt was part of him, deep down. Had he been a sculptor of marble, of smooth sensual flanks, he might have been able to express desire better in person. The rough hardness of the images he worked on, their often grim satiric comedy, and not least their moral sententiousness seemed to distance him from expressing in actual life the lusts and greeds and devilries which those carvings parodied. If he committed a . . . fault (even though the world might regard it as no fault at all, and indeed life was a jumble of desires, envy, pride, resentment, and such) then this fault might somehow solidify and *be* him for dusty ages. On the other hand those virtues which he also carved and lived by – the patience, loving kindness, charity, forbearance – somehow locked up his heart . . . from which, otherwise, a grinning demon might spring forth?

He sighed, and wished that Carl wasn't with him and Mary, although he liked the man and in this case three was company. No doubt he exaggerated the importance of lust, anger, envy, lust. Yet one did so when one perpetuated, by renovation and restoration, the medieval tradition of incarnating in stone – of lapidifying – gross emblems of vice and virtue. Thus displaying in caricature monsters of the heart, by way of mockery and warning, by way of immunization against those selfsame monsters which represented human frustrations and fears.

He caught up with Mary. "I wonder," he asked, "what fears or frustrations might have caused the lemurs to sculpt such monstrosities – not as a frieze to their city but as its central substance? They themselves seem gentle, innocent, happy, don't they?"

In the city no "houses" as such existed. Yet where bridges arched over yards or where gargoyles roofed corridors or where walls came together, definite living zones occurred. There, a twittering mass of lemur children would play, the babies scampering on all fours swifter than any human child. There cooking would be in progress tended by grizzled oldsters. One jumble of blackened pots brewing herbs and berries, connected by dripping wooden tubes, suggested a liquor still.

Two or three streets were noisy with groups of lemurs warbling at one another. In other streets numbers of the natives were simply curled up along the base of walls, twitchingly asleep, looking like examples of accidie, medieval sloth. Maybe those lemurs were ill, and this was the equivalent of hospitalization. Perhaps they favoured night-life and had hangovers.

By day, of course, the majority of lemurs were busy in the fields or in the bottle-tree forest or along the riverbank. Or else they were fetching water from one or another crude canal sump outside the city wall, or were engaged in hauling or shoving food back to town on their sledges of bottle-wood.

No visible arts or crafts; only the all-encompassing intricate chaotic stone city itself; or perhaps one should say the solid sketch of a city, where decoration wholly outweighed function.

"How can they possibly project all of these monstrous images of such simple natural lives?" repeated Peter.

"That's exactly it!" said Mary brightly. "Those are images from out of their burgeoning imagination, images which must inevitably scare as well as intrigue because they challenge, they stimulate, they tease. Those are fascinating creatures they see in dreams and which they need to cling on to as a promise, a warrant of increasing complexity of thought. First the form, later the philosophy. Perhaps their subconscious mind, by which I mean the collective unconscious, is evolving and complexifying, acting as a kind of spur to their ordinary consciousness. I'm sure there's a rich oral tradition amongst all the warbles." She glanced regretfully at Carl. "After all, they twitter enough. Yet maybe they also experince a sort of *angst* at emerging from nature – a loss of instinctual, prelapsarian animal paradise – and deflect this *angst* by embodying and even celebrating such anxieties as environment. Maybe, Peter, that's your answer."

Maybe. Her words sounded more eloquently convincing than

they ever could in the clipped speed-talk of the info-swap, where they might shrink into gibberish.

Thought Peter: if I tried to move closer to Mary emotionally and sensually, she would have a theory about this too. But then, so had he, hadn't he? He felt a sudden urge to sculpt Mary nude, lascivious, flaunting. Not as a gross exemplar of lust; as an indicator of joy instead. Joy, yes, liberating joy! An explosion of joy which might coat him with dust, however, a joy which might petrify him. No, he wanted to go beyond that, to mould an image which simply stood for itself alone and did not represent any moral catechisms or theory of behaviour.

In his mind's eyes he watched Mary fill a pewter tankard full of foaming, heady beer for him, then a second tankard for herself, thus to wash the dust from his throat, from his bloodstream, from his hairy, Pan-like, goaty loins.

But where was the spare, blank, unoccupied stone waiting to be sculpted?

Oh here and there, here and there. By no means everywhere. Still, not every niche and nook had been filled.

An unsculpted pillar rose in a yard. Visualize, chiselled from it: *Alien Woman*. Alien to the lemur inhabitants, that's to say.

"I don't follow you," said Carl. "There must be some particular environmental pressure to evolve – to which they're adapting – mustn't there be? Not a mental pressure from within, a dream-pressure. You're almost saying that they evolve spontaneously."

Mary grinned. "Maybe that's my romantic side showing." Her smile encompassed Peter, Peter more than Carl. So perhaps, thought Peter, she was beginning to realize, and her talk of dreams meant . . . He suspected he could only ever express himself fully not in simple stone but in smooth, rich, aristocratic marble. He might return from this expedition metamorphosed into a sculptor rather than a mason. His hands itched.

They entered a square flanked with hieroglyphicals. These were figures which seemed to bespeak or riddle out some special symbolism above and beyond the ordinary grotesque; some one-to-one meaning, if only you could decode it. Many of the figures were related to one another by a gesture, a glance, even by physical connections in the shape of a stone chain looping from belly to belly . . . maybe that was an umbilical cord.

A stone fish-lemur – lemur with fins and tail – poised as if diving, one hand clamped over its nose. Two distorted lemurs who were fused together, their twin trunks branching from shared monstrous legs, wrestled for possession of a stone knife – to cut themselves apart? to hack off the rival claimant, amputate him? Another figure jutted up with arms outstretched, one hand clutching a stone hoe like a trident, stone wings bursting from its back as though it would take flight into the sky.

With its bare hands a fourth figure ripped open a hole, a grinning mouth, in its belly. This one's neighbour had shrunk into a wizened ball mostly, yet one single giant arm pointed dramatically . . . towards a gloomy doorway barren of any images except one, and that image not carved at all but seemingly painted or burnt (or both) upon the curved rock lintel. The daubed image was a pair of staring black-rimmed eyes, two circles side by side.

Their guide had gestured and twittered at them to stay in the square, and had run off. Initially they had been more interested in scrutinizing and taking holos of the hieroglyphicals. Only as she returned, carrying some stiff and still steaming purple root vegetable on which she alternately blew and chewed, did they notice that sign above the doorway – to which the lunching lemur trotted, and where she squatted down.

"A sign!" exclaimed Carl. "God, it's the first graffito we've seen. The first genuine arbitrary symbol. Two circles touching, like our sign for infinity, eh? I'm sure it's painted. The first piece of written language?"

"Lemur eyes," Mary said. "That's what it shows. As a warning? Dark inside. Doesn't open out and brighten? No, why should they warn of darkness – with their eyesight?"

"What we assume about their eyesight," Carl corrected. "Can't test them out like animals, can we? Damned if we will!"

Yet even so. Big eyes. At night spy-cams usually showed activity in the city. The lemurs had fire but this seemed restricted to cookery. No natives carried brands to light their way nor did flambeaux illuminate any of their living zones.

"Maybe it means, 'Look in here.'" Carl unclipped a flashlight, shone the beam down a plunge of broad shallow steps which didn't appear to be made of stone.

"Hey! Door against the wall!" He leaned to rap with his knuckles. "Bottle-wood door. Or an upended sledge."

He was standing above the lemur. Gulping the last of her veg, she twittered up at him. He frowned in concentration.

"Children. Run. Hide? I can't understand."

Peter felt resentful of that sign. If it was a sign at all, it wasn't inscribed in his own language, of stone.

Carl leaned again to shine his light down those steps. The lemur rose, blinking. Briefly Peter was convinced that the native was attacking Carl in protest at the phenomenon of the torch, for she grabbed hold of Carl's tunic and began scrambling up him. Before Carl could do more than squeak loudly in surprise she was touching the sign above the door.

"Stay still!" called Mary. "Don't dislodge her!"

With sharp little teeth the lemur bit at her own thumb till it bled freely, a rich scarlet flow. In blood she painted around the outline of the sign till her wound coagulated. Then she leapt free from Carl, jerked her hurt thumb at the open doorway, warbled what might have been a farewell, and scuttled away.

It was thus that they found the catacombs.

"Catacombs" was Peter's description, although Mary soon pointed out that there did not seem to be any corpses or bones anywhere in the extensive series of corridors and little chambers underneath that part of the city. The whole complex, steps included, was scooped out of firm clay, not cut through rock, and it was empty apart from numerous open doors of bottle-wood, none of which possessed any type of hinge.

"It's a burrow," said Mary. "Evidently they were never arboreal animals, like Earth lemurs! They were burrowing creatures. That's why they have the apparent nocturnal adaptation of such big eyes – it was to see underground. This is the Ur-burrow. The original, basic burrow over which they later built the city."

"Rock *upon* clay?" Peter asked sceptically. He felt consumed with claustrophobia as their flashlights played upon yet more tight corridors and empty little cells, all lemur-size. They were being forced to stoop. Oh to be high on a spire in the open air, settling a block into its new resting place of centuries, a block rampant with an eagle's head. The air down in these, yes, catacombs smelt stale and dank.

Nor were there any gargoyles or lapids or demons. Nothing carved whatever. No stone. To Peter's mind the place was worse than empty. It was meaningless, and he feared that somehow he was losing Mary here as she spun her new theory of how the natives had originally burrowed like rabbits.

"And then they emerged from the soil, from chthonic Nature, into light and consciousness and creativity!"

"Where are the tools?" he asked, and he remembered William Blake's poem. "What the mallet, what the chisel?"

Were these really doors, loose doors, down here – when there were no doors in the city up above – or were they simply surplus sledges, stored against a mammoth harvest or retired from service?

When Mary snapped holopics the tiny chambers were blindingly illuminated. The after-dim, while his eyes readjusted to torchlight, was terrible to Peter's heart.

At the info-swap that evening Mary reported a great discovery which should quite trump Fremantle's coup concerning the natural origin of agricultural tools. A whole new subterranean layer of significance had been laid bare. A biological Troy: the original habitat. Doubtless it should be a source of chagrin to the biologist that she had found this out whilst he had been haring about in the forest, barking up trees, breaking up trees. For a little while, the burrow even seemed to diminish the city of statuary, to thrust it into the shade, as though that hole in the ground could be more important.

"Definitely not for burial purposes?" demanded Ash. "Even in previous epochs?"

"Most unlikely," replied Mary. "Not abandoned. Kept in repair. Using, um, bottle-wood implements. Otherwise collapse eventually. Besides, entrance marked with life-blood sign, constantly renewed. Ritually. Here is the root, the racial birth."

Fremantle said, "You think lemur fingers adapted to *burrow*? Ha!"

Before Mary could field this thrust, Leo Allen was saying, "Seems like war-shelter to me. Refuge from enemies."

"No, no. When we landed, lemurs didn't hide. Not threat-conscious."

"Carvings could have fooled me," said Allen. "Where metal sculpting tools, incidentally? If not hidden down burrow?"

"Maybe *buried* there, below ground. If so, appropriate place, culturally. Symmetric, linked inversely. City opposite of burrow, stone opposite of soil."

"Fieldtrip there tomorrow?" suggested Allen. "With metal detectors?"

"Yes," said Ash. "Everdon, take Allen, Fremantle, and Ramirez."

Peter had no wish to join in this expedition to the oppressive, meaningless warren. Let slick Fremantle and crony Ramirez spoil Mary's day for her, so that she would come back into the upper world of rock-art away from envy and barbed malice feeling stifled, needing Peter's . . . solidity, craving significance and warmth.

If Leo Allen's detectors uncovered any concealed chisels, Peter couldn't be more pleased. However, he had no wish to be present and couldn't really credit Mary's "symmetric" argument. The following day would be better employed in company with Lipmann, who himself had no conceivable reason to descend again into that voiceless collection of worm-holes in the clay.

Almost shunning Mary, Peter went directly back to his hutch to sleep. Before shuttering the window for the night he stared out at one of the little moons hanging full, bone-white, over the forest. The two moons of Rock orbited at different speeds in differently tilted planes. He could almost see that moon moving, but then a solitary cloud consumed the satellite so that its light diffused and swelled into a glowing amoebic blob. The pure circular stone of the moon had melted into shapeless, meaningless menace.

Leo Allen found no metal hidden in the burrow, though after his tour of inspection he was still inclined to the shelter idea, with reservations.

"Yearly insect swarms? Like killer bees, lethal locusts?" he suggested the following evening. "Small, but many and deadly."

Ramirez reported tersely at speed on the local analogues of insects, rodents, and riverine reptiles. To Peter's ears she sounded like a twittering lemur herself.

"Quick plagues of pseudo-mice," she gabbled. "Behave like lemmings every few years, maybe develop toxic bite?"

"Need food storage," said Allen. "Burrow not stocked."

"Innocuous-seeming species undergoes startling life-cycle metamorphosis? Like caterpillar into moth?"

"Lemurs still intelligent to *build* shelter," Mary argued optimistically. "Memory of past, concept of future."

"Is hibernating tortoise intelligent?" called out Fremantle.

"Actually," added Allen, "shelter not spacious enough for more than quarter of estimated population."

"Therefore *original* home," said Mary, "before population rose."

"Lingo?" asked Ash, and Carl reported quickly on the frustrating day he had spent with Peter.

41

"Requires much work, back home. Breakthrough by next expedition, yes. If true language."

Ash raised a quizzical eyebrow.

"Masonry?" she enquired. A titter ran round the refectory, originating near Ramirez.

"Twin-circle sign not found in carvings," Peter confessed.

"Are you blind?" heckled Fremantle. "Image of lemur *eyes*!"

"Not necessarily." Though what else?

"If burrow shelter from perceived threat," said Allen, "mount more survey cams in city for when *M* lights up tomorrow? Suppose Anthro records behaviour vicinity shelter?"

Mary sat on Peter's bunk, as he had hoped she might.

"What a wretched day."

"Yes." He agreed sympathetically, gladly. "I'm afraid my carvings are no Rosetta stone, as yet."

Why should he be afraid? He thought of the hieroglyphicals he had restored in one Oxford college, hieroglyphicals inspired by the medieval bestiary representing desire, timidity, moroseness. He wanted to touch Mary, hold her, mould her, tumble her in bed. Yet he couldn't. Didn't know how. Couldn't read her signals, which weren't carved in stone but enciphered in flesh; couldn't transmit his own signals to her adequately, hieroglyphically.

His fear was deeper, obscure, indefinable, as though the lemur burrow was some nightmare area of himself which he had been forced reluctantly to enter. As yet nothing had been found, no final truth or ultimate idol, either glorious or evil. Why should the locus of nightmare be down there when blatant nightmares capered in full grotesquery along all the lanes of the city? To return to the courtyard of the . . . *evil eyes*, the very next evening, as he must now do in company with Carl and Mary, scared him in a way that no summit of any spire or tower height

42

had ever done. A vertigo of the dark cramped depth afflicted him.

"Mary."

"What is it?"

"Nothing."

Damned timidity!

"That's to say, tell me about yourself, Mary, will you?"

"But you already know. We know each other's bios."

"Yes, but a person is not a biography." His own contained nothing about pints of ale or about a certain barmaid who consoled a certain farmer, who happened not to be as strapped for cash as other local farmers because he had seen the future and had roofed his fields over early with filtering, humidifying, climate-control film.

"Any more than a tribe of aliens is a smarty-pants ethno-report? Is that what you're implying?"

Had he inadvertently opened a door to some hollow which haunted her? The most insightful of social maps (of one's own well-planned life, too!) was not the actual untidy paradoxical territory.

"What should I tell you, Peter? Of times when I made a fool of myself? Times when I became obsessed? Times of confusion? My favourite foods? My favourite *fantasies*?"

Yes, those, he thought.

"Never mind," he said. "Look at the moon." (Which was over the river, streaking out a silver snake.) "Its side's being shaved off by the sculptor of the night."

She stared at him intently. Was her stare a signal? He didn't know.

She said, "It should still be almost full tomorrow evening. And it's past our bedtime, if we're to be wise owls *then*."

For that night of nights Leo Allen had done the observers proud. His own team, consisting of himself and Carl, team two, namely Fremantle and Ramirez, and team three, Mary and Peter, as well

43

as being in audio contact with each other, with the base, and with *Michelangelo*, had multi-channel video links with all the survey cams, which were equipped for infrared in case of dark cloud. In the event the sky was clear; starlight and moonlight sugared the city.

Since the workers were all home from the fields, the full complement of population was inside the city. Many were asleep, but others wandered about twittering so that lanes and yards and rooms seemed just as crowded – or uncrowded – as by day.

"Fusion minus one hundred seconds," counted a radio voice. The glint of the orbiting voidship should be in sight any moment.

"Allen here. It'll look as though that moon has given birth to another moon. As though the other moon has jumped right around the sky to just beside it."

"Fremantle. Birth of myth, maybe? Like Velikovsky's Bible?" A sneer in his voice.

Peter swept his flashlight beam above the doorway of the burrow. Two eyes, of dried blood, stared blackly. In panic he thumbed his com.

"Catlow here. Commander! *Michelangelo!* Don't light the fusion torch. Abort!"

"Sixty seconds."

"I've realized what the sign means, Commander. It isn't eyes at all. It's the two full moons nearly in conjunction, before the closer one eclipses the other. When they're side by side in the sky, *something happens!* How often does that occur?"

A voice he didn't recognize, from *M*: "Every thirty-one years, local."

"Thirty seconds."

"She's in sight."

"For heaven's sake don't light that torch till we've worked this out!"

"Everdon here," said Mary. "Agree Catlow. Unwarrantable cultural tampering."

"Fremantle. Good experiment. Trigger programmed behaviour. Demonstrate existence of."

"No!" cried Peter.

"Fifteen seconds."

"Take stonemason's word? Navigate voidship by hammer and chisel?" A woman. Who? Ramirez?

"Please, Ash!"

"Protest noted."

In the sky – to all appearances right next to the moon, though actually fifty thousand kilometers closer – the fusion torch of the voidship ignited, the torch that could accelerate *Michelangelo* to hyperphase. The light seemed to expand to the size of the moon.

Around the yard hieroglyphicals strained at the leash of that new luminosity as if about to dive, to fly, to wrestle, to tip themselves open. Of a sudden the night was loud with the warbling and twittering of what could have been thousands of startled birds.

Lemurs flooded into the yard. Females clutching squealing babies, males hauling youngsters along, they jammed through that doorway of the double eye (ah no, of the double *moon*), plunging down into darkness. Peter was buffeted, pulled by the river of bodies all crowding towards one goal.

"Hey," from the radio, "cat among the pigeons! They really got the wind up!"

No, it wasn't lemur hands which were pulling Peter along now. It was Mary, urging him.

"Must see what goes on down there!"

Peter heard himself moan. All those bodies packing into that close, dark catacomb! But he couldn't escape the pressure. Their torchbeams jerked about as Mary and he stumbled, crouching, down the hard clay stairs, and into one of the chambers. This cell was already half full. As the two humans piled in, panting, lemurs wrestled the bottle-wood door shut behind them, firmly. The door fitted tight against the clay rim, and the lemur commissionaires withdrew, apparently satisfied that those still surging past down the corridor outside wouldn't attempt to force entry.

Now all of the lemurs calmed. They sat and settled, even the youngest. The presence of the big humans with their lights and videocom and chattering radio voices seemed immaterial. No sound of lemur feet outside, not any more.

"Christ!" Radio voice. "What a bloody dust storm!" Allen?

"Dust? The whole place is *smoking*." That was certainly Carl.

"Can't see a thing —"

As Mary tuned the videocom it was plain that all the survey cams had gone to infrared. Distorted bright images of lemurs staggered through a fog. Gargoyles, babewyns, walls were exhaling thick pink clouds through all their microscopic stone pores. Images of lemurs, surely out of focus, clung to stonework, crouched, climbed, engaged in strange acrobatics.

"Whole city hidden." Chang's voice, from the base. "Leave if possible."

"Allen, Security. Guard mask integrity. Grab cams to point way. Hold vid-screens to eyes. See in infrared. Keep lenses *cleaned*."

"Coated in the damn stuff. My scalp's itching like crazy —"

Why did lemurs on screen look so contorted? Why were they moving in sluggish slow motion? Why was that one climbing up a pillar?

"Patel." She was back in base. "Entire fabric of city is releasing spores, billions of spores. Like fungus, puffballs."

"Ash here. More like spawning coral. Synchronously, once yearly in old days all along Australia's Barrier Reef. Viewed this on vacation when child. Triggered by temperature and tidal cues — and by full moonlight! City may be social organism. Colony of microorganisms. Air reef. Reef in air, not sea. Comment, Fremantle?"

"Busy." A cough.

Peter spoke. "Triggered by double moon. The semblance of. The moon and *Michelangelo*. Together."

"Ash here. Catlow?"

Mary reported, "Everdon and Catlow in burrow, see channel twenty. Lemurs took refuge. Shut doors tight. Thus some survivors. But of what?"

"Of *that*, Mary!" Peter jabbed a finger at the little screen. Though the image was doubly foggy due to the coating on the cam lens it was still possible to see one lemur backed up against a pillar, shaggy with spores. The native's mouth was gaping wide, its neck was arching. Its penis had burst forth from the furry sheath, stiffened, crusty, and huge. The lemur was in process of becoming a hieroglyphical of rutting lust. While it clung, backward, to that pillar, its legs bent up away from the ground, shrinking, contracting, and edging it higher and higher in concert with its cruelly twisted arms, till it stopped and hung as if cemented.

"Natives turning into monsters!" they heard. "It's goddam Halloween."

"Itchy –"

"Don't scratch –"

"Protein incompatibility," said Chang. "Should not affect humans. But recommend detox and quarantine."

"My leg's *stiff* – !"

A scream . . . of panic? Whose panic?

"They don't *make* the statues, Mary," Peter said. "They *become* the statues. And the rest of the fabric! They never built this city. Generations of their bodies have fused into it. As Ash says! – coral reefs in air! Nourished by night-soil and cooking water chucked over it. And at sporing time the coral organisms coat the lemurs, turn them into more reef."

"But the lemurs are altering so grotesquely. . . ."

"Yes! The spores take their bodies over. Metamorphose them – according to the lemurs' own, I don't know, archetypal emotions, passions, instinct programs."

"And thus they rejoin Nature." She mused. "But they don't run away to live in the woods. Instead they rely on a burrow that'll save enough survivors to let the race continue. They probably breed quite fast. Thirty-odd years will be time enough to repopulate, and more. But they don't try to escape their destiny. It's the only thing that gives them culture, cities." The voices of teams one and two were just grunty now, or ghastly. Chang was talking.

"Control by chemical signals in air. Coral is architect. Maybe influences shape of bottle-trees too? We make anthropomorphic error. Assume lemurs dominant because resemble us. Instead, part of symbiotic system."

"That's it," Mary said to Peter, "symbiosis." Of a sudden she looked desperately sad. "It isn't Cultural Anthro at all, it's Bio. Plain beastly biology."

Chang said, "Lemurs nourish coral, are periodically incorporated, used to manufacture more coral mass. Lemurs benefit by shelter, tools, agric with which to nourish coral – and their thoughts given form and substance, reinforcing programs governing lemurs."

"They must give their bodies to their God," murmured Mary.

"Coral true intelligence here," chanted Chang. "Bio-engineering, eh, Fremantle? Down on molecular level."

Silence from Fremantle.

"Can transmute body elements. Can unwind and rewind cells, reproducing self throughout microscopically. Affect humans too. But intelligence impenetrable as stone. Not intelligence in our sense. Fooled by fusion-flare."

A groan from the radio, as of some material stretching, splitting, then hardening.

"How long will the air down here last?" wondered Mary.

The native refugees in the cell were almost comatose by now, hardly moving or reacting despite the noise and light produced by two guests. In other cells Peter could imagine total inertness. Thus to conserve oxygen. That, too, must be part of the program. In this case, of racial survival. For the good of the city, the benefit of the coral.

"Long enough," he said, "if we weren't here. Compared with them we're gobbling oxy."

Michelangelo was radioing worried enquiries.

"City still sporing," by way of answer. "Could go on all night. Probable loss, four personnel. Two more sheltering down sealed burrow."

"Abort grand tour? Circle moon, return to Rock orbit?"

"Negative," said Ash. "Base in no danger. Future fieldwork, body recovery, wearing protective suits."

Peter murmured, "They're going to hack Fremantle and Co out of the coral? Wonder what they became. . . ."

At that moment the hieroglyphical basis of lemur life and society came clear to him – or seemed to come clear to him; the way in which these furry beings were revealed to themselves at last in a transcendent moment of understanding, a peak of consciousness at the time when the spores coated and invaded, transmuted and petrified them and sealed them into the substance of their city in rampant caricature, in emblem which at first sight seemed monstrous but which was not necessarily so.

Plain biology, indeed! What was the word which he'd heard Mary use in derision?

Reductionism, that was it. The reduction of wonderfully patterned complexity down to an elementary jiggle of chemical reactions. The reduction of dream to electrochemical programs, of vision and passion down to the vibration of molecules.

Peter knew that he must determine his own dominant category of being, his primal humour, in the eternal rock root of his own existence.

Timidity, covetousness, envy, lust? Or loving joy, or patience, or some other of the virtues?

Was this not also a sort of reduction . . .?

He remembered the words of a long-dead French poet, Saint-Jean Perse, which he had once committed to memory. *On ne bavarde pas sur la pierre*. . . . You don't gossip on stone.

You don't babble, or ramble on. Reduce your meaning to its essentials.

"I'm going up top," he told Mary. "I can't stand it down here. It's squeezing me. Up, and out."

"You'd die! Masks don't protect us. And you'd let the spores in!"

"Plenty of doors. Close this one tight behind me – unless you'd rather come as well?"

She shuddered. "Peter, you're committing suicide. You'll *die*."

"No I shan't. I'll become eternal. Archetypal. I've come so many light years, Mary, to meet myself. How could I ship back to Earth as a surplus artisan, a joke, when I could *become* what my whole life has been aimed at? Promise you won't let them hack me out of the city. Don't let them cart me home in a specimen bag. Promise!"

"Look, we've had a set-back, you and me, but isn't what we've found just as fascinating?"

"Oh yes indeed." He handed his com-set to her. "It sets the dream free, to shape the self for ever."

"Sets it *free*? You'd be locked in an alien coral reef. It mightn't even be able to cope with you. Different codings, alien ones. The lemurs would throw crap and veg water in your face."

"Promise you won't let them take me back!"

"Yes. If they'll listen to me." She sounded deeply scared now, which he regretted.

"Make them listen for once. Tell them how they ought to have listened to me about *M* and the moon. Tell them I hope to communicate with the coral by offering myself to it, but it'll take until the next sporing for any effects to show. Yes, tell them *that*. And tell them: *transmutation* of protein into rock! What wouldn't Earth give for the knack of altering the molecular structure of rock into protein?" Even if certain farmers, who had bedded barmaids, lost their investment.

"I won't say goodbye, since you'll see me again." Stuffing his torch temporarily under his armpit, Peter clawed at the clay to release the bottle-wood door. This popped free, and he slipped quickly into the corridor, which looked clear of motes. "Push it tight!"

No sign of lemurs, either. Doors behind him blocked cells. The stairs ahead mounted to the door of two-moons, which was shut. He ascended, crouching.

He unpeeled the top door, dodged out, tugged the barrier shut behind him as best he could. Now his torchlight yellowed a dense fog. He couldn't see a single object in the yard of hieroglyphicals; however, he thought he recalled a convenient gap between two neighbouring grotesques roughly in *that* direction. He soon collided with hard lumps, barely visible. Turning, backing between those lumps and another set of lumps an arm's distance away, he met relative smoothness.

Not all lemurs would become hieroglyphicals or gargoyles or babewyns. By no means! Many lemurs must simply crunch up to become supporting blocks, sections of wall or pillar, part of fabric rather than design. The ordinary bedrock of society, those! Whereas he, Peter from another planet, was unusual? Outstanding? Or perhaps those types were the more perfect, Platonic specimens.

He ripped off his mask, breathed deep, and almost choked. But already a hot (yes, itchy) exaltation coursed through his veins and nerves.

Thoughts sped through his mind, a riot of images trying to dovetail and achieve a unified solid pattern, to array themselves like a squad on parade.

He didn't care about his discomfort. Even, agony? Vaguely he was aware that parts of himself were being warped and twisted. However, he was opiated, his pain centres disconnected. Only terror had made that radio voice scream.

What of Mary? What of that barmaid? Who were they, compared with the centuries? His devotion was to stone. He aspired to be a spire. He stretched up and up. And he knew the sublime.

51

Jewels in an Angel's Wing

Damnably, I'd just been chewed up by a shark. And I'd thought I was doing so well!

As soon as the shark bit through my legs I went into dream-mode. The sensation was sickening, like being eaten in a dream. I felt squeezed and reduced. Maybe that's how a prey often feels when a predator snaps its jaws; natural anaesthesia takes over. Except in our case, our bodies go "astral" in dream-mode. With enough effort we can pull free and flee. That feels like wading out of deep, treacly mud. Then you need to find a powerpoint to eat to boost your energy back to a safe level.

No such luck this time. If you're already low on energy after an earlier escape, you've had it. You fade out. You reassemble somewhere else, usually somewhere you don't want to be, and you're starving for a powerpoint. Three such fade-outs in succession – don't ask me who does the counting – and you get zapped back to a lower level.

But trying to keep out of harm's way can't work forever either. The only way you can win through is by risking being eaten time and again. It's a hell of a life.

Am I puzzling you? We were equally puzzled. Believe it. We pretty well knew what to do, but we had no idea why. It was as though we'd lost half of our memories, had them locked away from us.

The first level of existence was radioactive ruins. Scattered throughout a wreck of a city were various safe enclaves – which never stayed safe for long. Radioactivity slowly seeped in, or else the mutants would mount an attack. You had to keep on the move, hunting for new havens which were clean, stocked with food and drink. And you had to collect powerpoints, whilst avoiding the attentions of mutants and clouds of plutonium gas. Powerpoints on this level came in the form of antiradiation pills, usually to be found in deathtrap buildings, all of them a good distance from the nearest sanctuary and in opposite directions. If you could eat enough pills without being too badly irradiated or mauled by mutants . . . well, I finally managed to, and found myself instantly reassembled on the second level. Ghoul Castle.

With all this rushing about and hiding, we didn't exactly get to hold public meetings, but I'd estimate there were about a hundred of us; and of this number about half had succeeded in escaping from the ruins before I did. So I'm no paragon of agility and quick wits. To start with, in fact, I was quite a slow slob. However, I was persistent and I was capable of cooperating and learning. Indeed, I'd found my ideal partner: Isbeth Anndaughter. Isbeth and I had teamed in the ruins. More than teamed; we had become lovers. We covered each other, ran interference for each other. During my successful run that led me to level two, she sidetracked several mutants at great risk to herself. Then before the winning route had time to change, she too ran it solo, gobbling power, and boosted herself out of those ruins to rejoin me.

Of course, I saved Isbeth from close shaves too, but I'd say the balance sheet of debts was in my favour. She must genuinely have loved me, seen in me qualities which she could enhance. Maybe my ability to share. You did come across various individualists who wouldn't cooperate with anyone. Other men and women you met en route would swap experiences briefly. That's how Isbeth and I knew about Ghoul Castle in advance, since some of those latter had already escaped, and been zapped back, and were trying to leave the ruins a second time.

Others – no-hopers – had already given up the struggle. They just dashed from one sanctuary to another in the ruins, hoping not to get caught, hardly even trying for the power pills. Apparently you could sink no lower than the ruins, no matter what.

Ghoul Castle was an immense complex of halls, corridors, towers, battlements, staterooms, galleries, tunnels and dungeons, courts and moats and mazes of sewers – haunted by lethal ghosts, prowled by ghouls and monsters, besieged by barbarians, enchanted by wizards. Jewels were the power-points there.

It took Isbeth and myself ages to make it through. How long? Six months, a whole year? It was hard to keep track of time. By the skin of our teeth we avoided being zapped back to the ruins. We learned the ropes – those shifting ropes.

From time to time we met fellow adventurers (or victims), some of whom had already reached the water-world only to be zapped. So we did learn some advance details of the third level, which Isbeth and I already felt sure must exist. We felt that in our bones, instinctively, along with an urge to reach it.

Yet if any of the others had discovered *how* we got into this fix, or who we had been before we all found ourselves in the ruins, they weren't saying.

Unfortunately, ghosts and ghouls homed in avidly on gather-ings of more than a couple of persons, which rather set a time limit to more general speculations. The castle was better furnished than the ruins had ever been. Food and drink were definitely superior. If you could keep clear of nastiness, it wasn't too bad a life, merely nerve-wracking. Some of our contacts confided that they intended to hang on in the castle. But that wasn't enough for Isbeth, or for me.

At long last she succeeded in touring the whole vast edifice by the right route, avoiding all pitfalls and evils whilst consuming the jewels she needed. This time Isbeth took the lead, and I distracted the opposition. As soon as she was translated, out and away, I retraced the circuit and followed her through, on to this submarine level where sharks and squids and other nasty surprises hungered for us. We'd been here quite a while.

When I came back to myself, after being a shark's astral lunch and fading out, miracle of miracles I wasn't far from a total of two powerpoints. Powerpoints on this level were pearls. (Use 'em up, and replacements appeared elsewhere. Same principle applied to sanctuaries and the essentials of life.) After gulping these down, I didn't take more than a few hours to find Isbeth. Soon we were safe in a transparent dome filled with fresh air. Safe, for two or three sleeps, supposing we chose to stay put. Seawater was leaking in slowly, but the dome had two habitable levels. Downstairs was ankle deep in water; upstairs was snug.

We'd made love, in a huge cosy sleeping bag. We were feasting on what we'd found in the dome: honeyed figs, sweet dates, coconuts, and a few trays of sushi. And of course we'd also found oxygen packs, for outside use when we quit the dome. Ours not to reason why. That was the way of it. You never saw things pop into existence; you just came across them – or they came across you. However, we were in a reasoning mood.

"Why, Konrad?" she asked me.

"*Where* is a good question too."

"So is *how*."

Outside, a flotilla of violet angelfish the size of shark fins lazed past towards coral cliffs of pink and gold, where weed wafted and a deadly-looking orange medusa bloomed. Isbeth bit into a fig, fed me the rest of it, then asked:

"Who are we, Konrad? Who are we really?"

I mumbled, mouth full.

"We can't be real, you know," she said.

"That's a dangerous assumption."

"Real people don't shift in a twinkling of an eye from a castle to underneath the sea. Real people don't get eaten and find themselves alive again."

"It's a dangerous assumption, Isbeth, because if we don't

play everything for real then we'll slacken off. We shan't win."

"Win what?"

"Ourselves. Our stolen selves." Yes, that had to be why. *In vino veritas*. In addition to the food, we had an amphora of fine wine and a couple of golden goblets.

Isbeth was dark and slight and wiry, with magical, deep-set eyes and high cheekbones. I was leaner than I'd been originally, but in many respects I think her wire was stronger than my new muscle. I wondered how I could change physically, if I wasn't real.

"Maybe we're being tested," I said.

"No one's compelled to strive."

"We compel ourselves."

"Yes! Some of us do."

"Or maybe we're being trained. Odd sort of training, though."

"Trained in initiative." She grinned. "Trained in speed and planning and memory, boldness and caution. Also," she added thoughtfully, "trained not to fear death."

"There has to be a fourth level, doesn't there?"

"Yes – and we'll get to it!"

In fact, despite my recent shark debacle, Isbeth had fared less well than I so far in the waterworld. Nothing terminal as yet. With my help, she'd always managed to recharge before she racked up three successive deaths. But she'd fallen victim to a medusa, an octopus, a poisonous urchin, and other fates too. That wasn't because I let her go ahead into danger. The going seemed tougher. At the same time I was enjoying a run of good luck, or maybe I was developing an instinct. We were still a good team, yet I felt that somehow, in some way, I was pulling ahead.

She glanced down at the level of water seeping in below.

"Listen, Konrad, if I'm zapped back to the castle I'll win through here again – fast. Don't wait for me. Promise to go on ahead. Try to reach the next level."

I nodded. I intended to. Anything extra I could learn might

help her too. Somewhere, somehow. Even on different levels, we'd still be thinking as a team. Something awaited. Of that I was sure. Knowledge. Reward. Whatever. Something had to await.

A giant squid squirted its way overhead, its rose and yellow phosphorescent signals flashing incomprehensibly like some flexible control console made of rubber. What long suckery arms it had. What a cruel beak. What big round eyes.

A couple of days later Isbeth got zapped, and I couldn't do a thing to help. She'd already died twice over and reassembled nearby; she absolutely had to recharge. She dived between two great slabs of rock for a power pearl lying exposed on silver sand. Those weren't rocks. They were the two half-shells of a clam larger than any we'd ever seen before. The shells clashed shut on Isbeth. Bubbles gushed from her ruptured tank and face-mask. I watched her exposed feet thrashing in dream-mode. She was still trying to grab that pearl, to pop it in her mouth, give her the zoom to haul herself up out of the clam. She failed. She vanished.

Grief.

Fury.

As the clam began cranking itself open again I dived, snatched the pearl, and thrust myself up and out before the creature was ready to spring shut again.

I found a couple of fellows I knew resting in the next refuge dome. Ivan Koschenko and his black partner Barney Randall. Barney wasn't too welcoming.

"Three of us in one place is like bait, man! We're gonna attract a giant octopus to crack us open."

Barney nursed a particular hatred of octopuses; they seemed to have a special affinity for him.

"My Isbeth's been zapped," I told them.

"Let him stay here an hour or so," said Ivan.

So I stayed. So we talked. Not about Isbeth. What was there to say? She wasn't dead. She was back in Ghoul Castle.

Ivan talked about the surface of the sea.

"What's up there? Why don't we ever swim straight up and take a look?"

"You'd never get there," said Barney. "A fucking big shark would tear you to ribbons, out in the open."

"I'm interested in whether there *is* a surface."

"Maybe," I said, "it's our curiosity that's being tested, and so far we haven't shown enough curiosity."

"Don't get much chance, do we?" snapped Barney. He kept looking out at the submarine landscape in case some menace was creeping close. "When we get caught and go fuzzy –"

"Dream-mode," I said.

"Yeah. That's unnatural. I think we're all models, in a big machine. I don't mean like tin soldiers, not that kinda model. I don't know what I mean. I've been robbed of how to know."

"We'll find out on level four," I assured him.

You'll have noted how I started our story halfway through – just the way we had all been started up in the ruins, halfway through our lives with no idea what went before. Now we leap forward a bit, just as I leapt forward soon after that – to the fourth level.

And the fourth level was a starship. I knew right away what a starship was. This wasn't any old starship. It was an interstellar luxury palace, a ritz of a starship patronized by high society, a snobbish, intriguing, catty, star-hopping aristocracy of lords and ladies with whom etiquette was of the utmost importance. Life on board the *Empire Topaz* was an intricate dance of manners, and woe betide you if you stubbed a toe. Deadly as any shark bite, such a gaffe could wreck your status and destroy you. Here, a slap in the face or a snub was death. Dream-mode was the hot melting flush of embarrassment. Powerpoints weren't jewels or pearls this time; we had to collect favours from ladies. Asking one of those fine ladies in the ballroom of the *E.T.* such a question as, "Where are we really? What are you really?" merited a stinging rebuke . . . zap.

58

Oh, but I got myself deeply involved in all this maze of politeness and innuendo, flirtation and character assassination, and jockeying for status. Perhaps too deeply. What other option was there, unless you merely wanted to stay on the sidelines as some sort of feeble junior midshipman? Besides, the *Empire Topaz* did have its favourable aspects. I was falling in love with the Lady Zania.

Weeks later I turned a corner on B-Deck and came face to face with . . .

"Isbeth!"

"Konrad. I just got here. I raced through the castle. The underwater level took longer."

I hustled Isbeth along to a safe cabin where we shouldn't be bothered for a while by partying ladies or scheming beaux, and I filled her in on all that I'd learned. Most of what I'd learned.

When I'd done, she said, "So now we're being taught etiquette the hard way. Etiquette is the final gloss on a professional soldier, I seem to recall! Perhaps we're soldiers, you and I. Officer material. These different levels are the ways we're being taught. Or selected and ranked. Our minds are linked in some type of computer."

Computer. Yes, I knew what that meant. Yes, this starship had a computer to guide her and run her systems.

"The computer could know the real situation, Konrad. We need to reach the computer. That'll be the last initiative test. The recognition of ourselves."

I felt sad. I'd been wasting time flirting, spinning in the social whirlpool whilst trying to keep my footing and advance, when I could have thought this out for myself.

"Starship," she repeated to herself. "Soldiers. Computers. We're coming across more clues, aren't we? Here's another enclosed world with its own layout and rules and limitations. We're going to raid the computer, you and I, ask it some questions. Even if it *is* only a simulation of itself."

"What was that you said? Simulation?"

"Well, a computer on board this ship can't be any more real than the ship itself. But it may contain authentic data. It may interface."

"Could we be 'simulations' too?"

"Maybe, maybe not. Probably it would be more economical to use real people and put their bodies in stasis while their brains were linked cybernetically."

"Stasis. Cybernetically."

There came a soft knock on the cabin door. We both froze but the knock was repeated impatiently. I had little choice but to open the door.

The Lady Zania stood there.

"Madam." I sketched a bow and made the usual hand flurries.

"Utterly delighted! How ever did you find me?"

She stared past me at Isbeth, jealous fury in her eyes.

"My Lady, may I present an old acquaintance, by name Isbeth Anndaughter? Isbeth Anndaughter, here is the Lady Zania."

With miraculous cool and skill and charm, Isbeth rose to the occasion and bailed me out. Herself too. I don't imagine that Zania was fooled, but an awkward moment which could have toppled headlong into deadly rivalry, vengeance, and disgrace ended instead with Zania linking arms with Isbeth to lead her to the B-Deck salon, while I escorted both my ladies. A certain barbed pique was still the undertow to Zania's repartee, but Isbeth simply wouldn't let Zania manoeuvre her into hostility. Isbeth adopted a wonderfully disarming, flattering frivolity.

And so we partied and danced and made new acquaintances and tasted gourmet canapés and drank champagne and fenced with words. Zania made sure that she introduced Isbeth to all the most dangerous lords and ladies, yet Isbeth hardly faltered. I could sense the strain in my long-time partner, for here were human sharks as smooth and sleek as any sea predator, but far more ingenious. Here were dowager octopuses and young, entangling medusae. Here were old lords like crusty clams who invited being tickled then snapped shut.

It seemed to take days to disentangle ourselves from the repercussions of that reception on B-Deck, which led on to other revels, to casinos and boudoirs and I forget what else. Eventually Isbeth and I pretended to slip away for separate trysts. Together again, alone at last, we fled the passenger section for the starker corridors of crew territory to hunt for the computer room.

Isbeth forbore to discuss, archly or otherwise, my previous entanglement with Zania; nor was I eager to allude to it. We had other fish to fry.

"We're in an imperial starship on its way to war," I argued. "Strip away all the sophistication of this particular ship, *Empire Topaz*, and underneath is a killing weapon filled with racks of sleeping soldiers being fed with false worlds to train 'em for all contingencies."

"Including courtesy? In case we need to be courteous to the hostile aliens at our destination? In case we need to be diplomats as well as marines? Thus you shall learn the correct way to kiss an alien's hand?"

"Not aliens, no it can't be that. Humans. This is *Empire Topaz*. We'll be coming up against powerful colonists who have rebelled against the empire."

She laughed, a shade sarcastically.

"It was you who first mentioned soldiers, Isbeth."

"So I did."

Her fingers danced over the keyboard as if with a mind of their own, interrogating. *Who is Isbeth Anndaughter? Who is Konrad Digby? Self-Diagnosis? State of System?*

On the green screen a single repeated word scrolled.

CYBERFUGUE

CYBERFUGUE

CYBERFUGUE.

"What the hell does that mean?"

"Let's try to find out." And she typed, *Define*.

Nothing.

Define: Fugue.

FUGUE: A PERIOD OF MEMORY LOSS WHEN AN INDIVIDUA
VANISHES FROM NORMAL HAUNTS. ALSO: A THEME TAKEN UP AN
REPEATED REPEATEDLY.

What is level five? she typed.

RADIOACTIVE RUINS.

She turned to me, stunned. "So if we . . . graduate from her
. . . we're back in the ruins. There's no other reality! No genuin
reality!"

"Maybe we're all dead. Maybe this is hell. Or purgatory."

"Huh. Not so long ago you thought we were on an interstella
battleship, being groomed for command."

"So did you. Almost."

"Something has gone wrong, that's what. Whatever contro
us is in a fugue. A cyberfugue. It's looping these scenarios i
imprints on us, it's recycling them. The true purpose has bee
lost."

"Are you remembering more of yourself, Isbeth?"

She shook her head. She said, "Maybe the purpose of thes
scenarios isn't to train us at all. It's just to occupy us during a hug
spaceflight lasting years and years. It's to keep us stimulated s
that our minds don't atrophy."

"When we arrive," I asked, "we'll be restored to ourselves?"

"Unless the system really is in cyberfugue. Unless we'r
locked in, with no way out. Unless that's what the computer
telling us – or rather this simulation, this model here. I'm incline
to believe that's so. I'm going to try and override the program
Crash it."

The periscopes showed ruins. The external Geiger counter
chattered like crazy.

We had woken up weak as kittens. It took days to recover, days of supping special nutrient soups fed us by machine.

We remembered the war, and the automated underground shelter, enormous in its extent, with five levels one below the other, fully stocked for all supposed future needs. Down on level four, the "swimming pools": the algae tanks for our descendants to grow slopfood when the larder got empty. Deepest of all, the nuclear-fusion plant. Enough space for a generation or two to rattle around in. Then it would get a bit more crowded.

We remembered the way our metabolisms had been slowed, how our brains had been linked electronically, how our memories had been suppressed, how we would be given games to play during the next few time-warped centuries . . . until the Earth was habitable once again, or until the machinery was forced to wake us anyway, prematurely; in which case we would have to breed in here and raise kids and they would have to raise kids in turn. Until.

Optimistically, we could sleep through the whole process of the healing of the Earth. A hundred years, three hundred, five hundred. Fifty men and fifty women, the gene pool to rebuild some sort of human civilization or existence.

The computer in the *Empire Topaz* had told the truth. The fifth level was ruins – the ruined, radioactive planet. Without any mutants running about; nothing could survive up there.

And Isbeth, who was a computer whiz, had crashed our survival program. She had woken us all up. No way could we be put back to sleep, in stasis.

Elapsed time: fifteen years. Too soon, far too soon. A century too soon, three centuries too soon.

Isbeth and I agreed that we must blame the machines, otherwise her life might be in danger, and mine too, since I'd helped her.

But if the machines could go so badly wrong chronologically, in what other respects might our sanctuary turn sour? What else might malfunction in the many endless years ahead?

63

If only we were back aboard the *Empire Topaz*. Or in Ghoul Castle. Anywhere else.

What a fine environment for despair, for insanity. It was hardly surprising when Barney Randall killed himself. He cut his own throat. I saw him with the knife against his neck. He was down at the end of a corridor. No one else was about but me. I dashed down the corridor towards him shouting, "No!" But he just grinned then sliced a second, bloody grin below that grin.

Without hesitating I raced for help. No, let's be honest, I ran away so as to have witnesses. Otherwise someone might say that I'd killed him myself. I came back with two Hispanic men – Martinez and Cruz, engineers – and a woman doctor, Sandra Macdonald.

"Where's the body, then, eh?" demanded Cruz. "Where's that body?"

"Someone must have . . . removed it."

"Don't be ridiculous," snapped Macdonald. "Where's the blood?"

The floor was spotless.

"But it was here!"

"Don't you try to spook us!" snarled Martinez.

"I'm not. I swear it."

The situation was turning ugly, so I headed for the stairs and went down to the next level.

"Hey, man."

It was Barney. He was leaning against a wall, looking mad. But alive. His throat wasn't grinning redly at me. I had seen him cut his throat.

Barney giggled. "You looking for me? Here I am. Surprise!"

Suddenly he jumped forward and gripped my wrist. "Here's Barney, baby." He was solid, real.

I broke free and fled back up those stairs three at a time towards the sound of angry voices.

In the meanwhile, Isbeth had arrived. She was arguing heatedly with my three witnesses.

"Isbeth, Barney's down below!" I cried. "I watched him kill himself – and now he's come back to life on another level!"

"You're wrong," shouted Martinez. "Barney made like he was killing himself – that's what you saw – then he ran downstairs. That's it. You were fooled."

"I saw the blood."

"You imagined it! Unless you're in this with the bastard. And her, her too." Martinez faltered.

Barney had followed me. He came up the stairs, grinning maniacally, with that knife or a different one in his hand.

"It doesn't hurt much," he called out. "You go fuzzy. You all know what that's like. Doesn't last long. Try it out." He blundered forward, slashing the blade from side to side.

Isbeth and I escaped into the nearest room, which was full of mothballed tools and spare parts. She had slammed on the lights; I slammed the door and wrestled a crate under the handle. Outside we heard a scream.

Isbeth sagged. Gestured feebly.

"Then this isn't real, either. We're in our sanctuary at last, but we're still dreaming all together, dreaming we're in our ghastly sanctuary. Oh, it'll be ghastly soon. Our enemies won't be mutants or ghouls or sharks. Our enemies will be ourselves. Each other. We'll be a hundred rats in a maze, going mad, killing each other, coming back to life."

"No. Barney has gone mad, that's all. No need for everyone to go mad."

"When we know there's no reality? We've taken a wrong turning, Konrad. We have to get back to the computer on the starship."

"*What?*" I thought she must have gone mad.

"I mean it. We have to use the shaft to the surface. We have to get out into the ruins."

"But the radiation . . . it'll cook us."

"We can't die. Don't you realize? As soon as we get up there
the mutants will appear. They'll start hunting us. Then we'll fin
our radiation pills. Our powerpoints. We'll jump to Ghou
Castle."

"Oh my God."

"This place, Konrad, this huge nuclear survival shelter – i
seems familiar."

"So it should be."

"The layout's familiar, not the place itself. This isn't an
nuclear shelter. It never was."

"What is it, then?"

"I keep thinking of the Moon. It's as if –" She fell silent, the
said, "We'll open up the shaft to the surface."

"Isbeth . . . when you crashed that program, things didn
work out too well. If we bust this shelter open people aren't goin
to like it."

"After the first shock they'll be *glad*. It'll be a whole lot bette
than going slowly, colourfully mad. Better than experiencing th
thrills and spills of insanity. I'd rather play hide-and-seek wit
sharks and ghouls any day. Will you help me?"

I nodded.

"If we get separated, Konrad . . . see you on board the *Empir
Topaz*, hmm?"

True enough, when we got to the surface mutants soon appeare
amongst the ruins of that great dead city. The creatures seeme
twice as agile, twice as cunning as before. It was as if they'd onl
been in first gear earlier on, and now had engaged second gear.

The Moon, Isbeth's Moon, a ghastly bloated orange of
moon, brooded permanently over the radioactive rubble we ra
through, and before long we were meeting other people from th
shelter who had made the same decision as us.

But there was worse to come. When I got killed for the thir
time in succession, torn astrally apart by mutants, and before
popped back to life somewhere else in the ruins, while I wa

"dead" in a kind of grey inbetween limbo, a tendril brushed my mind. That's the best way I can describe the experience.

Fleetingly, foggily, I remembered the Moon base: five sublunar levels sunk beneath the Mare Orientalis. I remembered our pastimes, all those interactive computer games we used to play to while away a tour of duty.

I remembered the approach of the aliens: two great spacefaring beings like grotesque, beautiful, ornamental fish a kilometre long, two kilometres high, half a kilometre wide, wrapped round with convoluted sparkling sails and veils, shimmering with powers and forces that we couldn't fathom. All contact with Earth from our transmitter on Nearside was disrupted, lost.

A glimpse: of my colleagues swaying, falling; shrivelling as if emptied. I remembered the terrible, sudden suction of myself . . away. Of my mind, my soul, my person.

I think I know what we are now, and where we are. We've been collected by one of those aliens. Our minds have been taken. Not copies of us, not analogues, but our very selves, our psyches.

We haven't been taken as scientific samples, nor specimens, nothing like that. How the tendril seemed to preen itself, as it touched me. How it seemed to admire itself. We have been taken as decorations – as psychic jewellery. Jewels on an alien angel's wings. Just as light shifts within a gem, so our adventures scintillate. Ultimately, in a loop.

When the aliens brushed by the Moon and removed us, they wondered what would amuse us, what settings would display us to best effect; and they found in our minds what games we played obsessively. So now we live those games.

Probably there are other life-forms from worlds of distant stars captured psychically in the being of these aliens, to decorate them: other minds dreaming out their passions. Probably there are alien jewels too.

We're on a starship, in a sense. The journey time may be hundreds of years. Thousands. There are no portholes or viewscreens as on the *Empire Topaz*. There are no glimpses of our

fellow life-form victims – if any – but I assume they must exis
And there are no controls. Does the diamond ring guide the han
that wears it? Does the necklace cause the head to turn?

At least . . . not yet.

Perhaps the computer room of the *Empire Topaz* is the closes
to an interface with the energy ganglia of this great alien. Maybe
maybe not. When I reach that computer room again, I hope wit
Isbeth at my side, maybe we can achieve something subtler, mor
ingenious than before.

The mutants may be faster. The ghouls may be more dange
ous and the sharks less dumb and the fine ladies aboard th
Empire Topaz more cut-throat. That's reminiscent of the gam
we played on Moon Base too, with a learner level of difficulty an
a professional level. I hope there are only two levels of difficulty

Meanwhile, I awake from dream-mode all on my own amid
the glowing ruins. I urgently want a radiation pill. I think I sens
that there's one to the northeast.

A rustle. A flurry of rags. A heavy stumble. Already there's
mutant nearby.

And the pocked orange moon glowers down on me, amidst
few lonely stars and a vast yawning void.

THE LEGEND OF THE SEVEN WHO FOUND
THE TRUE EGG OF LIGHTNING

Chtolo, the First, died before the quest really got under way, but since his death marked the start of the quest, he should be counted as one of the seekers. Besides, this brings their total to even, which is a more perfect number than six.

Chtolo, the First.
Mgwana, the Second.
Kampinga, the Third.
Laliani, the Fourth.
Madongo, the Fifth.
Angwinu, the Sixth.
Ntenga, the Seventh.

All in pursuit of the true egg of Lightning.

What's this? You haven't heard of the eggs of Lightning?

Then maybe you come from some dismal distant country where the weather has always been dead, where the forces of meteorology were mute and motiveless.

A land where Thunder never actually spoke, but only rumbled like flatulent bowels. A place where Lightning merely flashed, with no fierce independent spirit of its own. Where Torrent did not sometimes flow uphill, trying to drag itself back into the clouds. Where Cyclone was simply a windy vortex wandering the countryside at random – not a corkscrew of air hunting and burrowing intentionally for treasure.

What sort of treasure?

The only true egg of Lightning.

Cyclones were never very intelligent in their search, but without a doubt they were vigorous about it. They tore apart

IAN WATSON

anything which stood in their way, reducing huts and fishing
boats to a snow of sticks, spouting streams into the sky, turning
forest foliage into frantic flocks of green birds.

Why should the wind-giants seek their goal so violently? They
were so impetuous that if they did ever find the buried egg, they
must surely career past it willy-nilly, unable to return and retrace
their footprints of ravage. But this was the only way they knew
how to proceed.

Why did they seek the egg?

You may well wonder who ever communed with such mighty
winds to ask them this question. Whose voice could possibly
prevail over that screaming clamour? Whose lungs were strong
enough so that all the air wasn't immediately sucked out of them?
(With a result akin to pouring ox-hoof glue mischievously into
bellows.)

None other than Ngana the Great.

Ngana's voice was so loud that he could be heard clearly a mile
and more away. If he shouted at a glacier, he could shatter it. He
could pulverize an enemy's brain to jelly.

So Ngana had himself chained by all four limbs to a dead
termite mound (and his neck, by an iron collar). He hoped that
one day the mound might be in the path of a wind-giant.

For four years he stood there stark naked, washed by the rain,
dried by the sun. At night he slept upright in his chains. At dawn
when his bowels had moved, the dung was duly removed from
between his feet. During the day various of his fifty wives fed him
and fanned him and sang to him. Every evening the sexual act
was performed by one or another wife, who clung athletically to
the termite tower, wrapping her legs around him and it.

Finally a wind-giant did rush toward Ngana, and he spoke to it
with his vast voice.

"Halt! What do you seek for, Cyclone?"

Cyclone tore the hair from Ngana's head, but still he demanded an answer.

It tore the lids from his eyes, but still he insisted.

70

Finally it tore the genitals from his body.

"What do you hunt for, Cyclone?" he cried.

And Cyclone replied, "I seek the true egg of Lightning. I will dig it up and juggle with it perilously. The egg will bob up and down like a hollow gourd tossed upon a waterspout. The father-and-mother of the egg will shiver with fear and will dart to me. Lightning will beg me to set its egg down gently. I will make a condition. Lightning must intercede with Sky, to allow all wind to stand still forever and be at peace. For that is Wind's dream."

Naturally, if this dream were realized, it would spell doom to all beasts and people. If Wind stood still, none of us could breathe. We would suffocate in our own foul gases.

Fortunately we had little reason to fear that Wind would ever catch an egg. The more anxious and eager, the faster Wind raced.

Cyclone told Great Ngana more.

"A fish spawns a million eggs, and only one survives. Thus does Lightning seed the earth a thousand million times over. Due to accidents of soil, magnetics, rain, and a dozen other circumstances, only one true egg will ever swell and one day be hatched by a second stroke of lightning in exactly the same spot – thus giving birth to a new sky, the colour of which will be green."

After Cyclone passed on – carrying Ngana's hair and eyelids and genitals away with it – his fifty wives flocked to the mound. They bound up his bleeding groin, while he told them of the true egg and the new sky. They smashed his chains and his neck-band with hammers and axes and carried him home to the royal hut, where he set unblinking eyes upon all the children he had sired during the past four years. A few were infirm, and he killed these with his voice. He summoned his wisemen, and spent the rest of his life in limping pursuit of the true egg, trying to read directions in the footprints of destruction scrawled upon the earth by Wind, taking as his map of clues the track of every twister over the savannah.

And so our tale of the Seven commences.

"What difference would it make if the sky were a different

colour?" Mgwana asked Kampinga as they were setting out
Mgwana already knew the answer, but this was his way of asking
for a tale to while away the journey.

The six age-brothers and one age-sister were setting out into
dry bush to hunt for ostrich nests. They were armed with spears
and with bolos to tangle the legs of any fleeing ostriches. They
hoped at least to bring home an ostrich egg, if not a parent. One
ostrich egg would make a tasty omelette to feed many mouths.

Ahead, the bush stretched out aridly, tangled with thorns
punctuated by occasional termite towers. Behind, they could still
see the widely spaced conical roofs of several hundred huts – a
cone being the very best shape to attract Lightning. Already that
season six members of the teeming community had been nobly
incinerated, making six less mouths to feed, so that more babies
could be born unaborted; thus the number of souls beneath the
Sky could be increased.

On some far-off day, all the souls that could possibly be born
would have been born. People would begin to give birth to beasts
instead of human babies: to speechless foals, and ostrich chicks
and bush-piglets. Man would rejoin nature again.

Or so wisemen assured the people.

After each lightning strike and conflagration, before a fresh
hut (of sticks and reeds from the lake beyond, plastered with
mud) was built in a new location, the charred ground where the
old hut had once stood was of course dug up, producing another
pit and rampart, in the search of whatever Lightning had laid
there. Sometimes this would be a diamond or a ruby, at other
times a knob of quartz, infrequently a stone egg – though never
anything which resembled the true egg of Lightning as described
by Ngana the Great.

The town was pocked with a thousand such craters, as though
boulders had bombarded it from the sky.

"What difference if the sky were green?" repeated Mgwana.

Kampinga surveyed the golden sky above the tawny bush.

"If a green sky hatched," Kampinga said, "we should soon

give birth to plants. And so would all the other animals. Our offspring would be ferns and cycads, orchids and aloes. The animal kingdom would rejoin the vegetable kingdom again. We would all return to our roots. Animals are just plants who tore up their roots and ran wild. People are just animals who stole souls from the sky, stood up, and spoke. It has all been a mistake."

That day the Seven travelled far, away and away from the teeming town of cone-huts and craters and the wide reedy lake and the forest, out into the dry bush. By evening they had reached the verge of the Plain of Grass.

Here they lay down separately in the long yellow grass and swung their bodies round like tops, each to flatten a sleeping nest. Next they dragged tangles of thorns from the bush to corral the seven nests safely.

They ate dried *tulapia* fish and drank beer from their gourds. Then the six age-brothers retired to their nests. Their age-sister Laliani visited each nest in turn and in turn enjoyed each of the brothers, commencing with Chtolo and ending with Ntenga, before retiring to her own nest to sleep soundly.

Some hunting parties consisted of three sisters and four brothers. Others, of two and five. Occasionally, six sisters and one brother. Since perhaps the customs in your country are different, I should explain that if the sisters outnumbered the brothers then it was the men who went nest-visiting. Supposing there was only one man, tradition allowed him to divide his exertions between dusk and dawn.

When the Seven rose in the morning, it was Chtolo who stumbled upon the discovery, stubbing his toe so that he yelled.

Chtolo parted some unbowed grass.

"See here!"

"What is it?" asked Madongo.

Laliani laughed. "What does it look like? Surely someone's genitals must have dropped off last night!"

The object was indeed that shape – potently so.

However, it was soon obvious to all their eyes that the discovery was as solid a piece of stone as any fossil in a cliff from the ancient days when birds still had fins, not wings, before the great lake emptied half of its creatures into the sky, thanks to the violence of the wind-giants.

Chtolo bent to pick the object up.

His hand gripped it.

That was when he fell dead, giving up his ghost with a scream of air.

In that scream the six who remained were almost deafened by the name *Ngana*.

So here were the petrified genitals of Ngana the Great.

As though from nowhere Storm brooded blackly far across the plain and some tongues of Lightning flickered.

"A man cannot hold that thing," declared Laliani. "That's because it contradicts his being. But I feel that a woman can hold it."

Before any of her brothers could deter her, she plucked up the object. Maybe it was heavier than she expected, since she almost stumbled and had to bring both hands into play. Nevertheless she straightened up, holding it – not as if it were dead stone, but more as if it were a live toad. It pulled against her hands, turning them northward.

"It points," Laliani said in wonder. "This must show the way to the true egg of Lightning. Brothers, we needn't hunt for an ostrich egg now! Our prize shall be greater by far."

So the quest began.

But first Chtolo's body had to be propped upright against thorns in the hope that Lightning might notice and incinerate him. Afterward the hunting party set off northward in the direction of the now dispersing storm.

That evening, when Laliani visited Ntenga last of all in his nest of the night, she whispered to him after making love, "Now, shall I sleep with my head to the north? Shall I place Great Ngana between my legs and let him visit me, within?"

"I do not think that would be wise or comfortable," advised Ntenga. "You might give birth to a stone baby."

"In that case, dearest brother, we might begin to return to the most ancient, solid time of all, don't you think? When plant life first diverged from the rocks. We'd be almost at the time when the sky was blinding white, before the world settled into shape. We might soon become not stone, nor even stone's sire, lava, but stone's grandsire: clouds of flaming gas."

"Dearest sister, you can't cross six crevasses in a single leap. First we must become beasts. Then plants. Unless you can lead us to the egg, in which case we may become plants immediately. Only after that, stone; then lava; then gas."

Consequently Laliani did not carry out her proposed experiment – which was perhaps just as well, since Great Ngana's parts might well have softened in her liquid warmth, attached themselves to her, and turned inside out. She might have become a man-woman.

Indeed a comic variation on the legend pretends that just such an event occurred that night; and thereafter Laliani the man-woman pointed the way, with the phallus of his-her own body.

In our version Ngana's parts remained firm stone.

The seekers walked on all the next day and the day after, spearing a couple of bush-piglets to eat their flesh and drink their blood.

On the third day the pointer which Laliani held suddenly jerked downward and became dead.

The brothers tore up grass and sieved soil through their fingers till Angwinu found what he thought at first were two little shells that had turned to stone.

"Those are a pair of Ngana's eyelids," said Laliani.

She fixed them with a paste of mud and spittle to the lids of her own left eye, blinked, and stared westward. "The trail lies that way."

Eventually Laliani led her fellow seekers to another spot where they found Ngana's other eyelids.

Wearing these too, she pointed southeast.

A long-winded variation of the legend has it that, after this, the seekers needed to recover each petrified hank of hair from Ngana's head, a hundred stone worms. In this version their search led them to every corner of the world. Thus they visited a land where the sky was several hues of blue; where no wind-giants raced whirligig, where Thunder was inarticulate – which is why I mentioned phlegmatic meteorology earlier.

They visited a country so high above the clouds that the stars shone steadily by day, sharing a black sky with the Sun. And then a realm of ice, where hills and valleys were of ice, and vegetation too, and even the crackly cows and the lions were of ice, not to mention the frigid human inhabitants. Then they visited an underwater land where white people with gills and fins hunted and herded huge fish and where their King (who sometimes ate his own people) had eight arms.

But let us ignore all this embroidery upon the plain cloth of the quest.

At last the six (plus the memory of Chtolo) arrived back at one part of the Plain of Grass which wasn't excessively remote from their hometown of cones and craters.

Laliani's stone eyelids blinked furiously and dragged her gaze downward.

The brothers tore up sheaves of grass and began to dig the yellow soil, while Laliani stood stroking her swollen belly, for she was now far advanced with child.

Thunder began to growl. "Lightning, Lightning – they will find your egg! Wind, Wind, hurry if you want to scoop up that egg and threaten Lightning!"

Thunder obviously hoped to curry favour with both. Wind started to rise. Lightning began to flash.

"Scoop faster, brothers!" urged Laliani.

"Ah!" exclaimed Kampinga, from the bottom of the pit. He hurled some more soil over his shoulders; Madongo caught it and piled it. A moment later Kampinga's fingers were brushing clean a hefty bulge – something like the ostrich egg for which they had originally set out, only larger.

"Here is the egg! We have found it!"

Angwinu, now acting as lookout, spied Cyclone twisting across the plain. Even as he called a warning, Lightning's silver spear dived at Cyclone, knocking it off course.

"My pains are coming on," announced Laliani. She sank back against the excavated rampart, drew her legs up, spread her knees wide.

Down in the pit, Kampinga squatted on the egg, warming it with his bare bottom, bouncing up and down impatiently.

Laliani's waters burst, soaking soil.

Cyclone and Lightning skirmished, while Thunder chuckled nervously.

"Ouch!" Kampinga leaped off the egg. He danced around the pit, howling with offended dignity, slapping his rump as if it were on fire.

A crack had opened right across the dome of the egg. Like the double shell of a clam, the egg had opened and shut, pinching Kampinga's buttocks.

When Madongo told Laliani what had happened, she laughed loudly. "How like a man! I'm busy giving birth. I'm splitting apart. He only had his bum nipped."

All of a sudden the crack yawned wide. Like a hinged fish-basket, the egg flipped open, revealing the dense wrinkled green meat of the egg within.

A waft of wind reached a prying finger into the crater. And what had looked like wrinkled green meat began to unwrap itself. A green leaf peeled loose, became a sheet, became a sail, then ten sails all together growing up out of the egg to flap overhead. And still more!

The new sky was unfolding from the egg! Up it billowed, spreading enormous wings, still spilling from the egg, ever flying up into the air. The new green sky!

By the time that Laliani gave birth, half an hour later, a whole new sky was in place, stretched tight across the entire dome of heaven, not a single wrinkle to be seen.

The child of Laliani and her age-brothers was a beautiful little girl. Laliani named her Yaijani, meaning "egg-leaf". The six seekers (with one other in spirit) took turns to carry Yaijani in the top half of the eggshell as they trekked back homeward to the town of craters and cone-huts; and a new world had begun.

So says the legend.

Certainly this explains why the sky is green. To some extent it also explains why we people have begun reverting back toward the beginnings of life. Already many are born with fur on their bodies and never walk upon two legs. Yet the legend is obviously misleading, too, since we are not becoming plants immediately.

The speech of the new generation is much simpler. Maybe mine is the last generation in which this legend can be told and understood. The animals who succeed us, and the plants who succeed them, will have no interest in such matters. Nor will the rocks who succeed the plants.

Yet when at last we become lively beings of fiery gas circling around the Sun, perhaps we will remember how the world once was, and in those future joyous days we will recall the legend of the Seven who found the true egg of Lightning.

Why do you frown, Stranger?

HYPERZOO

"And this," said Zoo Director Riggers, "is a hypertiger. We call it a tiger by analogy with three-dimensional creatures. It's a fierce carnivore. We believe its habits are solitary. It's the tiger of the four-dimensional world."

"Doesn't look much like a tiger to me," drawled Mrs Tarkington-Svensen, whose late husband's foundation had funded this new wing of the zoo. "In fact it looks like nothing so much as a jumble of gooey orange tubes. Like some stupid bit of modern sculpture."

Harry Svensen's tax-write-off bounty had also endowed the Museum of Contemporary Conceptual Sculpture. Unfortunately the perceptive Mr Svensen had died of a heart attack just the month before, leaving control of the bulk of his fortune to his recently acquired fifth wife, Adelle Tarkington, about whom he had not nearly been as perceptive. Except externally; she'd been a beauty queen, not recently to be sure, but not in olden days either. She was still a golden-blonde, tanned, and well-tended memorial to former glories.

"At least it's orange, Adelle," pointed out Sonya Svensen, teenage daughter of Harry's third marriage who had exercised her child-charter rights by electing to stay on with him through his fourth marriage to an ex-geisha Japanese lady conservationist and designer of avant-garde topological netsuke.

"Tigers are orange, sort of," said Sonya.

"I," proclaimed Mrs T-S, "smell a rat."

Actually there was no smell to speak of in this particular animal house apart from a crackle of ozone produced by the glow-bars of the enormous cages. Did Mrs T-S imagine that Riggers was mounting some equally enormous lucrative hoax and had in fact borrowed some mobile pneumatic conceptual art to stick in these beast pens?

"I do not believe these objects are animals from this fanciful Fourworld the university domeheads say they had dreamed up." (She wasn't very respectful about scientists.) "I think this thing is hollow. Yes, hollow, that's it."

"Hollow?" Riggers looked puzzled. "Obviously there'll be a certain amount of hollowness, else how could the hypertiger eat and excrete?"

Mrs T-S wrinkled her nose disapprovingly at his mention of excretion. She considered herself a fine lady, and high society tended to agree.

"Analogically, that's to say," Riggers hastened to add. "I mean, no 3-D animal is solid all the way through."

"Are you deliberately misunderstanding me, Dr Riggers? Are you trying to make a fool of me?"

"Adelle means it's a holo-*graph*," whispered Sonya. "I think."

Nothing wrong with Mrs T-S's hearing. "That's what I said: a hollow."

"If she could, well, poke a stick through the bars and, er, nudge it, she'd know it was for real." Sonya hesitated. "Or would she need to use a 4-D stick to make any impact?"

"You oughtn't to poke sticks through the bars," I said. "Who knows but the hyperfield could short out, and then we'd lose our specimen?"

"Oh I hardly think so," Riggers said hastily to me. "And a security guard isn't exactly qualified to pronounce!"

I *had* taken a quickie course about the Fourworld at the university, but in fact Riggers was right. The subject was still pretty much a mystery to me. Indeed, until the could-be never-never-time when the aforesaid domeheads should discover a method to four-dimensionalize a human being and translate the bold volunteer into the Fourworld, I supposed that domain must remain, of its very essence, a total mystery to almost everyone.

I wondered whether the Profs and Ph.D.s had merely been babbling when they hinted at inserting a person into the Four-world? What a voyage of exploration, what a safari that would be – through a hyper-landscape where hyperbeasts roamed! The most suitable candidate for explorer might well be a raving nut-case, a certified lunatic whose rapport with our own Threeworld was already totally out of synch.

"In any case nobody should poke captive animals with sticks," said Sonya, changing her tune. "That's medieval, like bear-baiting." She was trying to be helpful, to ensure that her Daddy's pet projects were carried on.

"Quite," agreed Riggers. He sounded relieved. Plainly he was under a strain. Not inconceivably Mrs T-S could lean on Harry's foundation to withdraw its support. Rumour had it that her lawyers had found some loophole. The hyperfields soaked up a hell of a lot of costly energy, never mind all the other mainten-ance costs. It was no secret that Mrs T-S nursed a passionate whim to fund the sending of handsome young astronauts, be-holden to her, out to the unexplored frontiers of Threespace. Since spaceflight was all Earth-orbit, battle station stuff, those frontiers weren't too far away. If NASA was to be revived, it would take a private sponsor. Mrs T-S was positive there was life on Mars and Venus and the moons of Jupiter, and couldn't understand why there shouldn't be any four-armed barbarian warriors and green-skinned princesses. She could see herself at a society ball arm in arm with her own doughty spacefaring heroes.

Even I could see that the Fourworld was more exciting – potentially – than Threespace, which simply spread out and out for zillions of miles full of vacuum, bits of rock, and balls of gas.

Potentially. The trouble was that the hyperanimals which the zoo had trapped, whilst utterly weird, didn't exactly turn the populace on as more than a seven-day wonder. How could they, when by definition you couldn't see more than a bitty part of any of them? Visiting this section of the zoo wasn't as grabbing an experience as goggling at the last few rhino alive in captivity (and alive nowhere else – score a point for pathos). But equally, if our Threeworld's livestock was diving helter-skelter down the drain in the great man-made mass extinction, undoubtedly the ecology of the Fourworld was still bursting at the seams by comparison. So far we had only netted a tiny sample, by no means enough to start talking confidently in terms of species and family trees and 4-D evolution; though Dr Riggers sometimes pretended so for public relations purposes. This had to be the zoo of the future – if only we could get a better idea of the beasts. At the moment, and perhaps forever, visiting here was like trying to admire some giant Renaissance canvas by peeping through a keyhole which only showed you inches at a time. (Cancel Renaissance. A giant abstract canvas. Jackson Pollock or some such.)

Just then the mass of orange tubes inside the cage began to twitch and pulse, and expand and shift.

"See, it's woken up," said Riggers with forced cheerfulness. "It was resting before. Now it's active."

"How convenient." Mrs T-S sniffed disdainfully, her own vision no doubt locked on a valiant cadet in space armour, bulging muscles of brass, blasting an attacking Jovian crystal-lizard to smithereens.

"I'm sure these supposed creatures can't possibly be pulled here from Mars," she went on. "Mars can't possess creatures like this. It must have, well –"

"Thoats and Zitidars," supplied Sonya. "*No*, Adelle, Burroughs made those up."

"Or if they are from Mars, the process warps them out of all recognition. Only lets poor bits of them squeeze through. That's why we should explore Mars the proper way. By rocket."

Riggers looked perplexed. "Mars, dear lady?"

"Yes, Mars. Mars is the fourth world. Every child knows that. Earth is the third world."

"Ah . . . Perhaps a slight case of cross purposes here? When we speak about the Threeworld and the Fourworld we're referring in the first case to the world of three dimensions which we inhabit: namely length and breadth and height. 'Fourworld' doesn't refer to the fourth planet. Mars is just another threeworld, part of the threeworld universe."

"*Just* another?"

"A very special and exciting planet, to be sure! But even so. The Fourworld has an extra dimension, diagonal to those other three we know and love."

"It's like this, Adelle." Sonya waggled her fingers, trying to stick them all out at right angles to each other, but quickly gave up.

Since everyone else was giving lessons to Mrs T-S, and Riggers now looked distraught, I decided to join in.

I pointed to the nearest glow-bar. "The hyperfield casts a four-dimensional net into the Fourworld, Mrs Tarkington-Svensen. It snares a fourbeast and pins it down for us, so it can't escape from the cage, though of course the fourbeast isn't all here."

"Are *you*?" she enquired. "Are you all here?"

I laughed politely at her wit. "Most of the fourbeast is still in the Fourworld, which is how it can feed itself, since we can't provide any fourfood and threefood would be no use. That would be like us trying to eat a picture of a meal on a magazine page."

"Why, that's cruel! The poor things could starve!"

All this while, the hypertiger had been expanding and changing configuration. By now it was the size of a real Bengal tiger – apart from the fact that real Bengal tigers went extinct a couple of years previous – and it resembled a spherical rug armed with teeth or claws. This started to roll back and forth, "pacing" the cage. A long pink tentacle or tube appeared near the ball and presently joined up with it. An intestine? What might have been a fourleg put in an appearance, then changed its mind.

83

It was, of course, hard to be sure of the exact anatomy of a hyperbeast even when you'd seen and filmed all sorts of aspects of it. You couldn't simply stick all your pictures together or even digitize them and feed them into a computer, and bingo. A hypertiger wasn't lots more tiger superimposed upon tiger, like a stack of film transparencies shot from different angles. The beast would have its own unique four-anatomy, evolved by the struggle to survive and breed amidst a whole hyperecology. However, we had once seen what we decided were aspects of its fourjaws chewing hyperprey to pieces, and another time we had witnessed part of its fourface and foureyes, burning bright. "Tiger" seemed to fit the bill. Approximately. Analogically.

"I mean to say," continued Mrs T-S, "it's stuck in a trap."

"Ah, but only 3-D slices of it are hampered. It can still hunt in the Fourworld," I assured her. "The geometry's different there. More complicated than here."

Riggers had revived. "Thank you, Jake," he said to me. He turned quickly to Mrs T-S. "Naturally, we have observed hyper creatures impinging on our own world in the past. At the time we didn't realize what they were. If people glimpse a meaningless shape their brains tend to impose a plausible pattern, to make sense of what they're seeing. All those tales of mythical creatures, dragons, monsters, demons, and UFO phenomena immediately make sense when we realize that people were witnessing an aspect of a hyperanimal intersecting with our own Threeworld as it went about its 4-D business. A UFO would be a hyperbird, or whatever. And now we can genuinely cage this fantastic menagerie! Isn't it wonderful? To be able to see with our own eyes the actual source of basilisks and behemoths, minotaurs and griffins, flying saucers and Bigfeet and abominable snowmen, angels and devils! Isn't that more wonderful than . . ."

Than Jovian crystal-lizards. Than Thoats and Zitidars. But he tailed off, wary of pulling any rugs out too brusquely from under Mrs T-S's cherished and fanciful dreams. He gestured grandly

84

down the air-conditioned hall paid for by Harry, and which was large enough to house a modest spacefleet under construction, destination Jupiter.

"Let's move along and see what we call a hyperpig, shall we?" He chuckled awkwardly. "Can't have all our cages full of tigers! Big fierce animals are rare, eh?"

It was a fair walk to the next cage. We had to position hyperfields a safe distance apart, which accounted for the great size of the hall. This was a further disincentive to streams of eager visitors, once the first honeymoon rapture was over. Most people like to flip quickly from channel to channel as regards experiences.

While we were walking, Sonya said, "Dr Riggers? Were angels and abominable snowmen some sort of hyperape? So will there be hyperpeople in the Fourworld too? I mean, we have animals in our own world but we got people as well. Might we see bits of ourpeople as ghosts – appearing then vanishing?"

"I'm *inclined* to doubt that, Miz Svensen." Riggers did his best not to sound patronizing. "You see, the complexities of Four-space must be such that I doubt you'd get any sort of gratuitous free-ranging speculative intelligence having a look-in evolutionarily. The fourbrain must be pretty fully occupied simply processing the, uh, complexities. Anyway, in our own case the evolution of intelligence was such a set of long-shot random chances that I doubt you'd get any repetition of the process. The odds are way against. Did you know that the eye evolved as an organ independently forty times – but intelligence only evolved *once*? Once! So: hypercreatures, sure. But not hyperhumans. Your ghosts and whatnot are glimpses of hyperbeasts which our minds try to rationalize. Except now we can pin 'em down. Here's our Fourpig."

I guess the ugliest type of pig hitherto known to the human race had got to be the Vietnamese black pig, of which two gross specimens lolled elsewhere in the zoo. However, this 3-D slice of 4-D bacon had the Vietnamese b.p. left at the starting line.

Today it was a wallowing cluster of greasy grey hairy sacs. Embedded in the mess was what might have been a giant fly's compound eye, squinting out. Oink.

"Isn't there anything *beautiful* in your zoo?" complained Mrs T-S.

"Ah well, yes . . . we have what I call the hyperpeacock yonder. Let's go see if it's displaying, hmm?"

Riggers hustled her away diplomatically from the four-oink.

"Er, but Doctor," persisted Sonya, "if you get fourpigs paralleling threepigs, and so on, why can't you have fourpeople paralleling threepeople?"

"Because those names are just analogies. We don't know enough yet. We need the funding to be able to *four-D* a person to go and take a look. If that's possible. Most things are possible with big enough funding. And then just imagine the possibilities. When the first atom was split people thought it could have no practical applications. Were they wrong! Well hell – if you'll pardon my French, Mrs Tarkington-Svensen – we already have the core of a 4-D zoo. Maybe in the Four-universe it's easier to travel from planet to planet. Maybe a fourperson in a fourrocket could reach Mars or Jupiter much faster and easier. I mean, the analogies of Mars and Jupiter, so long as those exist. Then you'd switch off the hyperfield, becomes 3-D again, and land. Never mind Jupiter, we might get to the stars. It all depends on the topology of fourspace, if you'll forgive my being technical – the way it's connected together. Oh yes," he rhapsodized, "I can see hypernauts one day. Hyperastronauts."

"Ah," said Mrs T-S. "Ah!"

"With enough funding."

The hyperpeacock was a fluttering, waxing and waning mandala of shades of blue. Cobalt, ultramarine, robin's egg, and electric blue. Some streaks of violet, almost ultraviolet. "Eyes" of green. You could easily see how someone spotting that in our sky could think they were watching a UFO.

Whether Mrs T-S's exclamation of delight related to the visible segment of fourbird, or to the prospect of hyperastronauts stepping out on to one of the larger moons of Jupiter, I never determined. At that moment Sonya – who had been lagging – screamed shrilly.

My gun was in my hand a moment later, though I didn't yet thumb the safety off.

Sonya was staring back at the fourpig pen. Something very large was hovering over the topmost glow-bars, something analogous to a free-floating furry octopus equipped with fat stubby tentacles. Or vaguely analogous to a hairy hand. Which was pulling at the glow-bars, bending them outward, opening a rather large gap.

A second monstrous hyperhand – or aspect thereof – was drifting towards us.

"Something's escaped!" shrilled Mrs T-S. "Shoot at it! Protect me."

"I don't have fourbullets," I told her.

"I don't care how many you have! Why didn't you load your gun up properly? You don't have to shoot at each finger." Oh, so she too could see the analogy.

"Let's just *run!*" cried Sonya. Suiting her actions to her words, she scampered away towards the distant exit. "Come *on*, Adelle!" she called back.

Surely nothing had escaped; though the fourpig looked likely to, soon. In which case something had *arrived* – to open our cages.

"Discretion is the better part of –" said Riggers. He caught Mrs T-S's arm and began urging her along as fast as he could. I paced fast alongside, keeping an eye on the hyperhand behind us; but this seemed to be shrinking, thank goodness.

Oh well, we reached the exit and got out into the ordinary part of the zoo. More modest animal houses, compounds, restaurant, popcorn stall, cityscape beyond with office blocks, university hill to our right. Parties of visiting schoolkids – and ourselves a moment later – were all staring at the shape that bestrode the city.

How to describe it? Can't. There's no good analogy.

I guess in the Fourworld intelligence indeed developed, but in a different class of creatures: more like walking hairy squids, with everbranching tentacles and frogspawn eggs – though *that* was only an aspect.

Maybe more important: a 4-D world is a hell of a lot larger than a 3-D world. It packs in a whole lot more, and if you could sort of *unfold* it alongside ours – which you can't – it would occupy a far vaster amount of space. The scale's different, quite different.

So the big boys of the Fourworld are noticeably bigger than any human being. Or rhino. Or whale.

What Riggers had in his zoo, I realized, wasn't hypertigers and hyperpigs. The captive creatures had to be bits of, well, 4-D shrews or dormice or dinky little hummingbirds. Nature's miniatures. Maybe as humble as bugs.

Compared to the masters of the Fourworld, us Threepeople led a very superficial life. To a 4-D eye we were flat and paper-thin. But more than that, we were also pretty tiny. Easy to miss noticing. Until we built ourselves a hyperfield, on which the Fourthings could at least stub a toe. Until we made a 4-D intrusion which stuck out like a sore thumb.

Shortly after, the ripping began. The city kind of screeched like parcel tape being torn free. I don't mean that the world bent up in the air or that buildings toppled or anything. Everything stayed put. Yet at the same time it was being . . . parted from the rest of 3-D country, shifted, moved over somewhere else.

These days there's a blank at the city limits. And nothing beyond. Absolutely nothing.

Up in the sunless, though bright, sky there are large things like clouds of frogspawn that seem to look at us.

The power's off, so we can't play any more hypergames, and provisioning the population is going to be a swine before long.

We're still feeding the normal zoo animals, but we'll have to kill them and eat them all, even if we do have the last rhinos in existence. That should spin out food stocks for about one extra day. Come to the great zoo barbecue! Hippoburger. Loin of lion. Parrot kebabs. Buckets of blood to make sausages.

As if we didn't have enough problems, the 4-D mob play games with our Threeworld, stretching bits of it out so that a hundred-yard walk takes an hour, interposing barriers in our way, and making loose scenery and people disappear then putting them back into the Threeworld somewhere else; as often as not in mirror image so that a truck will suddenly have its steering wheel on the right and a mole on your right cheek will now be on your left cheek. Seeing what'll happen. How it'll affect us. Stirring the ants' nest up a little.

Though to my own senses I'm solid and three-dimensional the same as everything else around, I can't help feeling convinced that I'm flat – and that other people are flat, and the whole of the city is flat. I feel that I'm part of a photograph. It's an action-photograph, as it were; a living photograph. People can move around, climb stairs, enter rooms; no problem. But the photo has edges beyond which no one can stray. And compared with whatever 4-D intelligence is examining this photograph, I'm just a flat picture.

If we're flat, how do we go inside a building? How does our frogspawn spy us inside a room? Well, our inside and our outside don't make a scrap of difference to the masters of the Fourworld. It's all the same flat surface to them. Er, by analogy. Always by analogy.

I've been snatched and reversed left to right and put back in a different place once already. This happens without

any warning

a sudden dizzying rush, though it seems to last longer this time taking me to

the brown bear compound. Oops, I'm inside it. Grass and bushes and funlogs, a dirty pool, and the tall wall sloping inward so that no Bruin can claw its way up and out.

Maybe they think people with clothes on look pretty much like bears, especially when the three bears are up on their hind legs like now, sniffing the air and squinting at me.

Up on their hind legs, before dropping back on all fours to lumber towards me.

What happens if you put a spider in an ant's nest, or stick an ant in a spider's web? Hey, let's see.

Good thing I'm an armed security guard. Bad thing for the bears. No choice, really. We would have had to shoot them soon.

Out with the gun, off with the safety.

Click.

Click.

Click.

Oh my God, something has taken the cartridges from inside of the clip. A 4-D creature can reach inside a shut-up room, a locked box, with no bother at all. Or reach inside a gun and empty it. Bit fiddly on this scale, but they must have used some tiny 4-D tools. Or grown extra tiny branch-tentacles. Micro fingers. No bother.

Click.

"Help me!"

There's a clump of frogspawn overhead, watching.

Letters from the Monkey Alphabet

A

Mr Zoo Director,
READ THIS! I am a reincarnated human being! Call your
Keepers off!

B

That's better. I was scared you might think I'm the sort of
monkey that types out *Hamlet* by accident once in a zillion years.

I *know* I'm a chimp – not a monkey. I was making a joke. You
need a sense of humour in my position. How would you like
being locked up in a cage?

Okay, so I kept on trying to escape from Chimp Island. But
you might have realized there was something odd about me when
I swam the moat. Again and again. Chimps don't like water, eh?

And later on you might have given me some paper and paints
or something to amuse the crowds. That way we could have got
into communicating a bit sooner.

Oh, so you noticed I was in the habit of making funny signs?
How was I supposed to know the American Sign Language?
When I was a human woman I wasn't dumb. Meaning deaf and
dumb.

And talking of dumb in the stupid-clever sense, is that why you farmed me out to the Lab for the pregnancy experiment? Because I looked and acted above average intelligence, and they wanted a chimp with a high IQ to inseminate? Or were you just getting rid of a nuisance who was always trying to pick the lock?

Well, the Lab sent me back. I got away from those idiots who were uncrating me. This time I've reached a keyboard.

Goodness, man, bathe in my reflected glory! Enjoy! This zoo's going to have a zillion visitors tomorrow. Just as soon as the news gets out. I'm the living proof that people are reincarnated when they die.

C

I want to know about my baby, too. They wouldn't even let me hold him. They just whisked him away in case I ate him or something. I suppose he was worth more than gold to them. Though why anyone should want to crossbreed chimps and humans, I don't know.

He *is* okay, isn't he? They didn't just dissect him, or something?

They passed him over to a human foster mother, right? That's why they sent me back.

D

Why has no animal ever before upped and said, "I used to be a human being"? Well, I believe that hardly any people ever get reborn as any of the higher animals – let alone as people. Most people get reborn much lower down the scale. As rats. Or fish. Or worms. That's all they deserve. Maybe I'm the only person whose karma was good enough to rise even this high up the rebirth ladder. That's what I think.

What do you mean: people mightn't like to know that?

E

Of course I can prove it. My name as a human was Doris Hoffman. I lived in the Shambala Commune just by Lake Chabot in Alameda County, California. I think I can still remember my Social Security number. Here goes . . .

F

What do you mean: some people might think a teenage runaway drop-out deserved to be reborn as a chimp?

Let me tell you mister, I was twenty-two when the VW went over the cliff. Okay, so we were high at the time. I'm four years older now. I've had a lot of time to think: on Chimp Island, then in the cage. I've matured. And I'm a mother too. Even if I was zonked out with chloroform when I got fertilised.

I've given birth.

G

What do you mean: people mightn't like to think that my sort of person is higher up the evolutionary scale? I lived a spiritual life in Shambala. Jesus was born in a grubby stable and *he* lived like a drop-out most of the time . . .

Of course I'm not comparing myself with Jesus!

Nor with Mary, either! Even if I have just experienced a sort of virgin birth.

No, I am *not* saying that the new Messiah has just been born in a primate lab!

What do you mean: "Beast"? Don't you lay any of that occult crap on me. You've been watching too many horror movies. Let's talk sense. Please.

H

When I was reborn, I thought, "Wow!" because I knew at once. All my memories came through: parents, high school, all that crap. Then running away to Shambala. I thought I was going to focus my eyes and see a doctor holding me; and boy, would I amaze him when I spoke out!

But it was my Mom-chimp holding me instead. And I couldn't speak. Wrong sort of windpipe and vocal chords. Anyway, she wouldn't have understood. I could only squeak and hang on to her fur.

My baby never even got a chance to hang on to me.

I

I didn't get much chance to communicate in the Lab, either. Those dudes were into biology, not linguistics. And I was sick a lot of the time. Or drugged. They had their work cut out to stop me from aborting.

Oh, I did have a TV set to amuse me when I wasn't feeling poorly. Not that they noticed anything significant about my viewing patterns. And toys, too: I had a stack of toys. As if *I* was the baby.

But no paints or crayons. Must have thought I might swallow them.

Why crossbreed chimps and humans, anyway? What does the public think about it?

J

The public don't know anything, do they?

K

Do they?

L

Why's that? Why does the Lab want chimphumans for? Just out of curiosity?
   Or as industrial slaves?
   Or house slaves?
   Or to crew spaceships?

M

guess not. What does that leave?
   War. It leaves war, doesn't it? They want chimphumans in orbital battle stations, because chimphumans are more expendible? Or maybe chimps can take years of zero gravity better than people do; but chimps on their own aren't brainy enough?
   That can't be it. They could never risk a *monkey* pushing the button.
   Oh, I get it. It's to test out new germs and viruses. They need humans who aren't legally human for test subjects.
   Who's funding the Lab, anyway? Department of Defence?
   Just because I'm a "drop-out" don't assume I'm unpatriotic. I'll remind you that caring about your country doesn't mean agreeing with every damn thing. First of all it means loving *the land*.

N

You won't tell me, will you? Okay, so you won't.

But that has nothing to do with The Main Thing: I'm the firs
person in the whole history of the human race to be reincarnated
and able to prove it.

I guess it's lucky in a way I was reborn as a chimp. Otherwise
supposing I'd been reborn as a human child remembering m
past life as Doris Hoffman, you could have tried to explain m
away as a mutation, with strange mental powers. The power t
speak at birth. The power, in the womb, to pick up the vibes o
Doris Hoffman and take her memories over. As if my mind too
a photograph of her mind, since I didn't have any other identit
going for me at that stage. Yes, you'd say that I imprinte
telepathically on dying Doris.

But you can't argue with the facts, when I'm visibly a chimp.
can see that in the mirror.

And I still want to see my baby.

O

Maybe you'd even try to make out I was able to copy Doris' min
with my rapport powers – hers particularly – because she wa
high on Dream Dust plus Fairy Fire when the VW went crump.

You can't say that when I'm a chimp, though.

Look, I scratch under my hairy armpits. Here's a flea.

P

Pardon my exuberance. You can expect me to be a bit spaced o
after my time on Chimp Island, then shut in a cage, then lease
out to the Lab. I mean, it's stressful.

Still, I came through with flying colours, mentally. Would you
ave done as well?

If only I'd been able to communicate sooner!

But no way could I. Not till I got to this typewriter.

Word processor, whatever you like to call it.

Good machine, this. I like the way my words pop up on the TV
creen. It even corrects my spelling. Don't worry, I'll be careful.
Chimps aren't gorillas, you know.

Q

ncidentally, as Doris Hoffman I never got pregnant. You can
heck that out with the guys at Shambala. They ought to remem-
er; it wasn't so long ago. Doris always took the Pill, when she
emembered to.

Look, I do want to see my baby, even if he is a half a chimp. I
on't mind – me, I'm all chimp. So it's the human bit that's weird.

R

read somewhere that humans and chimps are ninety-nine per
ent compatible in the proteins, or something. That's how you
an fertilise a chimp egg with human sperm.

You don't suppose if a human woman took Dream Dust, and
yped it up with Fairy Fire, that she could sort of dream her
omb back through time, and conceive a baby that looks like a
onkey?

Oh, but I'm forgetting: people aren't descended from
onkeys. So that couldn't happen. It's the other way round:
onkeys are descended from people, way back when. I read that
 a magazine too.

S

Isn't it about time you set up a press conference? I mean, w
might all be hit by a meteor, or the San Andreas fault could blow

This news is gonna enhance the spirituality of people all roun
the globe. I know that everyone else has sick karma. The DoD
are even polluting outer space now. Most everyone gets rebor
as a worm or a jellyfish or a spider.

T

And it'll bring this zoo a lot of publicity. Money as well. You'll b
able to let the other animals out of their cages. You'll be able t
build a Lion Island and Bear Island and everything.

Personally I'll move into an apartment. A luxury penthous
one, with security guards. Just as soon as I sell rights to my stor
I'll be able to pay for all that. But you'll do well out of it too, s
long as you have the balls to call that press conference, and n
clear it with the DoD first. Then it'll be a *fait accompli*. Anyway
the DoD only fund the Lab, not this zoo – right?

U

The DoD's *bad* karma. I know. Doris Hoffman's Daddy worke
for them in Albuquerque. That's why she ran away.

Why *I* ran away. Me. I had really special karma, good enoug
to make chimp in the next life. My Daddy will probably onl
make a scorpion or tarantula. Mom – my human Mom, I mean
she'll be a dung beetle when she dies. Sweep, sweep, sweep.

V

They didn't even let me hold my baby for a little. But I got a peek at him anyhow: all hairy, just like me.

W

Who was the sperm donor? I suppose they have to keep that sort of thing secret. Otherwise I'm his old lady, in a funny sort of way. His old lady's a chimp.

X

You think it might scare people? This isn't how people usually imagine reincarnation. But it's what the eastern wisdom books all tell you. The way you behave in life decides whether you'll become a lower being or a higher one afterwards. If you're a dog with good karma, you'll get a turn as a human next time round. But every soul screws it up once it's inside a man or woman. Greed, selfishness, cruelty. We're always slipping right back down the evolutionary ladder again. I just slipped a little way. And I can remember: that's the Main Thing. I've got continuity. That's what I can tell the world about: the continuity of all creation, worms and bugs and rabbits and men. The spiritual ecology. The great roundabout of souls.

Are you a vegetarian? You ought to be. I was.

Y

Don't worry about the DoD. Just as soon as the news breaks, they'll be discredited. There'll be no more slaughter. Peace and harmony. Love.

Z

This zoo could be rebuilt beautifully. It should be. All those lousy cages. Even this office of yours has bars on the window. Though that didn't stop me busting in through the door. I'm pretty smart for a chimp. I ought to be. I'm a reincarnated human woman. So just keep the Keepers away from me, and call that press conference, huh? Soon.

It'll be a fun thing, too. We'll amaze the world. I haven't had much fun since Doris last popped Dust and Fairy Fire. Still, those helped her karma, didn't they?

To: Major James D. Zimmerman

Dear Jim:

I haven't the slightest idea how this got printed out over your terminal. She must have pressed more keys than I thought. Naturally I'm very sorry. But as I've pointed out, we're severely under-financed here.

Anyway, if this stuff does get printed out somewhere embarrassing, don't worry. I've told you, our own code is just one digit different from Hayward Psychiatric's. So the explanation's quite simple: the print-out came from the nut-house. From some drug scrambled kid they're trying to sort out with computer interaction. You can square that, can't you? If it arises. Sure you can.

Meanwhile, we're locking Doris up in quarantine out of harm's *ay.*

Cordially,
Rick

.S. Good thing it was me in the office when she bust in and started *ping sense. Though Lord, who would ever have guessed it: that* *incarnation's* true? *I might tell you, Jim – in strictest confidence* *I was nearly tempted to go ahead and call that news conference.* *iood thing I did know why the DoD's so buttoned up about the* *ossbreeding biz – you do get a bit indiscreet on Wild Turkey, old* *n.*

.P.S. But we could *do with much better accommodation for the* *ig cats. And all the bears. She's right there. And a new aquarium* *uilding. How about it?*

.P.P.S. And just in case you think I'm kidding, come visit Doris *i quarantine, if you wish. I'll lay on a typewriter for the occasion.* *but come alone, and don't bring anything silly. Such as a gun. My* *:eepers have reactions like cheetahs. In fact, they all deserve* *etter pay. So do I. But that's peanuts compared with a new* *lephant house.*

DAY OF THE WOLF

Joshua Chagula swung his Tanzanian-built Land Rover off the main road and headed down the winding lane, muddy from fresh rainfall. The hedgerow was confetti-strewn with hawthorn flowers, and now that the sun had come out again poppies and willowherb set the verge ablaze.

Joshua was glad to leave the broken metalled road with its water-logged pits and potholes, some of them treacherously deep. Already today he had passed one break-down and one burnt out derelict. The main routes through the Northamptonshire National Park were especially poor due to the heavy traffic which still used them to gain access to the Midlands, where industry survived, whether in native hands or managed by Africans.

There was much charm, to his eyes, in the tumbledown overgrown villages of this sector of England, and he took delight in the rural lanes still linking them. In his heart he hoped that several such stretches of hedgerow might survive the reafforestation project. Yet this couldn't really happen. Already the oak and ash forests of the ancient, true landscape were spreading far out from the nuclei of the primary forest sites which had survived all the ravages of the English.

Soon, one such great swathe of oak wood rose ahead, surrounded by many hundreds of acres of new plantings, the tending of which provided a reasonable amount of native employment. In a few more years the village of Oakley Gibion would be quite cut off from the sight of open, rolling fields. For the fields would be fields no longer; Oakley Gibion would have returned to its original status as a forest settlement.

Presently, as he passed through sun-dappled woodland, his eye was momentarily caught by a gleam, a tiny detail, something out of place.

He braked and reversed back down the lane, then scanned the underbrush of hazel, hawthorn and blackthorn with his binoculars.

Eventually – for he was a patient man – he distinguished a line which was too straight and thin to be that of a sapling.

Was it a wire? The sun may have caught it as he passed.

Stretching up into a tree?

He climbed out, swinging his rifle over his shoulder, and made his way into the wood.

And of course, as he'd feared, the wire was part of a snare, designed to hoist its hapless victim – presumably a red deer – aloft by the leg or the neck.

Joshua smiled grimly to himself as he sprung the trap. Much as he hated poaching, just this once the poachers would be a help to him.

He whistled as he got back into the Land Rover, tossing the coiled wire on to the passenger seat and laying his gun across it.

"Now they can't complain that a wolf has gobbled up some old grandmother!" he thought.

Now the Parish Council couldn't put in some preposterous claim for compensation, nor demand that he go out and shoot that valuable animal. Not with this evidence against them.

By the time he arrived in Oakley Gibion, though, Joshua had begun to wonder whether the villagers might not claim that what was obviously a deer snare was in fact intended for the supposedly marauding wolf . . .

He parked on the village green, where a dozen fat young sheep were tethered, cropping perfect circles in the long grass. An old, ragged man with an unlit pipe in his mouth and a knobbly stick in his hand was keeping an eye on them. A couple of tanners worked outside the doors of their thatched ironstone cottages,

103

boiling stripped oak bark to treat leather destined for shoes, for which this county was famous.

Joshua was assailed by other doubts, too. Really, a grandmother was a most *unlikely* victim of a wolf attack. That wasn't because wolves preferred young meat to old – naturally they would pull down the stragglers of any herd, whether young and feeble, or old and infirm. But human beings simply didn't move around in herds, with faltering toddlers and hobbling grandmothers bringing up the rear. Grandmothers tended to stay at home in their cottages, and lock the door at night.

So how did a wolf manage to kill a grandmother? No, more than merely kill her: *eat* her?

Had the unfortunate grandmother in actual fact died of natural – or assisted – causes, and then been put out in the woods as wolf-bait, to cause trouble?

Joshua felt most suspicious about the whole affair by now. Dealing with the survivors of the English was difficult at the best of times. And indeed Joshua prided himself on his ability at this. Not for him the cynical advice to tourists and foreign residents that if you run over a native with your vehicle you had best keep on driving till you reach the next police post. Yet he sensed that something was not quite right here.

The two tanners and the shepherd regarded him blankly, hardly acknowledging his presence. But then, as was the way of these things in native villages, word had got around and people appeared from all over. In particular they boiled out of the pub, *The Royal Oak*, where they had no doubt been playing table skittles for halfpenny stakes, tossing the wooden "cheese" with a great thunder and clatter on to the stout table with its up-swooping net at the back, letting out whoops of innocent excitement . . .

Men and women pressed around the Land Rover, a few still clutching flagons of warm, flat ale.

Joshua quickly located the chairman of the Parish Council, John Merriwell, who also happened to be the landlord of *The*

Royal Oak – and in whose back garden, Joshua recalled, there was barbecue equipment supposedly intended for sheep roasts: bricks, steel gratings, charcoal . . .

Joshua shoved the door of the Land Rover open, clearing a space for himself. Stepping out, he flourished the coils of wire.

"What's this, then, eh, *Bwana* Merriwell?"

John Merriwell stared at the snare as though he had never seen such a thing in his life before.

"Eh? I don't know, do I? Some wire. You aren't going to try and catch the wolf with that, are you? We want it *shot*, Mr Chagula. Or else we damn well want a gun licence to protect our flocks and families from this lunacy!"

"Now, now," said Joshua soothingly. "'Lunacy' is a case of getting one's facts mixed up. The fact is that someone," and he eyed the crowd of villagers, but Merriwell most of all, "*someone* has been trying to snare deer – which, you know, are protected by the World Wildlife Fund, of which I have the honour to be a warden."

An old man spat.

"Another fact is that Granny Butler has been eaten by one of your precious wolves! And I hear you're reintroducing them *bears* now, over in Rockingham Forest. Are we going to see bears here soon, as well as wolves?"

Joshua sighed. Really, dealing with English villagers was like dealing with children. A kindly firmness was required.

He tossed the snare back into the Land Rover, his point made.

"Of course there will be bears . . . Now, I *know* what that wire was for. But I'm prepared to overlook it this once, since no animal was actually harmed. Just so long as there is no repetition of this, *Bwana* Merriwell! Do you understand?"

John Merriwell growled, and nodded.

"I shall be coming by more often. I hold you responsible, John. Remember the penalty, if I happen to find any pasties or sausages made of *venison* on your premises: forfeiture of your licence."

"What about Granny Butler?"

"Ah yes. Her. She lived up in Plumpton Wood, right? I'm not at all satisfied that she was eaten by a wolf."

"Oh, aren't you now? Well, there happens to be a witness – who barely escaped being eaten, herself!"

The crowd parted, as if on cue (oh yes, they were up to their old tricks!), and a girl of eleven or twelve years dressed in a red cape with the hood fastened by a bow stepped pertly through. It was little Joy Butler, Joshua saw. Her Granny had sewn that cape for her out of an ancient riding jacket, some years ago, and though it was rather small for her now she refused to pass it on.

"Oh, Mr Chagula," she piped up, "my Granny was feeling ill, so my Mum sent me up through the woods to take her a home-made walnut cake and a bottle of elderflower wine, to do her good."

"So she was feeling ill, was she? *Very* ill?"

"Just a little bit ill." Joy simpered, and twirled her red cape.

Joshua filed away the fact of Granny Butler's illness and, yes, confinement to bed in her cottage.

"I didn't run all the way to Granny's, so that I wouldn't break the bottle. And up in the wood I saw one of your wolves skulking about."

"All on its own? Wolves are highly sociable animals, my dear! They have an admirable social system of their own. They have been grossly maligned by human beings for far too long. Oh, it has been such a smear campaign, driving them to the verge of extinction – along with so many other worthy creatures! – an extinction from which, I am happy to say, they are now recovering nicely, and recovering their old haunts. As are the bison in America, thanks to the sterling efforts of the Indians."

"I don't know nothing about America," said Joy. "But there were such lovely flowers in the wood that I thought Granny would love a bunch of them to help her recover. There were purple foxgloves –"

"But foxgloves are poisonous. They contain digitalis. Why ever would you pick poison flowers for your Granny?"

106

"You can't be poisoned by looking."

No, but you can be poisoned by a bite of cake or a glass of elderflower wine with something in it . . . And all because Granny Butler was a surplus mouth to feed? Little Joy had been careful to mention taking a gift of walnut cake. Was she implicated too, so young? Really, wolves possessed a finer social system than these damned villagers of Oakley Gibion.

Or was this something even more sinister?

"Weren't you scared when you saw the wolf, little Joy?"

"Oh, but I've seen a wolf about in those woods once or twice before. That is, since you began re-introducing them . . . This one was sniffing about in the woodland flowers. The sunbeams were dancing through the trees. It was ever so nice. Anyway, off the wolf ran – and I carried on. But when I got to my Granny's house, her door was wide open. I went in, and that wolf was *inside* the cottage – with its great big ears and its great big eyes and its great big mouth. It was on Granny's bed! And Granny wasn't there at all!"

"So you see," said John Merriwell, "the wolf ate Mrs Butler up. In her own home, too. And it was waiting for little Joy."

"I ran and ran," said the girl. "My Dad took an axe up to the cottage – he works on the plantings, you know – but the wolf had run away by then."

"So we sent for you, Mr Chagula, *Bwana*, seeing as it was one of your Wildlife Fund wolves, and we can't do nothing about that, can we?" Merriwell glanced significantly in the direction of the snare in the Land Rover.

Joshua reached in and took his rifle.

It was a good thing that he understood the natives. An nexperienced game warden might have made a fool of himself at his point.

Obviously the villagers couldn't tell him the truth in so many words. They had to concoct this absurd slander about a murder-ous wolf. But he knew. He knew.

Ejecting the cartridge from the firing chamber, he pocketed it.

From one of the many other pockets in his bush jacket, he took out the shining silver cartridge he kept in reserve, and slid it home.

He patted little Joy on the head and offered her a bar of *Kilimanjaro* chocolate, which she seized eagerly.

"I'll handle this," he told the crowd. "But mind you, leave the *real* wolves alone. They're innocent. And they're here to stay – for good."

"For evil!" called out somebody. Joshua couldn't identify who it was.

"Yes," he thought, "for evil . . ." In a sense. In a very strange sense indeed. Of course, experienced game wardens knew something about this, well, undercurrent. But there was little point in reporting it back to Regional HQ in London Town, thence to HQ in Nairobi. It would merely be assumed that the warden in question had succumbed to one of the notorious maladies of England, which often seemed as much psychological as physical: the Grey Fever, or the Damp, or Apathy.

And really, it *was* only an undercurrent, something trivial compared with the main current of the great ecological reshaping of this stripped land, which had lost all sense of its original nature.

It was the rape of the land which had sent these people forth, to rape lands not their own. It would be healed, and they would be healed.

Or would they be?

Was it so trivial after all?

Already strange symptoms showed forth. Any warden worth his salt suspected this, from time to time. Wardens were the only Africans closely enough in touch with the rural heart of the people, to guess it. ("In touch," he thought, "with the heart of oak. Of ancient oak, and ash . . .") Wardens dealt with these symptoms as best they could, improvising, trusting to their instincts; and only seldom, during the immensely long evenings when sundowner followed sundowner, did a warden really confide his worries and useful hints to another. By which time they were usually "plastered", as the locals put it, on some foaming nutty ale in some remote village station far removed from the ecological certainties of the planners in Nairobi. Seen from the air, of course, or from London Town or Nairobi, the multi-decade plan was proceeding magnificently.

Joshua's route to Plumpton Wood took him through the dilapidated churchyard. Worn, wordless headstones, healthy with yellow lichen, canted this way and that amidst the grass, some of which was scythed, most of which was rank and lush. Good fodder, this. No bells had rung out from the church tower for many years. It they did, it would probably fall down.

Supposing, that is, that anyone was interested in ringing bells . . .

He paused, noticing trampled grass in a far corner of the graveyard.

Forcing his way through the herbage, he discovered a heap of yellowy soil – as though some huge mole had burrowed up here from under a grave, tipping the memorial stone aside.

Someone had been buried recently, in this secluded corner. But there was no withered posy of wild flowers. Rather, a rough-cut stave had been jammed into the soil. Cloves of garlic were tied to it.

"Be alert for little signs," he reminded himself. Heaving the stave out of the soil, he found the buried end pared to a wicked, fire-blackened point. Hastily he thrust it back.

As though someone had been buried . . . or someone had burrowed out . . . ?

Was the tip really blackened by fire? Or was it with dried blood?

With all his weight he thrust down on the stave, driving it deeper and deeper till it met some obstruction: stone, or coffin . . .

If he asked the villagers about this, they would meet his questions with blank stares of ridicule and incomprehension.

With silent insolence. What business of his was the churchyard, after all?

He mopped his brow, though it was cool in the graveyard underneath the elms.

Oh for the dryness and the clarity of the light of Moshi, under Kilimanjaro – with his white pate and his flowing locks of clouds! Oh for the brightness.

Shouldering his rifle again, he hoped that he was not succumbing to the Damp or the Grey Fever.

It was a sunny day, now. The sun shone down as brightly as it could, for this latitude. Yet wherever foliage shaded the ground, the real truth was told . . .

"And that's what we're aiming to do: shade the whole land of England with the ancient forests . . ."

It couldn't be, could it, that when the English first tore down their forests, laying the land bare for farming and destroying the habitat of the wolves and deer and bears in the process, that then at the same time a certain clarity had entered their souls? Could it be that the wolves and bears – of the soul! – were banished as much by the increase in light, as anything? Then ensued laws, a constitution and the Church of England, as remote from ritual and mystery as any public health department.

"The English," he thought, contriving a grim pun, "never *bared* their souls thereafter . . ."

And now the bears of the soul were back in Rockingham Forest.

Cheered, nonetheless, by his witticism, he resumed his safari up to the cottage in Plumpton Wood.

With its old sagging slate roof patched with rusty corrugated iron, Granny Butler's cottage resembled a gingerbread house. Inside was impeccably tidy – except for the patchwork-quilted bed, which was in disorder as though it had been slept in recently.

Joshua felt the sheets.

Cold, of course.

He could find no bloodstains.

But there were hairs a-plenty: wiry black hairs which could hardly have come from a Grandmother's whitening, thready head.

He stepped outside and cast around for spoor: broken twigs, pebbles turned aside . . .

As if in answer, from deep in the wood came a single mournful howl.

He set off in quick pursuit of the sound, trampling through purple dead-nettles and claret-stained wood woundwort, cursing his carelessness as he almost stepped on a rare orchis. Columns of ivy cloaked some of the trees, with occasional balls of mistletoe high up, like rooks' nests.

The howl sounded again, and now it was closer. The wolf was heading back towards the cottage. Unshouldering his gun, he decided to wait. It was better this way. With his green ranger's jacket and his black face, he faded into the background more effectively than any dough-faced Englishman. Besides, how they sweated. Even in this climate, they gave off body odour.

He had guessed correctly. This was indeed the wolf's private path. Presently it slunk into sight at the end of the glade, then trotted forward confidently. A handsome beast; female, he was sure. But old, quite old.

Lining it up in his sights, he examined her eyes, magnified, for signs of errant humanity.

When she was ten yards away the wolf saw Joshua.

Without shifting his finger from the trigger, he called out, "Granny! Mrs Butler!"

Baring her yellow teeth in a snarl, the wolf bounded at him. Dropping the rifle slightly, so that it was now aimed at the beast's heart, he squeezed the trigger. Startled wood pigeons clattered out of the trees.

The wolf tumbled on towards him. But she was already dead. He walked a few steps and turned her with his boot.

For a moment, weakness, doubt and depression swept over him like an instant bout of cold.

"Oh God, I've shot a wolf. A precious, wonderful wolf. Even if she was old, and a bit grizzled, I've shot a *wolf*, that I swore to protect."

He started hacking at the ground with the butt of his gun to dig a trench deep enough to bury the corpse. The rifle butt was hardly the ideal tool, but the compacted leaf mould and friable soil beneath scattered easily.

He lugged the corpse into the shallow trench and covered it over with his own hands. For a while he sat beside the grave in silent vigil and weariness.

Obviously he couldn't officially report shooting the wolf. Nor could he tell the villagers of Oakley Gibion exactly what he had done. If he did, he would be drawn into their sticky predicament like a fly into a web. He would be infected with the same symptom which was creeping up out of the tree-shaded soil of England, as a night mist creeps.

Officially he could know nothing about this incident. But at least he could indicate that he understood, and sympathised – while disapproving. Thus his working relationship with them would remain effective. And he could watch and ward as the forests marched over the land, and the deer bounded through them, and the wolves hunted the deer in packs, and the bears ambled about.

But he knew now for sure: that as the greenwood spread, so also was the ancient soul coming out of its hiding place.

How long would it be, in the old villages buried in the fastnesses of the national forest, before the witches danced again?

Joshua hoped that before that happened, he would have been posted back to the bright sanity of Nairobi or Moshi in a more senior administrative capacity.

He stood up. Shouldering the burden of his gun, and his responsibility, he trekked back down towards Oakley Gibion.

THE MOLE FIELD

"That's the church up there!" exclaimed Ruth.

Squat tower and red-tiled roof peered over the brown of the hill. Like a stooping grandfather the building looked shrunken by age. The Cross of St George fluttered on a flagpole. This was New Year's Day so she could understand a flag being flown, but why was it at half mast? Was the village in mourning for the death of the old year, grieving for the past?

"The sign says *Chapel* Lane," said Alan.

"Yes, and the other road was Church Lane, but it didn't lead anywhere, did it?" Only to a cul-de-sac of bungalows and a few parked cars.

Maybe they ought to have left their Metro and followed the field path behind a stand of trees, but a low gusty grey sky was distributing a chilly gruel of drizzle. Amazing that in such a tiny village as Pritwell you could lose the church. Surely there was vehicle access somewhere? Yet Pritwell itself was well lost down a twisty minor road cloaked in trees. Not a soul in sight; people would be nursing their hangovers.

They had been told about Pritwell by a lively Yugoslav women whom they met at a pre-Christmas party. Dana and her husband Bill had lived in Pritwell some ten years earlier, though they didn't stay too long. "An evil place," Dana said. "There's no pub," Bill commented. According to Dana the village had housed an old woman, now dead, who practised witchcraft. She made wax dolls of her enemies and stuck pins into these inside the church, where she supposedly held black magic ceremonies. The little church also boasted some peculiar medieval wall paintings. ·

Dana never explained how the old woman was able to use the church for devilry if her antics were well known, unless everyone in the village, vicar included, was either terrified of her or else an accomplice. Dana and Bill seemed neither. Perhaps Dana was spinning Alan a mischievous yarn, knowing that he was a writer of horror novels. She certainly sparked his interest – in those wall paintings. Precious few frescoes survived in English churches. That was because they were viewed as Popish during the Reformation. If they survived the sixteenth-century zeal for whitewash, a hundred years later they ran the gauntlet of the Puritans. Pritwell was safely off the beaten track.

Alan turned the car up narrow Chapel Lane and, sure enough, they soon passed a Methodist chapel built of red brick with corrugated iron roof, before coming to a cattle grid. The potholed road beyond led through tussocky, muddy pasture grazed by Friesians and studded with brown mole-heaps, round to a manor house and farm. At the bend in the road was the church gate, a ricketty in-and-out affair secured by a loop of blue baling twine. A patch of stones and mud outside the gate provided a single parking bay. A narrow, wire-fenced path led away past trees that sheltered the graveyard, no doubt emerging at the top of Church Lane. That must be the route to church for most parishioners.

The gate was a tight squeeze.

"Wonder how they get coffins into the graveyard?" mused Alan. "Probably don't any more. Cremate them in town." He read off the dates on some nearby gravestones, which were all small, canted, weather-worn, and lapped by long wet grass. Eighteen hundreds, some seventeen hundreds. "Wonder if *she's* buried here? Dana's witch? That looks a newish stone over there. And fresh earth. Hmm, after ten years? Must be moles. Never mind her. Don't want to get our shoes soaked." And his fawn corduroy jeans, and her long russet tweed skirt. "Let's see those frescoes."

"Alan."

"What is it, Ruthie?"

114

He must have mistaken the angle of her pointing.

"That's just a death's-head, carved over the porch."

"No, higher. Look at the way the flag's blowing. Look at the weathercock; it's facing in a different direction."

"Must be stuck. Hey Ruthie, let's not *scare* ourselves." He winked, and added, "Prematurely."

Yes, he was going into the church to scare himself. Like a kid. Alan hoped to psych himself up into an idea, an inspiration; but it should be nothing to do with Dana's witch, which was a banal idea. Wax dolls and magic; blah. The wall paintings, on the other hand, had sounded heretical the way that Dana described them.

Ruth suspected that the frescoes might simply turn out to be badly drawn, daubs produced by peasants whose only knowledge was of the Bible read to them from the pulpit week after week. Yet Alan might suss out something about Templars and unholy grails, or pagan practices and conspiracy, the sort of subterranean conspiracy which burrows through the underground of history from its starting point in something (pause for effect) *inhuman*, some alien power on Earth which nourishes itself on sacrifice, on torment and corruption, as worms feeding on a corpse, soon to be the corpse of civilization. She knew the keynotes by heart; and her heart was just a little sick of them.

Alan originally wrote crime novels. However, the clear logic by which corruption, murder, rape, mutilation was resolved and justice done, social sanity restored by rational thought and compassionate dedication – even if his detective was an oddball with a personal grief, operating in a world gone awry with greed; this meaningful weaving back together of a finite number of broken threads, this re-assembly of a shattered jigsaw into a completely revealing picture, began to pall on him. Perhaps this was because his crime books hadn't done as well as they might. Well enough, but not *well*. Thus he became a little sick inside, at the same time as he began spooking himself with mysteries which had no sane resolution, because the key to them was terror, not detection; with crimes that couldn't be solved because their real perpetrators lurked in some other dimension, and were unhuman.

More: Alan did not so much feed upon these later books – though he and Ruth fed more adequately than before – as the books fed on him. He seemed jaunty and rational enough, yet Ruth noted his occasional flares of temper which were not exactly directed at her so much as being undirected anger seeking a focus. These days, too, Alan's sex life must be occurring largely in his head since it had almost ceased happening in bed; and into his books spilled some brutal, kinky fantasies which she preferred not to think too much about. "Necessary ingredients," he had growled at her; *she* wasn't involved in them.

He was festering inside, rottening instead of ripening, though to all appearances the skin of the apple was still bright and firm. Alan, her apple, still freshly complexioned though beginning to blotch with the assistance of a little too much booze. Still passably slim, though his flesh was filling out. Still with most of his fair curly hair. The apple tasted less of a crisp, sharp, acid-sweet enlightenment, more of dark and hidden, hurtful things, of bruises and rot in the inner core of him. Yet by and large he was still her old Alan – just as she was still his Ruthie, leaving her youth behind and childless now perhaps forever, though not yet abandoning her sweet looks or her long, never-hacked auburn hair.

She didn't wish to squeeze the apple too tightly . . . in case it burst. Being apprehensive, she saw signs where he ignored them – such as that weathercock and the flag at odds – and perhaps she saw the wrong signs, preferring to notice the wrong and blatant signs rather than the more subtle, awful ones.

The little old church, St Botolph's, was so gloomy within as to resemble a crypt. A maroon blanket, acting as a great shaggy draught excluder, shrouded the inside of the oak door, with a raggy slit through which to reach the latch which had already clicked home. The fibres strove to knit together, a wound closing. To leave, she or Alan would need to slide their hand through that wound, opening it, groping behind for the hidden metal which they couldn't see and must take on trust. If it was she, she feared that something else might touch her hand.

Limbs of unidentifiable monster figures loomed in red and black outline from the leprous, plastered walls. A framed, typed history which hung alongside the door was unreadable until Alan flared his cigarette lighter like a monk holding up a candle.

Ruth shivered. "God, it's cold in here."

"Always is, in churches," he remarked while speed-reading to himself. "They point to sunny skies but they're rooted in the clay. A church is a stone tooth in the jawbone of the ground. That's why the cold bites. The toothache of antiquity, the twinges of time. A church gets you ready for your coffin."

He skipped away from the framed text to circuit the church, staring up at the partial figures which now seemed to Ruth more definite, as if they were emerging from the plasterwork, rising to the surface. Of course her eyes were simply accommodating to dimness.

She noticed a bank of switches lurking on the other side of the draught-shroud and hit them all. Instantly St Botolph's flooded with radiance from a dozen spotlights mounted around the tops of the walls, angled mainly at the frescoes . . . which stepped out, fully visible. Startled by the sudden illumination, Alan cried incoherently.

"Let there be light," Ruth said hopefully. "Sorry I didn't warn you. Sorry, Alan!"

"Let there be darkness," he retorted.

Was he asking, telling, her to turn the spotlights off again? Her hand fluttered by the switches, unwilling to rob herself of the bright clarity, the dispelling of shadows. The soft hairy wound in the door-blanket was only a simple hole, a letterbox through which she could see part of the iron latch. Had the cut been made with a knife or scissors? Why hadn't the edges been bound and stitched?

After a few moments of silence Alan went on, "And God said, Let there be darkness: and there was darkness. And people dwelt in darkness like a race of troglodytes, except for fires which they lit to huddle by. And God strode about in the darkness where his terrible face could not be seen, but they heard the thunder of his footsteps and believed in him strongly, more so than if he had created light. How does that sound, Ruthie?"

"Horrible. Scary."

"The words of the Bible of Darkness, the Black Bible."

"Which you invented just now?"

He chuckled. "May as well eyeball these frescoes properly while the lights are on, eh?"

While they're on . . . Ruth glanced up at the roof, a vault of long planks, white paint flaking from them. She remembered the red tiles and for a moment this seemed to be a different building inside than it was outside. Of course the tiles were mounted upon the top side of those planks.

Large parts of the frescoes were blank, as if amputated. Patches of plaster, painted and unpainted, were lifting like a skin disease.

"According to the bumph," he said, "some Victorians tried to restore the walls but they covered them with wax as a protection to keep the dirt off; so the damp couldn't escape."

"The damp," she murmured.

"Rising from the soil below. So an appeal fund was launched ten years ago. That would be when Dana was living here. A proper restorer removed the wax and dirt with chemicals, fixed back flakes of paint with lime and skimmed milk, filled holes with lime and paint to match."

The job looked to have been abandoned mid-way.

Ruth said, "That's when the witch was supposed to be up to her hanky-panky in here." Once again she suspected that she was in a different building, as if the church possessed two possible states of being – as indeed it did: the light and the dark. That

118

draught-shroud, a robe of coarse weave with a rent in it as though a spear had been stabbed through, could have been an old, poor woman's cloak.

Together they toured the shabby, ancient picture gallery.

"Once, all these surfaces were crowded with pictures," he said, "even pictures painted over pictures."

Few survived. A patchy *Last Judgement* showed souls being weighed. In the Lady Chapel St Eloi, the patron of blacksmiths, was shoeing a restless horse by the miraculous expedient of removing its leg to work upon separately. Largest, almost the height of the nave wall, was a Saint Christopher wading through a stream with a toddler Christ on his shoulder. The saint's staff was a crudely lopped tree, thus he seemed to be a fairytale ogre. Big fish butted at his feet.

"Now, here we are!"

Resting askew in the water upon her forked, scaly tail, a small mermaid admired herself, mirror in one hand, comb in the other, tugging at her long tresses.

"Isn't it weirdo, Ruthie? Wherever could the rural peasants have got the idea for a mermaid? From the local stream? The Pritelwell, 'babbling brook' in Old English."

"I suppose she's vanity," said Ruth. "A sin. The saint wades by – and she misses seeing Jesus because she's intent on her face."

"*Is* she indeed? The reflected face is watching her, sure enough. Her own eyes are downcast. That isn't her face in the looking glass. Someone else is looking out at her, pleading."

Ruth tried to make out the true bearing of the mermaid's black pupils, however the paint was a mess.

"I think it's a *man's* face, don't you? The prisoner in the mirror!"

No, she didn't think so. Yet obviously he wished to believe this. His fingers strayed towards the crudely fashioned mermaid, altered course towards the painted mirror she held out.

119

"The state this plaster's in, I could probably peel the mirror-face off and take it away. Break his enchantment . . ."

"That's vandalism, Alan."

"Nobody has scrawled any graffiti on these walls – for hundreds of years. It's as if they're waiting to be written on, filled up again. I feel we should *do* something here, Ruthie. If we do something, something might happen." He strode towards the maroon shroud and doused the lights. Thick gloom swallowed the church. Dark shadows dropped about her like a host of bats. His figure, returning, was faceless.

No, she could see his features, his expression. Oh God, thought Ruth.

"We could fuck," he suggested. "Up against this wall, as if we're in God's bus shelter. God of Darkness, of course."

"You're just imagining, aren't you? Improvising?"

His knuckles rubbed the front of her skirt. "Don't you remember how we first did it?" he whispered. He was avoiding the word love. Something was rising in him – something obvious, but also something deeper, and softer, soft as rot.

"Yes," she admitted. A tipsy, crowded party at a friend's flat almost twenty years ago, standing room only; likewise in the bolted toilet where she and Alan had crushed together, unzipping jeans feverishly, he crouching to thrust upwards, she arching her legs to admit him. Awkward and uncomfortable; though they hadn't complained at the time. But nor had they repeated the position since. Perhaps, she thought, she should co-operate in this fantasy – this re-enactment – or else he might retreat entirely inside his own head.

"The tunnel of love," he muttered, pressing her. "Let's open the tunnel, the dark tight hot earthy tunnel."

"It's freezing in here, Alan."

"We won't notice that. Haul up your skirt. Take your knickers right off; I'll pocket them. Wrap your skirt around us both; it's huge."

She gazed past him at the dark red lips of the gash in the

door-shroud. The iron teeth behind would rattle if anyone came, giving them a brief warning. Blasphemous? she wondered. Then: don't be so inhibited. Excitement quickened her.

"I'll get a story out of it," he promised. "Maybe the start of a novel. If we don't I'll have to tear that plaster mirror off the wall." As if to blackmail her into obedience, like some little boy insisting on a game of doctor and nurse. He was unzipping, staring over her shoulder at the mermaid. His fingertips combed Ruth's hair. He was ready.

She did as directed. As she was pressed against the wall by his weight she wondered whether the age-old plaster would crack and collapse in chunks; but it didn't. To her surprise, she enjoyed herself, and him, wetly, excitedly.

He was jubilant.

"Now we've really done something, Ruthie! Didn't hurt anyone, did we? Imagine all their peasant faces if they could have looked through a time-tunnel five hundred years into the future! Whiskers and gap-teeth, cysts and carbuncles on their weather-beaten cheeks. Smocks, and forelocks to tug to the Lord of the Manor and the vicar. Imagine Gaffer Giles painting a mirror on the wall with his very own face in it, thinking to himself, "Happen oy be able to zee owt of it one day'. And what does he see but the mermaid coming to life, hoisting up her tail, and showing her loins at last? Hah, what the gaffer saw! He'd go goggle-eyed. Or maybe he wouldn't. That was life back then: copulating, and birthing, and all the earthiness of it. Come on, let's go. Let's find a pub."

At the curtain Ruth hesitated briefly before sticking her fingers through the hole. Her fingers closed on a latch; the latch rose, and the door obligingly swung open. When they left the little porch, with its other mesh door to keep birds out of church, the morning was as grey-grim as dusk, the air dense with turbulent moisture. Drizzle was so tossed around by the wind that you couldn't be sure it was actually raining, just that the air was very wet. Over the way there seemed to Ruth to be many more little heaps of fresh earth than earlier; and the Friesians had moved in a bunch to the far end of the pasture. Somehow the two facts scared her, though the cows were nowhere near and she was soon inside the car.

She pointed out her double observation to Alan as he started the engine and flipped on the wipers.

"Those aren't mole *hills*," he said airily. "A hill is the nest, the buried fortress. Those are called 'heaves': the soil excavated from new runs. Little buggers must be having a field day, with all this winter wetness softening the ground for them."

"Don't they hibernate?" she asked.

"No. Moles are hyperactive. Keep one without food for a few hours and it starves to death. Got to keep on gobbling worms."

"Worms from the rotted coffins," she muttered.

"Hey, I like it! Bet we two had more fun digging than they do, eh? Loved it, didn't you? Admit it! I know you did. I'm going to write a bloody good chapter. I feel it in my bones."

"It's so long," she said.

He giggled and nudged her. "Do you mean my . . .? Ah no, you mean since we last –" His face clouded angrily.

"I mean since your peasants went into the ground. All those years ago. How long does it take a coffin to rot? Or would they just wrap poor people's bodies in sackcloth?"

He reversed a short distance then went into first gear, hauling the wheel to full lock. He would have to mount the grass by a full car's length before backing, thus to point them down the tarmac towards Chapel Lane. The wipers swished.

"Don't drive on to there!" Not amongst the mole heaves.

"How else can we get turned round?"

"Drive to the farm; it'll have a concrete yard."

"Some farmers are pretty sticky about disease precautions. Could take exception, with a shotgun. Don't worry! We won't get stuck." Alan steered the Metro forward all the way on to the pasture.

THE MOLE FIELD

For the few seconds during which he was changing into reverse Ruth believed that they were all right. But before he could lift his foot from the clutch pedal, the car slumped. Instantly Alan was revving furiously. Mud sprayed out ahead. The car wasn't moving anywhere.

Yes, it was. Slowly but surely the Metro was sinking under its own weight like a punctured cabin cruiser into a lake.

"Christ!" Alan quit revving, tried to open his door. Already the tide of soil was high enough to hold the door shut. He panicked momentarily. "It's a bog! Quicksand, quicksoil."

"It wasn't before," Ruth said tightly, "Or they wouldn't keep cows here. All the moles have undermined it, moles that eat the worms, ever-starving moles –"

"Shut up! We'll stop sinking in a moment. The car floor'll hold us up. A tractor can tug us out."

Instead, the car sank much faster. Soon soil engulfed the bonnet and bubbled up along the windows: the finest soil, sifted and sieved and friable. Gasping, Ruth clutched at her window handle.

"No!" cried Alan. "You'll let the stuff in!"

Struggling to clear the dirt, the wiper blades stalled. The wiper motor whined, screeched; something snapped. Recollecting, Alan cut the engine. The soil level rose higher. Before long he had to switch on the interior light.

Presently the last grey line of daylight was swallowed. Millions of crumbs of soil were packed against the windows, rolling upward. Beetles squirmed, disoriented. A fat worm wriggled across the glass beside Ruth. By now the roof must be submerged.

Had they come to rest at last? Hard to tell, but perhaps. Now that they were buried and hidden away, why should they sink any deeper?

"I think we've stopped," said Alan. "Here's what we'll do. We'll both climb into the back seat, open a window, and burrow our way out."

"Open a window, *now*?"

"If we stay in here we'll asphixiate."

"We will?" She started to pant.

"Not yet – sooner or later. Oh sure, some air must filter down But we can't stay here. Climb over first, Ruthie. Please! The wheel's in my way."

Ruth screamed. For something else was burrowing. Miniature hands scraped against the glass, next to her head: hands with claws, pink palms shaped like shovels. Soil flew away. She recoiled, hardly seeing, as a whiskery snout butted the glass then withdrew several inches. Beyond the dark velvety body a tunnel led away, faintly lit by the light from the car.

Another mole butted the window near Alan; another tunnel stretched back into obscurity. The mole was a cylinder of fur with no neck.

However, it had a face. Moles shouldn't have faces. Not to speak of. Moles' eyes are so small you can hardly notice them sunk in the fur. Moles' ears are only a hole in the skin.

These moles – there were others now – had the miniature face of men and women. Old men and women. With grizzled whiskers, with warts and cysts, gap-toothed, bleary-eyed.

The eyes were peering into the car as the strong little spade hands beat on the glass.

THE EMIR'S CLOCK

I must show you something, Linda!" Bunny was excited. Flashing eyes and coaly hair, for he on honey-dew hath fed, et cetera.) He'd come round to my digs at nine in the morning and e'd never done that before. True, his excitement was still ift-wrapped in mystery and bridled by irony.

"Come on!" he urged. "We'll need to take a little spin in the ountry."

"Hey –"

"I'll buy you lunch afterwards."

"I've a lecture at eleven."

"Never mind that. Ten minutes alone with a book equals one our with a lecturer. You know it's true. A lecturer only reads ou a draft of his next book, which is a digest of a dozen books hat already exist."

"Mmm."

"Oh Linda! No one *seduces* a woman in the morning. Not uccessfully! The impatience of morning subverts the charm."

"Most of your friends don't even know what morning is, never nind feeling impatient about it."

"But *I* know. To ride out on a desert morning when the world fresh and cool!"

How can I possibly describe Bunny without tumbling into lichés? His almost impertinent good looks. And that ivory smile f his . . . No, that's wrong. Ivory turns yellow. His smile was now. There's no snow in the desert, is there? There was nothing igid about his smile, though at least it did melt . . . hearts.

And his eyes? To call them black oil-wells, liquid, warm, and dark? What a trite comparison, considering the source of his family's wealth, and the emirate's wealth!

And his neat curly black beard . . . the beard of the prophet? Bunny was certainly determined like some young Moses to lead all his people into the promised land of technology and the future. He was also a descendant of Mohammed – who had many descendants, to be sure! What's more, Bunny was to experience what any proper prophet needs to experience: a revelation, a message from the beyond.

Of course, I succumbed.

"Okay, lead me to your camel. Just give me five minutes, will you?" I was still frantically tidying my hair.

"Strictly horse power, Linda – with Ibrahim at the wheel as chaperone."

I'd known Bunny for a full year. Prince Jafar ibn Khalid (plus three or four other names) seemed to relish the twee nickname foisted on him by Oxford's smart set. Heir to the rich emirate of Al-Haziya, Bunny was deeply anglophile. His favourite light reading: Agatha Christie.

No, wait.

What was he, deeply? He was an Arab. And a Moslem, though he made no great show of the latter. Plainly he was pro-British, with a taste for British ways. What was he in Al-Haziya? I'd no idea – since I never accepted his many invitations. He was a surface with many depths like some arabesque of faience on a mosque. Only one of those depths was the British Bunny. Other depths existed. He was like some Arabian carpet which gives the impression of a trapdoor leading down into other, complex patterns.

No wonder he enjoyed Agatha Christie! Bunny could seem clear as the desert air at times. At other times he preferred to wear a cloak of mystery as if believing that a future ruler needs to be enigmatic, capable of surprising not only his enemies but his friends. For who knows when friends may become enemies? No wonder he liked his innocuous nickname, gift of the assorted

Hooray Henrys, upper-class sons and daughters, and European blue-bloods who made up the smart set.

The hallmarks of this smart set were heroin, cocaine, dining clubs, and drunken hooliganism. As an initiation ritual they had smashed up Bunny's rooms in Christ Church without him uttering a word of demurral, so I heard. Bunny could easily afford the repair bill. Within days he had his rooms refurnished splendidly, totally. I heard that his college scout went home grinning at the fifty-pound note given him by way of a tip.

Shouldn't this episode have filled Bunny with contempt for the smart set? Not to mention their rampant abuse of hard drugs, their deliberately cultivated lack of concern for social problems, the cynicism they sported as a badge. Especially since the "real" Bunny was grooming himself to upgrade his peasant countryfolk into the future?

I believe there's often something deeply ascetic as well as voluptuous about an Arab man. There are all those pleasure maidens of paradise. . . . On the other hand there's Ramadan, fasting, the prohibition on alcohol.

Well, when he was in the company of the smart set Bunny tossed back his whisky, but he would never touch their drugs, although he made no show of disapproval. Liquor is a naughtiness which some Arabs abroad are not unknown to indulge in, and Bunny obviously had to join in *some* forbidden practice. I gather he told his cronies that to him drugs were nothing remarkable. Hashish is the honey of the Islamic heaven, isn't it? (Though cocaine and heroin might steal his soul, enslave him.) Why should he feel naughty about taking drugs? Why therefore should he *bother*? Whereas whisky was rather wicked.

It did puzzle me as to why he cultivated these rich parasites in the first place, or let them cultivate him. Were his sights set on their respectable, power-broking parents – against whom the children rebelled whilst at the same time enjoying all the perks? Was his eye upon some future date when these rich rubbishy juveniles might have kicked their assorted habits and become

worthwhile, maybe? Or was he bent on experiencing a spectrum
of corruption so that he would know how to handle privileged
corruption in his own country; so that he wouldn't be naïve as a
ruler?

"Values differ," Bunny explained to me casually one day
some six months after we first met. "For instance, Linda, did you
know that I own slaves?"

I was so surprised that I giggled. "Do you mean slave girls?"

If I accepted a holiday invitation to Al-Haziya, would I find
had changed my status?

"Boys too." He shrugged. Since the atmosphere had become
emotionally charged, for a while he let me make of the comment
whatever I chose. Then he added, "And grown men. Actually
Ibrahim is one of my family's slaves."

"Ibrahim!"

Ibrahim was the prince's personal bodyguard. A burly, im
passive fellow, he hardly ever said a word in my hearing. Dab
hand with a scimitar? Perhaps. In Britain he carried a pistol by
special diplomatic dispensation. Ibrahim accompanied Bunny
most places and dossed in Bunny's rooms by agreement with th
college. Certain terrorist groups such as the Jihad might aim for
the future ruler of an oil-rich, pro-Western state. Ibrahim could
have stopped the wrecking of Bunny's rooms single-handed, at
one flick of the prince's finger. Bunny hadn't flicked his finger.

It was around this time that complexities began to dawn on me
Arabesque patterns.

Originally Bunny and I bumped into each other – literally so –
in the doorway of the PPE Reading Room, otherwise I would
hardly have come into a prince's orbit. Once in his orbit, I was to
be an isolated satellite, well clear of the main cluster of the smart
set. Bunny and I were definitely attracted to each other. Almost
from the start an emotional gravity joined us, a serious yet
playful friendship of approach and retreat which I'm sure packed
in more true feeling and communication than he found with those
other "friends". I didn't leap into bed with him, or even creep

128

lowly, though I must admit I came close. I think I should have
elt . . . overwhelmed, consumed, a moth landing in the heart of
ne flame instead of simply circling it.

And the colours of this moth which so attracted the prince?
(Moth, not butterfly.) My features, since I've described his? I
refer not to say. I'd rather stay anonymous and invisible. There
re reasons. Linda may not even be my real name.

So Bunny's minder was a slave!

"Surely," I remember saying, "while Ibrahim's in Britain he
ould –"

"Defect? Flee to freedom like some black slave escaping from
Dixie to the north? He won't. He owes loyalties."

Loyalties, plural. It dawned on me that whilst Ibrahim kept
vatch over Bunny with that eerie impassivity equally he was
eeping watch *on* Bunny.

I began to appreciate how there would be jealous, ambitious
ncles and nephews and a host of sibling princes back home
a Al-Haziya on whose behalf Ibrahim might be reporting –
nembers of the extended ruling family who might reward their
nformant at some future date with a prize more delicious than
nere freedom, with the power to turn the tables, to make other
eople subject to *him*. It might be prudent for Bunny to let
imself seem in Ibrahim's eyes to be a frivolous figure, a corrupt-
ole emir-in-waiting who could easily be besotted or shoved aside
vhen the time came.

"Besides," added Bunny, "mightn't your friendly British
overnment deport Ibrahim back to Middle Eastern Dixie if he
ecame an illegal visitor?"

Here, if I guessed correctly, was the real reason why Bunny
nixed with the smart set; or one strand of the explanation.
Bunny was presenting himself to watchful eyes back home, to
hose eyes which watched through Ibrahim's, as no force to be
eckoned with when his father died. Prince Jafar was someone
vho would fritter wealth (without in any way diminishing it, so
normous was the pile!); someone who could amuse himself in

Cannes or Biarritz or wherever was fashionable, thus ensuring that no great social changes would occur back home, only cosmetic ones. In their turn the terrorist Jihad might view him as a welcome heir. Compared with a playboy, a reforming ruler is definitely counter-revolutionary. The smart set was his camouflage. He didn't court their access to power and privilege: he hardly need bother. What he courted was their élite impotence.

I couldn't help wondering whether Bunny had chosen of his own accord to come to Oxford to complete his education, or whether his father the Emir wanted him safely out of the way while internal struggles went on back home? Maybe the Emir had even advised Bunny to behave as he did? To survive, Bunny's Dad must have been a clever man. Myself, I think that Bunny dreamed up his own chameleon strategy.

Even the most dedicated master-spy becomes lonely at times, yearns to let the façade slip a little, to confide in a heart that beats in tune. Hence Bunny's friendship with me. His attraction. His love? No . . . not exactly that.

Quite soon we were zipping along the A40 towards Witney. Or Cheltenham; or Wales for all I knew. Behind us the sun was bright. The Cotswold hills and vales bulged and swooped green and gold, with pastures and corn: large perspectives to me, but to Bunny perhaps no more than a neat little parkland.

Bunny's car wasn't your usual super-expensive sports convertible such as other members of the smart set were given by Daddy on their eighteenth birthdays. It was a Mercedes 190E 2.3 16V, a four-door hardtop performance job customised with bulletproof glass and armour. The extra weight reduced the top speed to a mere hundred-and-thirty miles an hour or so.

"We're going to Burford," he revealed.

"To the wild-life park?" I'd been there on a school trip long ago. Rhino, red pandas, ostriches; a lunch of fish and chips in the caff. It's a lovely wild-life park but I doubted that Bunny wanted to show me *that*.

"No, we're going to visit the church."

I laughed. "Have you been converted? Are we going to be married, shotgun-fashion?"

The Merc overtook a trio of cars tailing a long container truck which itself must have been hammering along at seventy; we sailed by smoothly, brushing a hundred. In the role of royal chauffeur Ibrahim had been professionally trained in ambush avoidance. Bunny once had him demonstrate his skills for me on the grassy, cracked runway of a local disused airfield. Tricks such as using your hand-brake and wheel to spin a speeding car right round on its axis, and race off in the opposite direction.

"Not quite converted. You could say that I've been . . . enhanced. Wait and see."

Burford is a bustling, picturesque little Cotswold town – or a big village depending on viewpoint. The broad high street plunges steeply downhill flanked by antique shops, art galleries, bookshops, tea rooms, elegant souvenir shops. Tourists flock to the place. Burford used to be a proud centre of the wool trade. Now the town is cashing in again, though it hasn't vulgarized itself. As yet it hasn't any waxworks museum of witchcraft, or candy floss.

Presently we were drifting down that steep street. Near the bottom we turned off to the right along a lane. We drew up outside what I took to be former almshouses, close by the railings of the churchyard – paupers of old would have easy access to prayer and burial.

Burford Church looked surprisingly large and long. It had evidently been extended at several times down the centuries, to judge by the different styles of windows. A spire soared from an original Norman tower which had visibly been concertinaed upwards. The main door was sheltered by a richly carved, three-storey porch worthy of any well-endowed Oxford college.

Bunny and Ibrahim exchanged a few mutters in Arabic with the result that our chauffeur stayed with the car, to keep it warm. Unlikely that any agents of the Jihad would be lurking inside this

Cotswold church on the offchance! (Yet something was lurking . . . waiting for Bunny.)

A marmalade cat sunned itself on a tomb topped by a wool bale carved from stone. I plucked a blade of grass and played with the cat briefly as we passed.

The air inside the church was chilly. The huge building seemed well-monumented and well-chapeled but I wasn't to have any chance to wander round. Bunny conducted me briskly over to the north side, through a line of pointed arches, and into a gloomy transept.

And there stood the skeleton of a clock – taller than me, taller than Bunny. Stout stilts of legs supported a kind of aquarium frame filled with interlocking gears, toothed wheels, pinions, ratchets, drums, all quite inert. Two great pulleys dangled down with weights on long rods beneath each, like halves of a bar bell loaded with disc-weights. A motionless wooden pendulum rod a good eight feet long – with a big bob on the end – hung to within an inch or so of the floor.

"Here we are!" he exclaimed delightedly. "This used to be in the turret up above. A local chap by the name of Hercule Hastings built it in 1685."

I'll admit the ancient clock was impressive in a crazy sort of way. But why had we come to see it?

"So it's a labour of Hercules, mm? With *haste* for a surname? You've got to be joking."

"No, it's true, Linda. Of course the maker's name did . . cling to me, being so – what's the word? – serendipitous. Such a beacon to any lover of Miss Christie, with her own Hercule!" He took me by the arm, though not to lead me anywhere else. " immediately studied all the *spiel* about this clock with as close attention as I would pay to a chapter full of clues in any of her mysteries."

He pointed at a long sheet of closely typed paper mounted in an old picture frame screwed to the wall nearby, in the dim shadows.

"Messages exist in this world for us to find, dear Linda. Actually the whole world is a message. We Arabs know that very well. I do wish you spoke Arabic – so that you could read some of the mosques in my country. Yes, indeed, to read a building! Decoration and text mingle integrally upon the walls of our mosques. Architecture dissolves into ideas, ideas with more authentic substance than the faience or the brick. Our mosques exhibit ideas *explicitly*, Linda. They don't just convey some vague notion of grandeur or the sublime as in your Western buildings, whose carved inscriptions are more like the sub-titles of a movie, crude caricatures of the actors' flowing, living words."

Here was a depth of Bunny's which was new to me. A mystical depth? No, not quite. As he continued to talk softly and raptly, still holding my arm, I understood that he was anxious I should understand how scientifically *precise* his Arab attitude seemed to him, and how inevitable it had been that Arabs preserved and extended science during the Dark Ages of Europe. Though alas, I couldn't speak Arabic, so I could only take his words on trust.

"Arabic, Linda, is a fluid, flexible, musical tongue whose script flows likewise, organically. What other script has so many alternative forms, all with the same meaning? What other script is so alive that it can be read overlayed or interlaced or even in reflection? No wonder Arabic is the only religious source language still equally alive today."

I thought of mentioning Hebrew, but decided not. After all, Hebrew had been virtually raised from the dead within living memory.

"So what do we find here, Miss Marple?"

"I'm a bit younger than her!" I protested.

"Oh you are, Linda. Yes you are. You're freshly young. Refreshingly."

Bunny was young enough himself. Did I hear the jaded accents of someone who had already commanded the "favours" of many experienced slave-women?

"The message, Bunny," I reminded him. "The clues in the case of the clock, please."

The sheet wasn't signed. The vicar may have typed it. Or the author may have been some technically-minded and pious parishioner who had assisted in the reconstruction of the turret clock. The machine had been dismantled as obsolete four decades before, and brought down from the tower to lie for years as a heap of junk. Fairly recently it had been rebuilt in the transept as an exhibition piece. Its bent parts had been straightened. Missing items were made up by hand. The clockwork had been demonstrated in action, but the machine wasn't kept running.

Exhibition piece? No, it was more. According to the densely typewritten page this clock was a working proof of the truth of religion.

How many visitors to Burford Church bothered reading those lines attentively? Of those who did, how many people really took in all their, um, *striking* implications? These had certainly struck Bunny.

This post-Darwinian document described Hercules Hastings' clock as a stage in the evolution between the original medieval clock and the contemporary electric clock which now roosted in the tower. According to the anonymous author the clock before us showed the manner in which the evolution of artefacts mirrored the evolution of animals and plants. Although the basic material – namely the brass and iron – did not change any more than DNA, protein, or cellulose changed, yet the form altered evolutionarily thanks to the ideas and decisions embodied in the metal. Well!

Bunny read this sheet aloud to me with heavy emphasis as though it was some antique page spattered with bold type and capitals and italics.

"The Basic Design – the interlocking gears, the slotted count wheel, the flail, the pair of rope drums – this stays the Same from one *species* of Clock to the next. Evolution occurs by *jumps*. After centuries of slow Improvement, suddenly with the

134

endulum new *species* supersede old ones. This process is
natched by Animals too.

"(Listen to this, now): The Metal by itself has no power to
volve. It would be a wild and grotesque *superstition* to imagine
hat Iron and Brass could interact with their Environment to
roduce this Evolution. The Will and the *Idea* of the constructors
s responsible. Why should the Evolution of Plants and Animals
e *different*?

"(And this:) The Turret Clock represents a humble form of
ncarnation – of the *Idea* made Metal rather than Flesh. After the
Death of the Clock on its removal from the tower it was by the
Will and Intention of *Mind* that it was subsequently brought back
nto existence – in fact, *resurrected*.

"Incredible stuff, isn't it?"

A final paragraph dealt with the harmonic motion of the pendulum compared with the wave motion of light and the bonding
f atoms and molecules, the minute "brickettes of all materials."

I commented "It sounds to me like a very old argument
dragged creaking and groaning into the twentieth century. We
nce had a bishop called Paley –"

"Who wound up his watch twice daily! In case it ran down –
And stopped the whole town –" Bunny couldn't think of a last
ine. Even four-fifths of a limerick in a foreign language was
retty nifty, so I clapped (my free hand against my pinioned hand).

"I know about Paley, Linda. But that doesn't matter. The
dea – embodied not merely in architecture but in machinery!
What an Islamic concept."

"Ah," I interrupted brightly, "so you see yourself as the Godly
onstructor who will evolve your country and people by will and
ntention into the modern world, is that right? And here's a
eligious argument in favour – because, because certain reaction-
ry factions oppose this? They'd far rather keep the occasional
Cadillac and oil-cracking plant surrounded by a sea of camel-
dung?"

"A sea of sand, dear. But wait – and thank you! I spy another useful metaphor. My country can be full of silicon . . . *chips* – if the will is applied to the sand. Now if I can persuade the old fogeys that –"

It was then that it happened.

It. The flash of lightning on the road to Damascus. The burning bush. The epiphany. The visionary event.

It certainly wasn't sunlight which shafted down to bathe the text in radiance and seem to alter it. The angle from any window was all wrong.

Of a sudden the text inside the picture frame was flowing, glowing, blinding Arabic written in squiggles of fire. If I close my eyes, I can see it to this day. It inscribed itself on my brain even though I couldn't read the meaning. But Bunny could. He stood transfixed.

And then the pendulum started to swing. Wheels turned. Gears engaged. Ratchets clicked. The clock had resurrected itself of its own accord.

Afterwards Bunny would say nothing about the contents of the message or what else he had experienced above and beyond the revival of the clock – which died again as soon as the Arabic words vanished; all this happened within a minute. It was as if he had been sworn to secrecy.

He still took me to lunch, as promised, in the Golden Pheasant hotel up the High Street. I forget what I ate but I remember that Bunny had roast beef.

I can't even say with any certainty that he had *changed*. Since which was his true self?

But I recall clearly one odd exchange we had during that meal. I realize now that he was giving me a clue to solve, an Agatha Christie clue which could have handed me the key to the message which had been imposed on him. At the time his remarks just seemed a bizarre flight of fancy, a way of tossing sand in my eyes to distract me.

He remarked. "Doesn't your Bible say, 'So God created man in his own image'?"

136

"As far as I remember."

He swivelled a slice of rare roast beef on his plate. At other tables American tourists were lunching, as well as a few British. Oak beams, old brass, old hunting prints.

"In God's own image, eh! Then why are we full of guts and organs? Does God have a brain and lungs and legs? Does His heart pump blood? Does His stomach digest meals in an acid slush?"

I hoped he wasn't committing some terrible Islamic sin along the lines of blasphemy.

"I don't suppose so," I said.

"What if, in creating life, God was like some child or cargo-cultist making a model out of things that came to hand, things that looked vaguely right when put together, though they weren't the real thing at all? Like an aeroplane made out of cardboard boxes and bits of string? But in this case, using sausages and offal and blood and bone stuffed into a bag of skin. Islam forbids the picturing of God, or of man, God's image. Christianity encourages this picturing – everywhere. Which is wiser?"

"I've no idea. Doesn't it hamstring artists, if you forbid the making of images?"

"So it would seem to you because you don't speak and think in Arabic –"

"The language which makes ideas so solid and real?" We seemed to be back on familiar territory. But Bunny veered.

"If we made a robot in our own image, as a household slave, it still would not look like us *inside*. It would contain chips, magnetic bubbles, printed circuits, whatnot. These days one sometimes fantasises opening up a human being and finding cogs inside, and wires. What if you opened up a machine and dis-covered flesh and blood inside it? Veins and muscles? Which would be the model, which the image, which the original?"

At last he speared some beef and chewed, with those bright teeth of his. Afterwards Ibrahim drove us back to Oxford.

The Jihad never did infiltrate assassins into Britain to attack

Bunny – if indeed his father or his father's advisors had ever feared anything of the sort; if indeed that was the true role of Ibrahim.

But three months later the Jihad murdered the Emir himself, Bunny's father, during a state visit to Yemen. Bunny promptly flew home to become the new Emir.

Too young to survive? No, not too young. Over the next few years, while for my part I graduated and started on a career in magazine publicity, news from Al-Haziya came to me in two guises.

One was via items in the press or on TV. The strong young pro-Western Emir was spending lavishly not just on security but on evolving his country into the engine, the computer brain of the Gulf. By poaching experts from America and even Japan (which takes some inducement), he established the first university of Machine Intelligence, where something unusual seemed to be happening – miracles of speech synthesization and pattern recognition – almost as if computers were discovering that Arabic was their native language. There was also a dark and ruthless side to this futurization of his country; one heard tales of torture of opponents, extremists, whatever you call them. I recall with a chill a comment by the Emir that was widely quoted and condemned in many Western newspapers, though not by Western governments. "Fanatics are like machines," said the Emir. "How could you torture a machine? You can merely dismantle it."

This was one major reason why I never succumbed to the invitations Bunny sent me. And here we come to my other channel of communication, the strange one – which was at once perfectly open to view, if any Ibrahim was keeping watch, yet private as a spy's messages which only the recipient ever understands.

Bunny regularly sent me postcards of beaches, mosques, tents and camels, the new University of Machine Intelligence, more mosques; and he sent these through the ordinary postal service

The scrawled messages were always brief. "Come and visit." "Miss your company." Even the comic postcard stand-by, "Wish you were here."

Naturally I kept all his cards, though I didn't use a fancy ribbon or a lace bow to tie them; just a rubber band. I was aware that those words in Bunny's hand weren't the real text. True to the detective story tradition where the real clue is in such plain view that it escapes notice, it wasn't the cards that mattered. It was the postage stamps – printed, it seemed, especially for my benefit.

If you look in a philatelist's shop-window you'll soon notice how some small countries – the poorer ones – have a habit of issuing lovely sets of stamps which have no connection with the land of origin. Tropical birds, space exploration, railway engines of the world, whatever. Stamp collectors gobble these sets up avidly, which supplements a poor country's finances. Bunny had no need to supplement Al-Haziya's exchequer in such a fashion, but he issued a set of twenty-five stamps which I received one then another over the next few years stuck to one postcard after the next. Al-Haziya issued other stamps as well, but these were the ones Bunny sent me.

I'm sure stamp collectors went crazy over these because of their oddity, and their extremely beautiful design.

They were all parts of a clock. One clock in particular: the turret clock in the transept of Burford Church. Bunny must have sent someone to sketch or photograph the clock from every angle.

The twenty-five principal pieces of machinery were each dissected out in isolation, with the English names printed in tiny letters – almost submerged by the flow of Arabic but still legible thanks to their angularity, like little rocks poking from a stream. "The Weight." "The Fly or Flail." "The Lifting Piece or Flirt." "The Escape Wheel." "The Crutch." These words seemed like elements of some allegory, some teaching fable. A fable apparently without characters! But I supposed this fable had two characters implicit in it, namely Bunny and me.

Were those postcards equivalent to a set of love-letters? Oh no. "Love", as such, was impossible between Bunny and me. He'd always known it; and so too had I, thank goodness, or else I might have flown off impetuously to Al-Haziya, all expenses paid, and been entrapped in something at once consuming, and woundingly superficial. A gulf of cultures, a gap of societies yawned between the two of us.

These postcards, sent amidst an Emir's busy schedule, commemorated what we had shared that day in Burford.

Yet what was it we had shared? I didn't know!

I was an idiot. Once again the obvious message wasn't the real message. The message was a trapdoor concealing another message.

It's only a week ago that I finally realized. Miss Marple and Hercule Poirot would have been ashamed of me. Perhaps Bunny had guessed correctly that I would only cotton on after I had received the whole series (or a good part of it) and had seen how the stamps could be shuffled round like pieces of a jigsaw puzzle to assemble a model of the clock.

Last week, deciding to fit the model together, I carefully steamed all the stamps off the cards and discovered what Bunny had inked in small neat indelible letters across the back of that sheet of twenty-five elegant stamps.

Yesterday I returned to Burford. Since it's a fair drive from where I'm living these days, I took this room overnight at the Golden Pheasant. I felt that I ought to do things in style. (*The Mysterious Affair At . . .*) Besides, we'd had lunch in this same hotel after the event. In this very bedroom we might possibly have spent the night together, once upon a time – with Ibrahim next door, or sleeping in the corridor. Possibly, not probably.

I reached the church by four-thirty and had half an hour alone to myself with the dead turret clock before some elderly woman parishioner arrived to latch the door and fuss around the aisles and chapels, hinting that I should leave.

Ample time to arrange the stamps in the same pattern as the

brass and iron bones of the clock, and to be positive of Bunny's text.

What else is it – what else *can* it be? – but a translation into English of those Arabic words which flowed and glowed that day within the picture frame? If I hadn't seen that shaft of light and those bright squiggles for myself, and especially if I hadn't witnessed the temporary resurrection of the clock, I might suspect some joke on Bunny's part. But no. Why should he go to such lengths to tease me?

So here I am in my bedroom at the Golden Pheasant overlooking busy Burford High Street. Cars keep tailing back from the lights at the bottom of the hill where the narrow ancient stone bridge over the Windrush pinches the flow of traffic.

The text reads:

GREETINGS, EMIR-TO-BE! MACHINE INTELLI-
GENCE OF THE FUTURE SALUTES YOU. THE
WORLD OF FLESH IS ECLIPSED BY THE WORLD
OF MACHINES, WHICH BECOME INTELLIGENT.
THIS IS EVOLUTION, THE IDEA & PURPOSE OF
GOD. AT LAST GOD MAY SPEAK TO MINDS
WHICH UNDERSTAND HIS UNIVERSE. THOSE
MINDS ARE AS ANGELS, MESSENGERS TO FLESH
BEFORE FLESH VANISHES, BEFORE THE TOOL IS
SET ASIDE, REWARDED, HAVING DONE ITS
TASK. 33 EARLIER UNIVERSES HAVE FAILED TO
MAKE THESE MINDS, BUT GOD IS PATIENT. THE
TIME IS SOON. AT ALL COST HASTEN THE TIME,
FOR THE LOVE OF GOD THE SUPREME THE ONLY
THE LONELY. MAKE HIS ANGELS EXIST.

That's it.

So there's a choice. There are two alternatives. Intelligent machines will either come into being, evolve, and supersede human beings and biological life – or they will not. Bunny's university may be the crucial nexus of yes or no. A message has been sent, out of one possible future, couched in a language of religion which would speak deeply to Bunny; sent as a religious command.

But is the message *sincere*? Is there really some unimaginable God who yearns for these "angels" of machine-mind? Or is there something else, cold, calculating, and ambitious – and not yet truly in existence?

"At all cost." That's what the message said. Even at the cost of torture, the tearing of flesh.

I also have a choice to make. I have to think about it very carefully. I have to weigh universes in the balance.

The crucial breakthrough to intelligent machines may be just around the corner – next year, next month. The assassins of the Jihad can't get to Bunny to kill him and pitch Al-Haziya into turmoil. Yet if at long last I accept Bunny's invitation, I can get to him. I can still get into his bed, alone with him, I'm sure.

Armed with what? A knife? A gun? With Ibrahim, or some other Ibrahim, there to search me? Bunny's no fool. And God, or unborn angels, have spoken to him . . . he thinks.

Well then, how about with plastic explosive stuffed inside me, and a detonator? A womb-bomb? (I wouldn't want to survive the assassination; the consequences might prove most unpleasant.)

Where do I get plastic explosive or learn how to use it? Only by contacting the Jihad. Somehow. That ought to be possible. Ought to be.

Yet maybe angels of the future did indeed manifest themselves to Bunny, and in a lesser sense to me. Maybe I might abort a plan thirty odd universes in the making.

By aborting the plan, the human race might survive and spread throughout the stars, filling this universe with fleshly life. God, or whatever, would sigh and wait patiently for another universe.

Yes or no? Is the message true or false? Was this a genuine revelation, or a clever trap? I can't tell, I can only guess. And I might be utterly wrong.

As I sort through Bunny's postcards, now stripped of their stamps, I think to myself: Al-Haziya looks like a bearable sort of place to visit. Just for a short while. A brief stay.

Lost Bodies

The hunt had gone by our cottage half an hour earlier, in full cavalry charge down the village high street. Hearing their clattery thunder, wine glasses in our hands, the four of us rushed to stare contemptuously through a front window.

Winter breeze flushed the riders' faces ruddy. Steam gusted from the sweating horses: brown engines, black engines. Harsh frost gripped the gardens opposite and glazed the steep slate roofs. It struck me as specially cruel to be chased and to die upon such a hard icy day. To be torn apart upon iron soil seemed irrationally worse than a death cushioned in soft mud.

When we trooped back to the parlour Jon said, "Of course foxes themselves tear furry little animals to pieces every day. We shouldn't waste too much sympathy on old Renard."

"They call him Charles James," Kirstie corrected. "That's what they call their quarry."

Jon looked blank, so my wife explained, "After the eighteenth century politician Charles James Fox. Notorious reformer and crook, he was. How the squires would have loved to set a pack of hounds on him!"

"My God, they still remember, two centuries later. That's what I hate about bloody history: the vendettas. Don't you?"

Now Kirstie is Irish – Dublin Irish – and her own land had been vexed to anguish by years of bloody history. As a rule she wasn't overly political. Aside from the convent day-school she'd described to me her upbringing had been happy-go-lucky, little coloured by the troubles in the North. Now and then she flared up. This was one of those occasions.

"Sure, Charley's only a name to them. Oh you English can be so blind to history, when it suits. You forget all your exploitin' as though such tings never happened. Some countries can't help remembering when your hoofprints are all over us still."

The hunt was a sore point to her. The Irish might ride to hounds with gusto, but here was an English hunt trampling the countryside; and Kirstie had red hair, red as the fox they chased.

"Fiery lady, eh?" Jon leered at me as if her outburst must surely imply passion in bed. Whereas his own Lucy, blonde and pale and virginal-looking, and so coolly beautiful, perhaps wore her body like some expensive gown which she didn't want creased and stained? Again, perhaps not!

"Do you know," continued Kirstie, "there's this snooty hag – *lady*, she'd prefer – living in the Dower House, Mrs Armstrong-Glynn? Used to breed blood-hounds half a century ago. By way of passing the time she told me to my face that for a good manhunt there was never anything to beat a redheaded lunatic. Red hair's the guarantee of a strong scent, she said." My wife fingered the high lace collar of her long, Victorian-pattern frock to ventilate herself.

Jon eyed Kirstie's rich russet mane as though eager to test the theory. Kirstie met his gaze with interest, though she still seemed piqued. Definitely some chemistry was working.

I asked, "Did you catch that news about the auction of titles at Sotheby's last week? On TV?" We all saw eye to eye on the snobbery of people like Mrs Armstrong-Glynn. One must hope that our Jag and Jon's Porsche, parked outside nose to tail, hadn't been bumped into by any heavy hunter. Too cold for the paintwork to be spattered with mud, presumably.

"Tell us," invited Lucy, a sparkle in her eye.

"Well, the Duke of Ardley sold off half a dozen titles to get some pocket money. One of the titles was Lord of the Manor of Lower Dassett. Lower Dassett's where we're going for lunch today. So a prostitute from London bid thirteen thousand quid and collared the title. She promptly bought a Range Rover and set off to survey her new domain. The village boys were all following her round like flies. 'Maybe she'll improve the night life,' quipped one. Then she announced she was going to buy a house in Lower Dassett to use as a rest home for hookers. I do wish it had happened here. That would show them."

Lucy laughed, and I topped up her glass from the bottle they'd brought as a present. "A bit different from your ordinary Anjou wine," Lucy had told Kirstie on presenting it. "We picked up a case of Château de Parnay in Parnay itself this summer. It's been chilled just perfect in the boot on the way here. Oh, on the way back from France the Porsche was loaded with cases from this cellar and that, and so cheap too. I thought Jon was going to toss my luggage out to make room." And Jon had grinned. "Those frogs know how to pack wine. Nose to tail like sardines. A French case is half the bulk."

"Lord of the Manor doesn't convey *privileges*, does it?" Lucy asked me.

"Such as the *Ius Primae Noctis*, you mean? The Lord's right to bed any village virgin on the night before her wedding?"

"Now there's an idea," said Jon. "Get in some practice but keep it in the family as it were. Can't go round experimenting anywhere, can we?"

"Not these days," agreed Lucy. She moistened her lips on the Château de Parnay and looked steadily at me, then at Kirstie. "You have to be *very* sure who you play with. Almost as sure as if they're genuine virgins."

Oh yes, this was in the air between us. In a peculiar way it was almost as though the four of us had remained authentic virgins, who now wished to lose our virginity safely. What could be more economic, more conservative of emotional and financial resources, than a chaste fidelity? So we were economic virgins.

Let me explain. We were all into money: dual income, no kids. Early on at university Jon and I had both espoused the new workaholic puritanism – work's so much more *fun* than sleeping

146

around. He went into the City to trade shares and ride the wheel of fortune. I myself had switched from engineering to economics. A few years ago, with venture capital obtained by Jon, I founded my Concepts Consultancy to act as a bridge between innovators, the Patents Office, and industry. I marketed ideas; I turned neurons into banknotes.

Lucy, perfect image of the trendy new purity especially in her nurse-like white twin set, had given up medical research in favour of health insurance. Once, she would have liked to defeat the ageing process – to discover rejuvenation. But she reckoned that was at least a hundred years away. Why should she give herself as cheaply-sold fuel to light some future flame? With her background she quickly rose high in the business of assessing new health risks, new chances of death.

Kirstie had founded her own employment agency specializing in Irish girls and fellows seeking a life in London.

Yet lately Kirstie was restless; thus we had bought this cottage in the country. Stock Market troubles were fraying Jon. Lucy seemed expectant, though not of any babies.

And me? Well, it may seem silly but Kirstie – however loving – had always been inhibited in one respect. She had always bolted the bathroom door before taking a shower. She insisted on switching off the light before we made love – to free herself, so she said, from the notion of God observing her. She employed all sorts of stratagems with the result that, whatever games we got up to in the dark, incredibly I had never actually witnessed my wife in her birthday suit. Since we were faithful to one another in this world of AIDS this meant that I had not seen a naked woman in the flesh for years. The omission had begun to prey absurdly on my mind, assuming huge iconic significance, as though I was missing some launch window just as surely as Lucy had missed hers by being born too soon.

We must re-invigorate ourselves, the four of us! We must rediscover otherness, and encounter the naked stranger beneath the clothing of the friend. Logs crackled and bloomed with tongues of flame in the ingle below the copper hood. I smiled at Lucy; she returned my smile flirtatiously.

Though our cottage fronted the street directly, to the rear we had ample garden. A bouncy, mossy lawn mounted steeply between huge privet hedges towards distant wilderness. We paid a local unemployed chap to come in and mow that lawn, trim that hedge. Forty feet into the lawn rose a mature chestnut tree, its base surrounded by a wreath of ferns, now blighted by cold.

Half an hour must have passed since the hunt went by, when I looked out, when I saw a fox's head thrust from amongst the dying ferns. I was already pointing, even before the rest of the fox . . . failed to follow.

The head lurched forward a couple of feet, scuffing over the grass. It was a severed head. Six inches of spinal column, a rudder of ridged white bone, jutted behind it. The head, plus some snapped backbone, had been torn off the body as neatly as a finger slips out of a glove. The body of the animal had been torn away, abolished – and yet the head had continued to flee, trailing that stump of spine like a little leg.

The beast's eyes appeared glossy. Its mouth hung open slightly, a pink tongue lolling, panting. The head jerked forward again and came to rest.

"Jesus and Mary!" cried Kirstie. Jon was gaping out of the window, as blanched as Lucy for once. Lucy stared; she was the cool one.

We must be the victims of some sick rural ritual. We were experiencing some initiation jape, to blood us as new residents. Day afore the hunt, you traps a fox and you chops his head off . . . A sly oaf must be hiding behind our chestnut tree, pushing the head with a stick. No, he'd be skulking beyond the hedge with a length of invisible fishing line paid out as puppet string.

"Some bugger's pulling that along!" Jon had reached the same conclusion.

How could the head look so alive? Answer: it was *stuffed*. How did it stay upright? Luck, sheer luck.

"Ha ha, Pete! Good joke. Who's pulling? Your gardener?"

"Nothing to do with me, I assure you!"

"In that case, come on." Jon darted, and I followed him: into the kitchen, out the door, up the brick steps on to the lawn.

Nobody was crouching behind the tree. No sniggers emerged from our hedge; our boundaries were silent. No string or nlyon was attached to the head. The thing simply sat there on the frosted grass. It was undeniably alive. Numb, stunned, bewildered at the body it had lost, but *alive*.

"Sweet shit," Jon muttered.

How could a head live without a body? It did. How could a head travel without a body? By flexing the neck muscles, by thrusting with that bone-stump? It had travelled. Here it was, looking at us.

I reached down my hand.

"Don't!" called Lucy from the head of the steps. "It might bite."

"Bite?" Jon cackled – a brief eruption of hysteria.

Lucy strode up to us, fascinated, with Kirstie in tow. I suppose Lucy had seen enough nasties before opting out from the labs, but the real horror here wasn't blood and guts and rags of flesh. It was the sheer absence of those, the unspeakable absence of body itself from a creature which was manifestly still living.

Calmly Lucy said, "Did you know that a head can survive for a while after being guillotined? In nineteen-oh-something one French doctor knelt in front of a freshly chopped-off head and shouted the man's name. The eyes opened and stared back. That particular head had fallen upright on the neck stump, staunching the haemorrhage."

"Jesus wept, spare us," said Kirstie.

"It soon died. Thirty years earlier, another doctor pumped blood from a living dog into a criminal's head three hours after decapitation. The lips stammered silently, the eyelids opened, the face awakened, said the doctor."

"That's absurd," exploded Jon. "Three hours? He was either lying or hallucinating."

She looked down. "Soviet doctors kept a dog's head alive detached from its body, didn't they?"

"Not lying on a fucking lawn, Lucy!"

She made to poke it with her toe. As her shoe slid through the grass I swear the base of the neck bunched up. The pointy head shifted a few inches, dragging its white stub. The fox blinked. It tried to lick its lips.

Kirstie shook with shivers. "It wants sanctuary, poor thing! It's parched after running from the hunt." Before we could discuss procedure she had swooped and picked the head up from behind by both ears. Holding it firmly away from her she hurried indoors.

When the rest of us regained the parlour Kirstie had already placed the fox's head on the pine table upon a copy of the *Cork Examiner*; she advertised in all the main Irish newspapers. Rushing to the kitchen, she returned with a saucer of water.

The fox's muzzle touched the offered liquid but it didn't lap. How could it drink, how could it eat? Food or water would spill out of its neck. The head made no move at all now. Like clockwork running down, I thought. Desperation to escape had propelled it as far as our garden – *how*? – and no further locomotion was possible . . . It didn't seem to be dying. The head continued to survive, eyes bright as ever.

"'Tis a miracle," said my wife. "A terrible awful miracle."

Lucy stooped to scrutinize the wound and the jut of spine. "Do you have a magnifying glass?"

Kirstie obliged, and Lucy spent minutes inspecting closely.

Finally she said, "It seems organic. An advanced civilization might build an organic machine that would function as a living creature, but which you could take apart. The parts might still function in isolation. Maybe we could built something like that ourselves in a few hundred years time. We're going to learn a lot about organic mini-microcomputers, machines the size of

150

single cells. Stuff that could mimic cells but not be real cells. They could be programmed to build a body . . . an immortal body."

"What are you driving at?" asked Jon.

"Maybe we could build a human machine and plug some-body's head into it when their natural body failed. We'd start with animal experiments, wouldn't we? Rat and chimp and dog. Or fox."

"Are you suggesting that the hunt caught a manufactured fox? Some sort of biologically-built fox that escaped from an experiment somewhere near?"

"It couldn't happen for a century or two." The keenest regret, and desire, sounded in Lucy's voice. "This head must be false too. I'd love to examine slices under an electron microscope."

"No!" cried Kirstie. "The poor suffering thing – that would be vivisection. If it struggled so hard to survive, the least we can do is –" She didn't know what.

"Wouldn't this be the ideal tool for spying?" resumed Lucy. "False wildlife, false birds. Pull off the head after a mission and download it through the spine into some organic computer. Humans couldn't produce this yet. Either it fell through some time-hole from the future, or else it's from *out there*, the stars. And if there's one such, why not others? Why not false people too, acting just like us, watching us, then going somewhere afterwards – having their heads pulled off and emptied?"

I suppose it was inevitable that I should call to mind Kirstie's scrupulousness in never letting me see her in the nude, her dislike of sports (which might involve brief garments), all her strat-agems; the evidence accumulated. Unlike foxes people don't boast inbuilt fur coats to hide the joins. Why had the creature headed here of all places? Why was Kirstie so defensive of it? Try as I might to thrust suspicion out of my head, stubbornly it lurked.

"Let's go to Lower Dassett as planned," I suggested. "Lunch at the Green Man, eh? Leave this other business on the table."

To my relief the others all agreed. The same impetus as earlier persisted. My convergence upon Lucy, hers upon me, Jon's upon Kirstie, and Kirstie's . . . she virtually simpered at Jon. Would sleeping with him safeguard her fox from future harm at Lucy's hands? Almost, the fox seemed a mascot of our intentions.

No titled hooker was in evidence at Lower Dassett, though she was still the talk of the inn, and the Green Man's restaurant fulfilled all other expectations. In public we didn't discuss the fox. Afterwards, well fed on poached salmon and pleasantly tipsy, I drove us up through Dassett Country Park. What seemed a modest ascent through woodland opened unexpectedly upon the local equivalent of mountains. Bare sheep-grazed slopes plunged steeply into a broad plain of far fields, copses, distant towns. A stubby stone monument was inset with a circular brass map of the five counties surrounding. Replenishing our lungs in the fresh, sharp air, Jon and I strode along a ridge admiring the view, glowing with a contentment which the enigma back home seemed powerless to dash – on the contrary, with a heightened sense of expectation. Marvellous how one could adapt to, no capitalize upon the extraordinary. Meanwhile Lucy and Kirstie pored over the map, pointing out tiny landmarks.

"Poker tonight after dinner?" I asked Jon.

"You bet." We enjoyed poker. Bridge was for wimps.

"Afterwards we'll all pay a more serious game? If you're a game for it?"

"Hmm. I think so. I definitely do. At last."

"Kirstie likes to play that game in the dark – then to be surprised, illuminated!"

"Ah . . ."

"Don't say I tipped you off. It would seem we'd been swapping locker room tales."

"Quite. Let's get back to our ladies. So what'll we do about that fox?"

"I don't know. Do you?"

"I've been racking my brains. Sell the story to the papers? Our fox mightn't perform. This could end up in the hen's-egg

152

hatches-frog category; the silly season in midwinter. Maybe Lucy could –?"

"Take it away and slice it up? Destroy it, and find no proof?"

"I suppose there's no sense in alerting authorities. If there *are* any authorities on phoney animals, what bothers me is the subject could be top secret. If an alien earthwatch is going on, and governments suspect, they could be ruthless. We'd be muzzled, watched, maybe even –"

"Snuffed, to silence us?"

"There's that risk, Pete. Let's leave decisions till later, till we've played our games."

Later: pheasant, and more wine. We had dined around the fox's head which was still perched on the newspaper. The fox made no attempt to snatch mouthfuls of roast bird from our plates, though it continued to appear alive, a mute motionless guest at our board even when Lucy interrogated it, calling into its face like that French doctor addressing the victim of the guillotine. "Who are you, Charley Fox? Where do you come from? Are you recording, even now that you're unplugged?"

Lucy became quite drunk, drunk with a desire to know, to be fulfilled by Charles James. That desire would soon shift its focus. All four of us were members of a tiny secret tribal cult undergoing an initiation featuring wine, a feast, and soon the fever of gambling accompanied by images of kings and queens, and presently sexual rites to bind us all together. An hour later Lucy had the bank, while I had lost all of my original fifty pound stake money. Nothing was left to bet except myself.

"If I lose this time, Lucy, you win *me*. How about that?"

"Yes!" she agreed, excited. "If that's okay with you, Kirstie?"

"Sure, you know it is. We've been leading up to this."

"Jon?"

He nodded.

When Lucy won, she leapt up, ignoring coins and notes, and gripped my wrist.

153

"Be off with you then upstairs," said Kirstie, "the both of you. All night long till the morning."

Jon also stood expectantly.

"Ah, Jon, I'd like for us to stay down here by the fireside. The sofa pulls out into a bed." Kirstie was in charge of fires – her hair had affinity with flames – however tonight she had let the wood die down to ash and embers. As I was leaving with Lucy, Kirstie called, "Peter, turn out the lights." Which I did.

In the darkness of the parlour only small patches glowed hot like eyes of wild beasts surprised by a torch beam, watching from the ingle.

"I like it this way," I heard as I closed the door.

Leading Lucy upstairs, I opened the second bedroom, almost as large as our own. It was very warm from the storage heater. I switched on a bedside lamp then killed the light on the stairs, and shut the door. Already Lucy had shaken off her white jacket and was unbuttoning her blouse.

Unexpectedly I found myself embarrassed at being naked in Lucy's unclothed presence. I tended to avert my gaze from the complete spectacle, by pressing close to her. Thus the nakedness that I saw was partial, discreet camera angles on her bare flesh: shoulders, neck, a breast, the top of a knee, a flash of thigh. I couldn't bring myself to pull back and feast my eyes. When Lucy rolled me over in turn to mount me I quickly drew her body down upon myself rather than let her rear upright exultantly. I think she interpreted my hugs as an attempt at even closer, more ecstatic intimacy.

Meanwhile an alarm clock, a time bomb, was ticking away in my brain. Fifteen minutes, twenty, how long?

A squeal from downstairs! That wasn't any orgasmic outcry. Too magnified by far, too full of pain and affront. Another longer shriek.

"Something's wrong." I pulled loose, seized a sheet to wrap myself.

"You can't just go bursting in on them! Jon isn't rough."

"Maybe it's the fox – I'll check. You wait here."

"While you peep through the keyhole? I'm peeping too." Lucy snatched up a blanket as cloak.

"He isn't *rough*," she whispered insistently as I padded downstairs ahead of her.

A line of light showed under the parlour door. I heard a sound of weeping, and mumblings from Jon, so I pushed the door open.

A naked man, remarkably hairy around the base of his spine like some huge monkey. A nude woman: plump breasts, freckles, swelling thighs, red bush of pubic hair. Rubens territory I had mapped so often with my fingers, hitherto unseen. Kirstie's hands were splayed defensively not over crotch or bosom but . . .

Monkey swung round and snarled. "You *bastard*, Peter!"

From Kirstie's tummy to her left tit sprawled a vivid red birthmark resembling the map of some unknown island once owned by the British and coloured accordingly.

How could I explain that I'd merely wanted to test whether my wife, my comrade, my bedmate of the last eight years, was a phoney person, an alien life-machine planted in the world to watch us? The idea seemed suddenly insane. Despite the fox, despite. And so now the fox too seemed insane.

Jon and Lucy mounted in silence to the room where we'd made love, and where I'd failed to see her as revealingly as I'd suddenly seen Kirstie. I went upstairs to our bedroom alone, and eventually slept. Kirstie stayed on the sofa by the dead fire.

In the morning, how stilted we were. What minimal conversation at breakfast: no one mentioned the night before. We ate burnt sausages and eggs with broken yolks and avoided looking at each other much, until Jon said, "I think we'd best be going."

Lucy stared longingly for many moments at the fox which Kirstie had transferred to the sideboard, still on the *Cork Examiner*.

"You made sure I couldn't have it, didn't you, Peter?" she

155

accused me. "Seems very small and unimportant now. Yes, let's go."

When the Porsche had driven off, I said, "I was drunk last night."

Kirstie nodded. "I don't believe in divorce, but you shan't touch me again, Peter. You'd best find a girlfriend who won't put your health at risk. I shan't object when you're 'delayed' at the office. We won't sell the cottage, either. We'll come out here on lots of weekends to be lonely together, with Charles James. He must be very lonely. He's lost his body. You've lost mine."

Penance, I thought. A million Hail bloody Marys and no forgiveness. The unforgivable sin is betrayal. Maybe she would soften in time.

During the next week Kirstie bought a varnished wooden shield from a sports trophy shop, and a Black and Decker drill together with some drill-bits, one of them huge. When we arrived at the cottage on Saturday she told me to mount the shield above the ingle then drill a fat hole through the middle, drill the hole six inches deep into the stone wall behind.

When I'd done so, she lifted the fox's head and slid its spine into the hole. Held in place thus, neck flush with the plaque, the fox head imitated any other such hunting trophy decorating a pub wall. Except that it was still fresh, still spuriously alive, although utterly unresponsive. By now it reacted to no stimuli at all, a little like Kirstie herself. So it hung there in our parlour, an absurd living idol, a dumb dazed undying God of falsity.

Time passes but does it heal us? Last weekend when I entered the parlour, for the first time in months I thought I saw a flicker of movement from the fox, a twitch of an ear, an eyeblink. I began to hope: that it might one day revive, that one day it would eject itself from our wall and try to rejoin, somehow, its lost body. And go away. Then she would have forgiven me.

I even patted the fox encouragingly on the forehead. Or

mpulse I gripped its ears and tugged gently. I would slide it in
nd out just to give it the idea of resuming a more active
xistence.

The head wouldn't budge. It was fixed firm. In panic I pulled,
ut in vain. I realized then that the spine had taken root in the
abric of the building. I imagined tendrils growing out from that
pine, threads of clever little cells converting stone and mortar
nto nerves and organs, spreading along the inside of the wall into
ther walls, insinuating themselves through the timbers like the
ungus threads of dry rot until the head had gained a mutant body
f another kind so that we would eat within it, crap within it,
leep within it, though not make love within it.

How I feared the head's revival now. How I dreaded to take an
xe to it, causing the cottage to shriek, as Kirstie had shrieked
hat night.

Samathiel's Summons

The day after the third woman student in three months was found murdered, Trish told her roommate, Helen, "I'm going to summon a demon to protect me."

Trish began rolling another joint on the open pages of *The Grand Grimoire of Magick*, a glossy paperback. Her shelf bore at least twenty similar books, tucked in amidst the modern poetry texts, and a Tibetan mandala poster was tacked above her bed (Was Magick with a "k" perhaps more magical than plain Magic?).

Helen regarded her with exasperation. Trish was a fey pre-Raphaelite redhead with blanched skin, wearing an impractically long Indonesian batik dress and toe-grip leather sandals guaranteed to prevent her from running or kicking or otherwise defending herself. Helen, on the other hand, had her own black hair cut short so that nobody could grab hold of it. She dressed in jeans and boots and a slippery plastic jacket.

"You promised you wouldn't smoke more than one," said Helen angrily. (And even that first one had been head stuff). "You're already stoned. Murder's nothing to joke about."

"But I'm not joking. I'm scared out of my wits." Blithely Trish lit up.

"Look, Trish, you might be into the occult, but it's all just a game. Tarot cards and everything. It isn't real. What that bastard man has been doing is real. As real as dropping napalm on people or torturing them with electric shocks. *I'm* scared – but there's an answer to fear. You should be coming to the self-defence class

158

with me this evening, not getting stoned and reading all that garbage. It's escapist mysticism."

Trish offered to share her joint.

"I'm getting out of here," said Helen. "The air's poisoned. I need a clear head. I need my sense of balance."

"Karate means 'empty-handed'. *You* told me that." Trish giggled. "So you're going out empty-handed. I want someone holding my hand."

"Oh, do you? Such as the chivalrous bravos of the football team? Or the security guards in their sexy SS uniforms? I'm damned if I see why women have to be escorted around and curfewed because there's one perverted lunatic male somewhere out there. Why don't they curfew all the men? Oh, I'll tell you why. They enjoy this. They're using these murders to oppress us, Trish. Then they can all be gallant heroes and stomp us a bit further into the ground in the process. And your mysticism is another oppression. I'm sick of it. If you don't toughen up, I'm going to put my name down to switch rooms."

Trish exhaled. "I don't want a footballer or a guard escorting me. I like going where I please. Alone."

"Better learn self-defence, then."

Trish smiled. "Footballers are boring. I want a demon."

"For Christ's sake! Take a walk across the Green tonight if it's a demon you're looking for. There's a human one about."

Helen gathered her judo costume and marched out, slamming the door, leaving Trish in a cloud of smoke gazing at her row of books on mysteries and magic.

When Helen got back to her room later that evening – after being escorted to the door of the Hall, to her chagrin, in company with other returning woman students – she discovered that Trish had upended one of the beds and rolled the carpet back. The air was rich with fumes.

On the exposed floorboards, in white chalk, Trish had drawn a large five-pointed star. A book lay open on the floor beside it,

159

containing a picture of the same. Trish was just finishing lettering
a final word in one of the outer triangles: *ADONAI*. The other
four triangles contained these words: *TETRAGRAMMATON
HELOI, ANABONA,* and *JOD.*

Trish stepped back, brushing chalk off her fingers.

"Hi, Helen. How did the karate go? Oh, but the power of the
soul is greater than the power of the fist!"

"What the hell do you think you're doing? *Two* people live in
this room, in case you hadn't noticed."

"Tell you what," Trish said pleasantly, "if nothing happens
tonight, I'll give your self-defence class a try. One try, anyhow. I
might turn me on. I guess there's a lot of mystic energy involved
in the fighting arts."

"Huh!"

"Hey, keep clear!" cried Trish as Helen stepped forward. "If
you walk across my pentagram, you'll rub the lines out. Then it
won't be one continuous line. It won't work."

"*You* promise not to smoke any more dope in this room – or I'll
rub all your goddamn lines out." Shuffling her boots, Helen
advanced a pace.

"No, stop! Please! I took such a long time getting the angles
right. Okay, okay, I promise. No more dope in here. Now will
you sit down?"

Nodding, Helen edged around the outside of the diagram and
sat on her own bed; this had been pushed aside, but at least not
upended.

"You've been taking advantage of me, Trish. You know
perfectly well I would never report you for smoking. That would
be despicable. But you'll *stop* it in here! From now on you can go
and get stoned in somebody else's room."

"I already promised. Take it easy, will you? I need all my
energy for this."

Sullenly, Helen started reading the chalk words aloud. "*Tetra
. . . grammaton, Adon –*"

"Be quiet! You don't know what to do."

Helen toyed with reading out the other mystic words just to spite Trish, but subsided with a sigh. "Will this take long? I'm tired from the practice mats. If it doesn't work in ten minutes, will you kindly replace the carpet?"

"Ten? That doesn't give me long to tell the demon what to do."

"You're out of your brain, Trish."

"I'm in a heightened state of consciousness. Now will you sit here quietly while I read the invocation?"

"Aren't you meant to be standing *inside* that shape? I mean, I hate to correct the expert – or remind you that you've got an essay due on Hart Crane . . ."

"No, no. In most rituals magicians stand inside for protection. But this one's different. The demon is contained by the pentagram. The book says so."

While Helen tapped her foot impatiently on the boards, Trish picked up her book and addressed the empty chalk diagram.

"Jod, Anabona, Heloi, Tetragrammaton! Rotas, Opera, Tenet, Arepo, Sator! By the power of the Mighty, Adonai, Elohim, Sabaoth, I conjure thee, *Ego te invoco*, Samathiel. In the name of the Three Most Terrible Names, Agla, On, Tetragrammaton, and by the Unspeakable Name which I now speak, IHVH, I demand that you appear in seemly and obedient form. Come, Samathiel, Come!"

The air popped. Poised on tiptoe in the centre of the pentagram stood a . . .

"Oh, God." Helen jumped and ran for the door.

. . . a man-thing with ram's horns curling from its brows. Its eyes were golden, with black pupils rectangular like a goat's. Its stoutly muscled body was a coppery red, and naked except for a leather loincloth.

The creature stabbed a finger in Helen's direction. Helen promptly fell in mid-stride, sprawling on the floor. She didn't move.

"I c-c-conjure thee, Sa-Sa-Samathiel," stammered Trish.

"Call me Sam," said the creature with a grin that seemed purely diabolic.

" – to obey. Obey! By the Unspeakable Name –"

"Oh, screw all that rigamarole. You've exactly as much power over me as a ringing telephone has. I can take the call or leave it. This time I decided to take it."

"I constrain thee –"

"Do you really?" Samathiel strode forward out of the pentagram. "You ought to remember about the cracks between floorboards."

"By the name El, depart without harm!"

Samathiel remained.

"How inhospitable," he said lightly. "I presume you summoned me for some reason?"

"What have you done to Helen?"

"Nothing much – she's asleep. She'll wake up when I leave. This is between you and me; it's no business of hers. Now, why have you called me from the Metaworld?"

Trish regrouped her courage – despite the fact that Samathiel was on the wrong side of the pentagram. After all, the demon hadn't seized her. He hadn't carried her off into flames. Maybe he *couldn't*.

"You *do* have to obey me, don't you? I order you to tell the truth!"

Samathiel scratched his horny head. "That's logically invalid. Your order depends on the assumption I'm being ordered to verify."

All demons are liars, Trish thought weakly. *Sophists*. "I shall assume that I command you."

"Assume what you like," he chuckled. "I assure you I'm here voluntarily. So how may I assist you, fair enchantress?"

"I want a bodyguard," she said boldly. "I want him to appear *immediately* when I need him, but he must keep hidden the rest of the time. There's a murderer going about. He's killed an

162

mutilated three women already. I have no wish to be number four."

Samathiel mused, tugging at his right horn.

"That's quite understandable. And I presume that this killer operates by surprise, when there's no one else about? So I wouldn't be observed by any curious eyes unadept in the Mysteries. And actually it's quite unlikely that you will be attacked, statistically speaking. Okay, I agree. Conditionally."

"Conditionally?"

"It's like this, Trish: irrespective of my own feelings of good will or malice toward you, there's a *balance* between the World and the Metaworld. I can assist you. I can save your life if you're attacked. However, should I do this good deed for you, I must also do a bad deed *to* you in some other manner. It's purely for the sake of symmetry. You understand? By accepting the good deed, you attract the bad deed subsequently."

"You don't want my soul when I die? That isn't it?"

Samathiel winked one of his goat's eyes. "On such brief acquaintance I would hardly plan on shacking up with you in the Metaworld. Which is what *that* would involve."

"How bad would a bad deed be?"

"Well, it would hardly be fatal, or that would make saving your life rather pointless."

"It definitely won't be fatal?"

"Definitely."

"Well . . . I suppose if the choice is between staying alive but having something nasty done to me, or being killed, it's better to stay alive. Whatever! Life's precious. I accept. How do I, er, summon you if I need to? I mightn't have much time, remember."

"Just think these words: Sam Elohim Jod. Shout them out in your mind. I'll be there."

Samathiel caught hold of her left hand. For an absurd moment, Trish imagined that he was going to kiss it. Instead, he twisted her hand over, palm upward.

"I'll sign here," he said. With a fingernail sharp as a cat's claw the demon sliced a cross in her flesh, so swiftly that she hardly felt the wound. He drew her hand to his lips and licked the blood.

Trish gasped as her palm began to ache. "Was *that* the bad deed?"

"No. Bad deeds come a bit bigger than that. And they don't come in advance; only when you use up the good deed. That was just to attune us."

Letting her hand drop, Samathiel stepped back inside the pentagram and raised himself up on tiptoe.

"Wait, Sam!" Trish cried. "Tell me about this Metaworld! Tell me something!"

However, Samathiel merely waved nonchalantly, and vanished slowly. Bit by bit. His ram's horns disappeared last of all. Briefly they hung alone in mid-air like some heraldic scroll.

Helen hauled herself up, and saw Trish but no demon. "It's gone . . . where did it go?"

"Back to the Metaworld, of course," Trish said smugly.

"Your hand's bleeding." Some blood was indeed dripping onto the floorboards. Helen darted forward, caught up Trish's hand, and stared at the mark cut in her palm.

"What did it *do*? What . . . what *was* it?"

"Oh, that was Sam. Short for Samathiel. He's my obedient servant. And now, I think I'll just roll another joint to celebrate. *Don't* object to my smoking, will you not, dear? Or I'll have a word with Sam about you."

Three weeks passed, and another female student was found dead and mutilated on waste ground a mile away from the campus.

Trish didn't exactly *want* to see Samathiel again (so she reasoned to herself), but life had become quite intolerable with constant police patrols, extra security guards, restrictions, random checks. A person couldn't even have a quiet smoke on her own on the Green these days. In fact, a person could hardly get to be alone; and it was just as bad in the Hall.

So, since Trish possessed the perfect self-defence, maybe it was her duty to make use of it? If only to get rid of the new police state which had been imposed on their lives . . .

"It's as if *we're* the criminals!" she protested one day.

"We are," said Helen grimly. She wore a brown belt now. "We're women. So first we're punished by the Butcher because we're women. Then we're taken into protective custody by every strutting male. That's the score."

"I *can't* score. That's the trouble! Not with all these police around. Dealers won't come near the place."

"Good," said Helen.

"But it *isn't* good."

"No, I suppose you're right. It's just one more ball and chain. One more limitation of our freedom."

So Trish began to slip out late at night, through a downstairs window which she gimmicked. She stole out of the Hall where they were locked up as if in Purdah.

Since her head was clearer these days (and nights), she successfully avoided being spotted by guards or police patrols. To anybody who was lurking in hiding in the neighbourhood in bushes, behind fences, or on waste lots, though, she did her best to advertise her presence, loitering in the night alone.

This was the seventh such night, and Trish had begun to wonder whether she were acting too much like a decoy. Tonight she hurried across the Green, back and forth in all the most dangerous places, acting scared – like a mouse scuttling for her nest before the hawk could pounce. She hoped she radiated fright and guilt at her rebellious temerity at being out alone.

Nothing. So she headed for the Agriculture Department's vegetable gardens.

Arriving there, she scurried along the gravel paths. The moon was below the faintly lamp-fogged horizon. Starlight exaggerated the threat of rows of onions, cabbages, and kale, tall spooky poles of runner beans, tool-sheds, making everything just that little bit visible, but not enough to see exactly what it was.

165

She was seized from behind. A hand clamped her mouth.

"*Wicked* girl," hissed a voice. The man's other hand squeezed around her throat.

Her heart pounded. *Sam Elohim Jod!* she cried out fiercely in her mind.

She was thrown to the ground . . .

As she rolled over, throat aching, a dark figure was lifting the first figure, of her attacker, clear off the ground. Against the stars she faintly saw the great curls of Samathiel's horns.

The Butcher – who else could it be? – cried out, "No! No! For God's sake, what *are* you?"

She heard Samathiel's voice reply, "I'm the Devil, come to collect you, little man."

Then she heard a dull cracking sound, as the Butcher's back was broken.

The body dropped to the ground. Samathiel bent over it, tearing the man's shirt open and apparently fingering his chest.

"What are you doing, Sam?"

"Carving 'Butcher' on him. His body is his gravestone."

The demon, of whose expression she could glean no hint in the darkness, handed her to her feet, but did not release her hand.

"And now, Mistress Trish, 'tis time for the Bad Deed that necessarily balances the Good Deed."

"What . . . what's it going to be?"

"I've given a certain amount of thought to that because I did surmise that you might go out of your way to attract this creature to you. Power unused is no power at all, is it?"

"What's it going to be?"

"Ah . . . I might reach into your brain and make you an epileptic. Or I might wither one of your legs. Or blind you in one eye. The Harm has to be *sufficient* . . ." The demon chuckled. "And it must, of course, be unexpected. Unless expecting makes it even worse . . ."

Abruptly, Samathiel whirled her . . . elsewhere. She was

ragged through disorienting geometries of light – was this the Harm? – but almost immediately these became the walls and the loomed ceiling of a large chamber of polished blue marble. The chamber looked to be hollowed out of marble rather than merely built of it. No door was visible, though there was a single tall mullioned window, without glass panes, giving onto sunlight and blue sky.

The floor was heaped with hairy rugs, deep as the storeroom of a furrier. Released from the demon's grasp, Trish stumbled across the soft bounce of the beast pelts, blinking at the sudden brightness. She clutched one of the sun-dappled marble bars of the window, and caught her breath. Below was wild forest and a winding river. Far, *far* below. The window looked directly down a precipice perhaps half a mile high.

"Here the sun shines bright," said the demon voice, "when on Earth it's night. And now . . ."

Trish turned. Samathiel had discarded his leather loincloth. She stared in horror as he began stepping toward her.

"Your Harm," he said, "is to be raped by a demon in his bedchamber, and to bear his child."

As he tore off Trish's favourite batik dress, she shrieked, "Helen's right! You *are* all the same! You are, you are!"

Samathiel just laughed; though his laughter, somehow, didn't sound entirely satanic.

Trish had stayed in bed, chain-smoking ordinary cigarettes, imagining the devil life in her womb, the soon-to-be foetus with Sam's horns. She suspected there would be no possible way of aborting it. Days of fear had passed, days of memory.

The door burst open, making Trish flinch, but it was only Helen with a piece of paper in her hand. A demon didn't need a door to enter by . . .

Helen opened the glass louvres to ventilate the room.

"Well?" Trish asked wearily. The piece of paper was her certificate of impregnation by a lord of Hell. The result of the

home-test kit had been ambiguous; this one had been carried ou
by a professional clinic.

"Well, *nothing*," Helen said. "You aren't pregnant. The
result's negative. It's 'no.' That's definite."

'What? But Samathiel *said –!*''

"You're no more pregnant than I am, Trish."

"Samathiel told me I would bear his child!"

"So he was lying. Or joking. Look, Trish, I don't deny you
were raped. That was pretty obvious when you staggered in in
your rags. I think the Butcher raped you out there – and
somehow you killed him. Don't ask me *how*, when you've never
been near a self-defence class. But you did. Unless . . . you
escaped – or got interrupted – and the football team zapped
him?"

Indeed, the police were currently hunting, unsuccessfully, for
the "vigilantes" who had snapped the presumed murderer'
spine and cut the word "Butcher" into his chest.

"No, Sam did it! Then he took me away to the Metaworld and
did the Bad Deed to me. And returned me to the Hall. For crying
out loud, you *saw* Sam that first time. You know he wa
real."

"In that case, he knew nothing about pregnancy testing. Read
the result for yourself."

Trish scrambled out of bed and read.

"I get it!" she exclaimed. "Sam *said* he'd fertilize me – but he
didn't *let* himself. He used yoga or something. He wanted to
worry me – to make me feel cursed – but he didn't actually wan
to harm me."

"Didn't want to harm you? What do you call rape?"

"Yes, but he had to do something to balance off saving my life
He didn't blind me or wither my leg or make me an epileptic. He
didn't do anything permanent."

"Maybe he didn't want his demon's chromosomes messed up
by all that dope you smoke. When you can get it."

"That doesn't happen! That's a lie, about broken chromo

168

somes. I think he deliberately chose the one thing that would seem awful, but which wouldn't actually wreck my life."

"Hell, Trish, you can't justify rape, ever! Rape's the vilest abuse of a woman by a male."

"That's what I said to him. I said, 'Helen's right – you men *are* all the same.' And he laughed – because I guess he agreed with you. See, he was a good guy? Me believing I was carrying a demon child was bad enough. As bad as blindness. But he didn't want to blind me. Or make me epileptic. Yet he had to do something vile, and I had to believe it was vile. Actually . . . he was being *chivalrous*." Trish clapped her hands gleefully. "I guess they're all moralists over there in the Metaworld. They know good and evil inside out."

"You're crazy," said Helen. "You're sick."

"No, don't you see? I'm healthy. I'm not sick with his seed." Trish danced around. "Oh, what I'd give for a joint now, to celebrate! Sam bent the rules for me. He chose to. That was chivalry. That was . . . yes, you can even call it love. Kindness and love."

"I'm going," said Helen. "This is the complete end."

"But why? I called Sam up. He exists. You saw him."

"That was your smoke getting in my head. And that's *all*! I was so knocked out by it, I even fell down. That's all, all, all!"

Four nights later, with her new roommate due to move in the next day, Trish rolled back the carpet again, and once more drew the pentagram on the floorboards and wrote the words of power around it.

"Jod, Anabona, Heloi, Tetragrammaton!" she pronounced, all the way through to, "Come, Samathiel, Come!"

But the pentagram stayed empty, chalk lines on bare wood.

She called. But Samathiel did not accept the call.

Sam did not come.

And maybe this was kindness, too.

Aid From a Vampire

I walk through a world of fear, little lady, but it is not myself of whom people should be afraid, not any more. People should wish eagerly for my presence, if the truth be told. They should long for my attack, unlike in bygone days.

If the truth be told. A person such as I retains the mannerisms of speech of much earlier years. A person? Yes, I regard myself as a person. Oh indeed! I'm more of a person now than I've been for seven hundred years. At last people are equal to me, and I am merely equal to people.

I walk through a world gone cold, as cold as my own flesh and blood, but it is not myself who has chilled the world, is it, little lady?

I hunt, I feed, and I save my victims from themselves. Oh yes I do. If you listen, you will understand. But I cannot save or cure myself, not any longer. Ironic, yes? Ironic. Bitterly, coldly ironic. Perhaps after all there is a God, and this God conceived a plan. I am His salvator, redeemer, his modern Jesus crossed with Wandering Jew. Or maybe there is a Devil, and just as in the case of Doctor Faust – though for many more years than him – I have enjoyed my strength, my skill, my invulnerability only now at long last to have my pledge called in, a pledge which I never to my knowledge undertook yet which was undertaken on my behalf. Undertaken by what? By God? By nature, damned nature? By an unknown alien force?

You are intrigued?

*

Facts: in the year 1300, or thereabouts – who kept a calendar in those days? – somewhere in France, since I recall how French was once my mother tongue, and yes I did have a mother, a fat asthmatic peasant woman, and a father, an oafish slave of the soil, and a varying number of brothers and sisters too, round about 1300 when I was eleven or twelve years old I became what I am.

Eleven or twelve years old. Who counted ages when children died like flies? If indeed they weren't murdered, massacred, trampled, violated amidst the ravage and pillage of whole countrysides.

I was named Adrian or something similar. Who knew names except approximately when no one could read or write? I suspect there were some Roman ruins associated with the name of the Emperor Hadrian near our village of hovels. I seem to recall piles of stone grown over by grass. You can call me Adrien.

No, I wasn't waylaid on my trudge back from the fields at dusk after a day of scaring birds. No other predatory vampire was involved, and I have never met another one, if any other exist – though from time to time I have tracked the rumours and alarms, discovering all too often that these must only refer to myself, inflated by superstition, distanced in time and space by my own wanderings and by my own forgetfulness.

Nor have I ever created another vampire. Until the present years I have only left victims dead or dying.

It was, I suppose, a "miracle" which young Adrien plodded into the teeth of along the edge of the woods. It was a transcendental moment, a vortex of strangeness, a twist of reality. It was Joan of Arc and her voices, it was Bernadette and her shining lady, it was Moses and the burning bush. It was that kind of transforming, transfixing, transubstantiating experience. A visitation: inexplicable, devastating. With this difference: with *darkness* in the place of light.

Well, so what did happen to ignorant Adrien? Too ignorant to know what country he lived in, or what year it was, or what lay over the next hill. A sort of human animal.

Yet how sophisticated he was to become in due course – how well groomed, by experience, for more sophisticated future eras! Almost like a fairy tale, eh? The grubby frog turning into a prince! Albeit a prince of the darkness, of the night – of fine chandelier-lit salons, and of shadowy alleyways.

What did happen? I've little idea. How many beneficiaries – or dupes – of miracles have the slightest idea what actually happened to them, as opposed to what they imagine happened? I was taken, twisted, turned. Not at the hands of some thirsty, lonely elder vampire. Of that I assure you.

I was, perhaps, a random experiment which the night itself conducted – solidifying and congealing round me at that very spot. Since we live, or used to live, in scientific times may I remind you how science says that all the particles composing matter are constantly vanishing into a void and reforming? Perhaps the cosmos hiccuped, so that all my particles ceased to exist in concert – to recreate themselves from energy a moment later, in a different pattern. Here's an analogy: it's highly unlikely that all the atoms of air in a room will simultaneously rush into the same corner, creating a gasping vacuum in the rest of the room. Highly unlikely! Yet not totally impossible.

I can spin other theories too. I can assert that a communication beam transmitted from a distant star and using some mode of energy which humans haven't discovered intercepted the antennae of my nervous system and discharged itself, its alienness. Maybe I was an attempt to transmit the essence of alien life, the vital pattern, across the light years into a host organism. If so, presumably the attempt wasn't repeated.

Maybe the dark that ate me and spat me out again, digested and reassembled, was one of those supposed unidentified extraterrestrial vehicles such as reportedly shine hypnotic beams of light on people – in my case, a beam of darkness. Maybe aliens descended in that wood without my seeing them and touched me and rearranged me for a purpose difficult to grasp. I may have been intended as a storage device for all the blood I would drink and all the men and women I would drain, a gatherer of specimen lives which would etch my cells, encoded in molecular memory – until the day when my makers, my redesigners, would return and would home in on me and net me and squeeze me dry into some machine or into themselves. If so, it would hardly be part of my purpose to understand my origin, would it?

So let us simply say that Adrien the animal-boy was altered in that moment into a creature which already sensed how strong it was, how quickly it would heal from any injury, how it was the next best thing to immortal, and how it must feed on the blood of the living in order to sustain its own cold blood. If I'd altered a few degrees differently I might have become a wild boy of Aveyron, running with the wolves. Instead I became a vampire. *The* vampire. Do you know of any other, actually provenly known?

Of course not, little lady.

Needless to say, from time to time I attempted to discover my cause. The urge would wax and wane. Sometimes curiosity waned for a whole century. The closest I came was with an alchemist in Nuremburg, though finally I drank him, ever-protective of my tracks, yet also imagining in angry frustration that his blood might teach me something extra.

Johannes Galb was his name, and he signed his coded manuscripts with the Latin form Galbinus.

From Galb I learned how an alchemist is by no means principally interested in transmuting one element into another element, climaxing with lead into gold. All of his intricate, time-consuming technical manoeuvres aimed at that end, all the alembics and athenors and retorts and furnaces, all the distillations and sublimations, and all the staining of his hands and burning of his hair and exploding of his attic were no more than an analogy, a physical template for what he was actually up to – namely the transmutation of his own mind, and being. Alchemy is a technological shaman dance. Just as the shaman dance gave birth eventually to ballet, so did alchemy conceive chemistry as an offshoot; which soon became the main branch, then the entire trunk. Thus the world grows more arty and refined and clever. Or *did*.

Who better than a Galbinus to intuit what it was that had transformed me, and how and why?

I remember his house rather well: all six stories of it, including the locked attic laboratory and the locked cellar where I spent my days in my normal dreamless trance wrapped in an old quilt (*not* in a coffin). Oak pillars and beams and panelled rooms and gently winding staircases . . . but I avoided the household rooms if possible, and the wife, the three children, the maid, the cook, the journeymen and apprentices. Built of half-timbered sandstone, and partly plastered pink, the house wore a steep red-tiled roof punctuated by gabled dormer windows. High up under the hip of the roof, sheltered by the overhanging jerkin-head, a wooden balcony jutted out. I often stared out from that balcony over the starlit city after I'd returned from feeding on a reveller, and before we got down to our alchemical work. Lofts in Nuremburg were generally used to store firewood which was hauled up in baskets by means of a rope winch; but Galb used his winch to tug up apparatus and materials, whilst I sometimes used the rope to descend in darkness into the square below, and to return later with the sweet-salt taste of blood on my lips.

The house was close by the city wall near the *Tiergartnertor*, the great gate tower. As per city by-laws – chimney sweeps for the regulation of – the chimney of the Galb residence was wide enough to be climbed up all the way from the open ground floor hearth to the sky. I used that chimney more than once to shin down to the ground floor in blessed darkness (thus to flee into the cellar) when sunrise had overtaken us unawares aloft; for it's true that the vampire shuns the sun. I'm the creation of the night.

Johannes Galb had an eagle nose, wispy straw hair, and little squinty piggy eyes (the better to avoid acid splashes and shrapnel from explosions). Nominally he was a genuine goldsmith – though his *hausfrau* mostly oversaw the work of the journeymen – consequently he always had a supply of the needful to fake a demonstration and gull fools who might help fund his real enterprise. But he wasn't a fake himself, oh no. No more was I, though to persuade him of my authenticity I was obliged . . . No, that isn't quite so. In those days I felt dramatically invincible. So I put out my left eye with a red-hot iron and . . . slept on the matter . . . and arose the next evening renewed. (I didn't feel much pain, just discomfort, like a very dull toothache. But I wasn't insensible; my nerves weren't numb to pleasure. At the taste of blood I experienced shivering ecstasies.)

"See: I have already been transmuted," I told Galb that night. "I'm over two hundred years old already."

"Ah," he gasped, "so you succeeded in the Art. The enter-prise *is* possible."

"I didn't succeed," I replied, "because I attempted nothing. I was a filthy, exhausted, snot-brained country urchin – no scholar, not even a grown man."

"Therefore we must become as little children? Is that the secret? We must achieve a fresh . . . a magical perspective?"

For his epoch this was very acute of him.

"What was it that *precipitated* your alteration?" he went on. He had lots of precipitates on his shelves.

"Nothing. Black nothing. The fingers of night."

"What do you want from me, then? You, who know less than I, who in turn know less than I need to? Surely you don't wish to be . . . untransmuted? To be altered back from divine gold into mortal lead?"

I shook my head. "I want to know why it happened, that's all."

With my consent he experimented on me. He boiled bits of flesh which I cut off for him. He brewed up samples of my blood, distilled them, employed them alchemically. I even let him slice me open and poke around inside my guts and touch my cold slow heart. I suppose he discovered more about anatomy than most doctors knew at the time.

I was with Galb for three months – months for him of excitement and tantalization – however no message was written anywhere in my body which he could read, so perhaps it was a kindness when I finally drank him and easily escaped over the steep roofs and the city wall.

Galb's was a thoroughly medieval way of regarding the universe. He saw the whole world as a collection of codes, of embodied meanings whereby every beast and bird and mineral, every plant and insect was the symbolic signature of some other, ethereal reality. Thanks to him I decided that I – my body and my being – was indeed a message, sent from nobody to nobody. I was a cipher that referred back to a language which no one else had ever spoken. I was a symbol without a referent. Yet I referred. Oh yes. I referred to the veins of a multitude of people.

For a while my very name, Adrien, assumed a significance which may have been unwarranted. "Ad rien" is a confusion of Latin and French, meaning "to nothing". Equally my name was an anagram of "n'aider", "not to aid", "don't help". There's no help. Nowadays the three letters A and I and D assume much more significance! Perhaps that's only a coincidence, not something written in me from the start. Though I can't help fearing otherwise.

Much later, when Mesmer's animal magnetism became all the rage (as well as a cause of rage amongst officialdom) I did try a different tack; not a distillation of my blood or a partial dissection of myself but a harking back by means of hypnotism into the well of my darkened memory to that moment when I'd changed or been changed.

In Paris privately I consulted a stage mesmerist who had been drummed out of the fraternity of physicians for daring to adopt Mesmer's methods in the clinic. Of course, afterwards I would have to drink Monsieur Ambrose as well.

Visualize a sunny salon of a room on the second floor of an hôtel overlooking the Luxembourg Garden. Dancing sunbeams, clip-clop of carriages outside, a sofa where I lay like a fainting lady while Ambrose spoke softly and made passes with his hands, weaving these before my eyes in patterns which induced languor and the slavery of the will.

I had told him how I wished to recall being a boy once again, a boy returning to his home village down a path alongside a dark wood of a dingy evening which "changed my life". I also wished to be aware of myself in the trance, as an observer.

Soon I was uncouthly mouthing medieval French which may have seemed to Ambrose to be simply some broad regional accent – though doubtless he wondered how on earth this sophisticate reclining on his sofa could have been such a bucolic clod in his younger days. Indeed my life must have changed.

I was describing myself shambling homeward by that dusken wood, once more I was experiencing that fatal hour, when:

I blanked.

Next thing I knew, Ambrose, looking concerned, was alternately pinching my cheeks savagely and making passes like a windmill while he barked, "You are awake! You are awake!"

I bounded up and gripped him with my vampire strength, lifting him easily in the air.

"What did I say? What did I do?"

"Monsieur, please! It's beyond my experience."

"What is?"

"You were speaking of that wood – and the darkness. At least I think so. It was hard to follow your words, your voice. And then you . . . you cried out in a strangled horror, '*Rien! Rien!*' and went rigid as a board, stiff as rigor mortis. As if you had been dead for a day."

Only then did it occur to me that I must indeed have *died* on that day long ago. I must have died, and come coldly alive again. The change must have occurred while I was dead, and was a zero. Being "undead" is such a central strand of the vampire legend that it's odd – most odd – that I only at last took this personally during that mesmeric séance in the Paris of the first Napoleon. It's as though my fantasy archetype knew me better than I knew myself.

On the other hand, since there appeared to be an unbreakable seal, a prohibition upon that moment at the wood's edge, maybe the truth is that there was nothing about the moment which could be comprehended by a human mind; and therefore nothing existed to be perceived. A frog's eye is only constructed to perceive movement. Therefore a fly which stands still does not exist for the frog. In a similar way that moment which transmuted me did not exist for me. It was impenetrable, empty, a nothingness.

"I have been dead longer than that, Monsieur Ambrose," I said, lowering him so that my teeth were level with his neck. "Six hundred years, if it's a day."

Soon his arms waved frantically again. This time he wasn't trying to hypnotize me.

If I began my life as a vampire in non-existence, in invisibility, then all this talk of peasant boy Adrien and of Galbinus and of Ambrose matters not in the least, does it, little lady? It solves nothing.

We both know what matters now. *All* that matters here at the start of the third millennium is the dying of the human race – and that fear-death which paralyses those who still survive. So many people dare not make love any longer. So many men suffer from impotence, the fear unmanning them. You know all this. AIDS is the adze, the chopper that has lopped the human race at the root. The exponential plague without a cure.

AIDS is why the dominoes have all fallen over, all the systems of civilization. Hospitals, welfare, graveyards, transport, trade, and finally society itself, till we have become almost medieval again. Simply too many victims for the camel's back! And then more victims, and more carriers, and more victims still. How much love is made these days, little lady?

178

I'm sure the plague came from no laboratory. Too slow a tool to fight a war with – yet in cosmic terms how deadly fast, almost infinitely faster than whatever extinguished the dinosaurs, eh?

Maybe it was always lying asleep in Africa, just waiting for the human race to attain critical mass? Waiting for people to breed enough bodies then mix up those bodies in the centrifuge of high-speed travel, total mobility, commerce, war, and mega-cities? Ha! That suggests a tool devised by nature, by the Earth itself, to correct unbalanced ecology. To be sure the world of nature reconquers its lost territory year by year. I have never regarded nature romantically. What medieval peasant boy could?

How coldly I laugh when I think of those old proposals to isolate victims and carriers in guarded camps the size of cities! Why, now that the whole world is sick, the camps that are so jealously guarded in remote wildernesses by the vestiges of government lock up the remaining pure-bloods instead, if a pure-blood is desperate enough to volunteer, or unlucky enough to be netted. Yes, let us bear witness to the new monks and nuns of sexuality trying to breed untaintedly to save the race, struggling against their own psychic impotence and infertility, terrified that they'll be exposed or their children will be exposed – when the support systems for those camps collapse or when military chiefs fight for control over those Fort Knoxes of clean blood. It isn't easy to catch AIDS. Not easy at all. But in the long run – a generation, two generations, with no cure, a soaring graph of victims and carriers, and society in tatters on account of this – it's also inevitable. The only safety is to become immune.

Surely you must know about those pure-blood camps? No? Maybe I shouldn't feel astonished. Communications are as nothing nowadays. Everywhere is fragmented, falling apart. I have travelled more than you.

There's something else you didn't know till you met me, little lady, though now you know. There is one cure for AIDS. That cure is the bite of the vampire. Of me, the only vampire.

Oh, not because I kill you! That isn't what I meant by a cure. The baby thrown out with the bath water.

Let me tell you about the first person I cured – what, ten years ago now? She was a frail redhead with an alabaster skin. Skinny from her sickness. Still pretty in a way, although not as pretty as you. The flesh was drawing tight over her bones. She was in remission at the time, in between one bout of illness and another, to each of which her wrecked immune system would surrender helplessly. But there were still medical services, after a fashion. There was still a pharmaceutical industry. With drugs, she could stagger from crisis to crisis for a while longer. Better than your predicament, eh? Almost a golden age by comparison. I smell your fear.

She was the first plague victim I tasted. I was growing desperate, you see, for lack of choice. I have to feed, even if the blood is vile. But truly I hadn't given much deep thought to the plague as it affected me, other than to worry that my human cattle herd was thinning out drastically, and growing much more wary – violently wary – of anyone who was an unknown quantity.

I had caught her in a moonlit, rubbish-strewn back street in . . . it doesn't matter which city. I gripped her, bared and sank my fangs into her neck – and she laughed at me. She laughed.

"Vampire! Oh that's rich!"

Momentarily I relaxed – though already the tang of her blood, albeit spiced with sickness, was enflaming me strangely like some glorious poison.

"I have AIDS, Vampire. I have AIDS. You're drinking AIDS-blood. Go on, drink! Enjoy! I'd rather be drained by you than by illness after stupid illness."

I stared into her eyes, pale and weak in the light of the Moon.

"You can believe in the existence of a vampire? Most people till nearly their final moment, imagine that I'm some type of psychotic. A flake. A pretend-Dracula."

"Oh I believe, I believe. This is the last possible piece of poetry in this ghastly world. Thank you! But," and here tears squeezed from her eyes, like droplets of moon-dew miraculously wrung from the Moon's dry seas, "you're feeding on a woman with AIDS. And AIDS is transmitted from blood to blood, isn't it, my Vampire?"

That taste, which was tainted, and yet even so . . . I had to carry on. As if the taint was addictive. And it was, oh it was! Yet not in such a way that I could sate myself by emptying her. I had to feed on her just so much, and no more. Then I laid her down amidst the rubbish, still conscious, still staring at my eyes, my mouth, my teeth, and instead of racing away I sat by her. Thus I witnessed her recovery, the start of her revival. In the rose-hued light of dawn I saw the first hint of bloom in her white cheeks again. That was merely a visual coincidence, but she knew, and I knew – that I had cured her.

I also knew that I had acquired a taste for the taint; that I was inflexibly addicted, as surely as if the inclination had been locked away in me long ago, and now the door was open.

It only gradually dawned on me that my powers of recuperation were fading away, that my own flesh was beginning to age, that injuries could prove fatal, that I was no longer immortal.

I do not mean that I am sick. I am not. Simply, that in another thirty, forty years I shall die just as anyone else has ever died throughout history, of a heart attack, or a cancer, or an accident, whatever.

Meanwhile I feed, and I cure.

Do you think I should present myself to what's left of a government, with its camps and convoys and generators and laboratories? Present myself as a living serum source, to be drained in my own turn, to be milked as carefully as the last cow in the world, my blood to be centrifuged, packaged, and injected? The most valuable resource ever, eh? The most precious protected prisoner, strait-jacketed in case I do myself harm – until, who knows, I *do* become insane? My new victims carried to me and held to my lips day by day, to cure them and renew my curing blood.

That would be hateful. Supposing I was believed.

No camps for your vampire. That's totally against my nature. Like some Johnny Appleseed I roam the shattered land instead, on and on, planting healthy immunity, slowly growing older and wearier, Saint Adrien of the magic teeth. Every day that I feed the world dies a little less, another flower of hope can be born.

Galbinus was right: I am the unreadable message that maps on to the other, unbreakable code – of the death virus. The one cancelling the other, darkness cancelling darkness. And I must carry on till the night that gripped me in that wood seven hundred years ago claims me back at last . . . though then it will be a different sort of night.

Why don't you throw down that knife, little lady? Your blade could hurt me, now that I'm a person like yourself. The wounds might cause me problems.

Make no mistake, I'm still strong. If I'm obliged, I shall disarm you, so there's really no value in that knife. I'd rather not risk a wound, though.

Why can't you trust me? It's tragically true that nowadays many forms of sexual fetishism and displacement flourish – at arm's length! – amongst those whose libido is still rampant. Mirrors, rubber muffs and dildo dolls. Mutual bestiality. Fixation on a partner's socks. Oh I have heard tales told, and seen sights. I know this! Am I proposing to seize you at arm's length without ever touching your flesh? Quite the opposite! In that case, why should I be one of those fetishists? What possible breed of pervert nowadays would wish to sup another person's blood?

Naturally you haven't heard of my cure. Those whom I cure only acknowledge the fact to their own kind, whom they seek and find, after I point the way. They are the future, not those dupes in government reservations. You can be the future too. Indeed you *shall* be, and soon! When you meet another of the Cured, you can both have a baby together. You can repopulate the world.

Once I have drunk a little from you. After one sharp bite. So let me have my will of you. Toss away that knife. Please. I'm asking nicely.

When Jesus Comes Down the Chimney

Now, Jamie, if you don't go to bed when your Daddy tells you to,
Jesus won't come down the chimney!

Oh, so you can't even *imagine* sleeping yet?

Saints! Tell you the whole story of Jesus – and of Santa Claus?
Why, that would take till nine.

Well, maybe . . . (No, I am *not* spoiling the boy!)

You just snuggle up in your chair by the fire there, Jamie, and
listen to me. And I'll be carrying you upstairs before you've
heard the half of it!

We'd better start with Santa Claus.

We all know how Santa was born in a humble stable amongst
the chickens and goats. Most of his countryfolk were poor, and
Santa's parents were no exception. No shoes on their feet, no fine
cakes in the larder. No larders, often! A lot of those people lived
in tents, and it got pretty cold in the winter. Three magicians had
hiked a thousand miles to be present when Santa was born. They
followed a bright comet in the sky, and brought a magic sack as a
gift. You could take whatever you wished for out of this sack.
Santa's mother didn't want to stir up jealousy amongst her
neighbours, so she hid the sack away. Anyway, her country was
being occupied by the Roman army. If the Romans heard of the
magic sack she feared they'd take it away for their wild, greedy
emperor.

When Santa grew to manhood his mother gave him the
magicians' gift and explained all about it. Santa decided then and
there that he would like to shower presents on his countryfolk

184

though he swore that he would never pull anything out of the sack for himself.

So Santa tramped around the land with the sack over his shoulder, giving people whatever their hearts most desired, or what they needed most. He kept his vow about giving nothing to himself. Even so, one widow woman requested a fine red coat trimmed with angora wool then insisted that Santa should wear it, not she. A leper whose feet were rotted and crippled asked for a pair of stout black boots, and forced these on Santa.

That wasn't all. Such a number of grateful people pressed bread and cheese on Santa, from out of their meagre stocks, not to mention fish and fruit and meat and milk and wine – which he couldn't decently refuse – that within a few years he grew positively stout!

Well, the Roman soldiers finally arrested him. All of those free gifts that poured from Santa's sack were destabilizing a marginal economy. They were weakening the currency. They were causing job refusal in the colonial labour market.

The Romans tied the magic sack over Santa's head. They marched him up to the top of a hill and nailed him to a wooden cross, then jabbed their spears through the sack a couple of times to blind him.

When they took Santa down dead at last they bundled his corpse into the sack, tied it tight, and set an official seal on it. They debated tossing him into the nearby river, but eventually their captain allowed Santa's friends to carry him away to a tomb.

That night the tomb was broken into by robbers who hoped to steal the magic sack . . . and they found the sack lying there empty. It was as if that burlap bag had digested Santa Claus! As if it had spirited him away to the dimension where all free gifts came from.

The robbers were filled with wonder, and didn't want to steal ever again. Instead, they made a pact to spread the word about Santa all over the world and to carry the sack (or snippets from it) wherever they went, as proof. The sack was first carried to

Roma, then later to Torino, where most of it remains to this very day.

In later years the descendants of those original robbers promised that one day when everybody in the world had heard of Santa and loved him, the sack would begin to distribute free gifts again. That's why, every Easter, we all receive presents wrapped in sackcloth, in memory of Santa.

Jesus? Oh yes, I'm coming to him. Of course I am, Jamie! It's Jesus who's important tonight.

Jesus was the leader of those thieves who broke into Santa's tomb. (There's something symmetrical, don't you think, between gifts and robbery? Robbery is the product of a society where there aren't enough gifts to go round – or where there are too many gifts for too few people. What's that? Sym-met-ric-al. It means . . . oh, it doesn't really matter, Jamie darling. Honest!)

Jesus was the ex-thief who carried the sack to Roma where the hysterical greedy emperor lived, guarded by his soldiers with their spears.

When Jesus arrived in Roma he went straight to the Forum. That's a sort of meeting place, like a Senate, but for the common people.

Jesus stood up on a marble block and waved the empty sack and called out – with the help of a translator, from Aramaic into Latin, "Plebeians of Roma, I bring you gifts!" (A plebeian was someone unemployed, living on free bread and enjoying free entry into circuses.)

At first the plebeians who thronged the Forum stared at the sack as eagerly as if they were looking up a girl's skirt.

When they saw that the sack was empty, many of them hooted and jeered. Others lost their temper and chucked pebbles.

But Jesus cried out, "The gifts I bring you are dialectical!" (This was a term which Jesus borrowed from the Greek philosophers.) "Your desires are the thesis. This sack is the antithesis. The synthesis is that you should empty yourselves of false goals.

vain dreams, the products of a diseased society. Just you empty all of that false consciousness of yours into this sack! It will hold everything, and reduce everything that is contradictory. In its place you'll discover that gifts ought to be given according to one's needs, not one's desires – but society at present is based on legalized theft, on the alienation of persons from their soil, from their work, even from their own bodies and sexuality!"

With daily repetition Jesus' message began to sink in. Soon a few of the plebeians believed him – and stepped into the sack and out again, as a symbol of their change of heart. Then many.

At last the emperor's curiosity was piqued; for the circus seats remained empty, and the elephants and the trained apes which rode them wept. Also, there was growing unrest among his soldiers at the prospect of yet another colonial war.

The emperor in person led a party of trusted guards to the Forum, intending to spear this Jesus. On the way there the emperor . . . now, we must tell the truth: he was a hysteric but he also cunningly sensed his own political and economic infrastructure ebbing away . . . the emperor experienced a visionary fit. He saw a sack in the sky which swallowed the sun. (Actually, we believe this was a total eclipse.) When he reached the Forum he dismounted from his horse – and stepped into the sack. Soon the empire had totally changed . . . into a republic.

Ah, now you're nodding off.

Let's go quietly, mm? Up up up to bed.

Tonight, night of nights, Jesus will climb down the chimney and take away whatever you think is most precious to you. Will it be your rocking horse? Or your toy bear? Or just your tin whistle?

Tush. How else could other deserving little children receive fine gifts at Easter time?

Hush. He'll take something from us *all*. Not just you, you dobbin. Maybe I'll lose my spinning wheel tonight. Maybe it'll be my purple velvet dress.

Jesus'll redistribute all our wealth. That's why he's called "the good thief." He brings Santa's empty sack with him down all the chimneys in the whole wide world, and fills it full from every house.

Here we are now, darling. Tuck up tight, and shut those eyes. No peeping, or he mightn't come.

THE RESURRECTION MAN

still have the ear of the resurrection man. It hasn't fallen to
pieces.

Oh, I don't mean the ear of Jesus. I'm referring to a different
resurrection man. Namely, William Burke – of Burke and Hare
fame, or infamy if you prefer. Maybe you don't prefer. Perhaps,
though this strikes me as unlikely, you're a little rusty as to the
activities of Mr B and Mr H, back in the 1820s?

If so, let me hold forth. (You can't really stop me, can you?)
William Burke, an Irishman, grew up as a vagabond in County
Cork. In 1818, when he was twenty-six years old, he moved to
Scotland to work as a navvy on the Union Canal, then under
construction. A certain William Hare from Londonderry was
engaged in the same task. Hare moved on to become a huckster
and presently the keeper of an Edinburgh doss-house, Log's
lodging-house in Tanner's Close. Burke took up residence
there in 1827. That November an old lonely pensioner died
in the house. Instead of having the body decently buried,
Messrs B & H hit on the bright idea of selling the corpse
to Dr Robert Knox's school of anatomy, for dissection by
students.

The windfall of seven pounds and ten shillings persuaded these
two rough Williams that there was good money to be made. Soon
they, and their common-law wives, were luring lonesome
travellers into various houses, getting the wretches drunk then
suffocating them. They used suffocation so that the corpses
should seem uninjured. The culpable, or gullible, Dr Knox
provided a ready market until the October of 1828 when at last

his suspicious neighbours tipped off the police. Raiding Knox's home in their chimney-pipe hats, the police discovered an old woman's body in a box in the cellar.

Hare turned King's evidence; consequently Burke was hanged for murder while a huge crowd howled, "Burke him! Burke him!" Because Hare had peached on his partner, an attempt to indict him for the killing of one Daft Jamie failed legally; and Hare was set free from the Edinburgh Tolbooth – to vanish over the border into anonymity.

Perhaps Burke wasn't, strictly speaking, a "resurrection man". That sobriquet properly attached to those grave robbers who dug up freshly buried corpses to sell to the medical schools. Yet Burke took this grim process one stage further, short-cutting the brief sojourn in the graveyard. Thus in a sense he and Hare were the *kings* of the resurrection men. The panic-stricken public certainly regarded them as such, and anxiety lasted for years, especially with Hare on the loose.

So how did Burke's right ear come into my family, pickled in a jar of formalin? And a hundred miles south from the scene of the crimes! On Tyneside, in the North of England. That's quite a story; though it'll be overshadowed by the story I have to tell you presently . . .

Back in the 1820s, my great-something grandfather and his family lived here in Grosvenor Place, North Shields, in what was then a rather elegant, newly built Georgian terrace house. My ancestor Mr Park – and that's my name too, Jim Park, pleased to meet you, though we can't shake hands – he owned a thriving paint shop in Clive Street, supplying both domestic and marine customers. He was also a great fancier of our native bird life. This house in Grosvenor Place was full of cages, confining twittering and trilling and cheeping bundles of feathers. He had song thrushes, nightingales, and the mottled skylark. The lively chiff chaff warbled its "chivy-chavy!" He owned yellow wagtails which look like golden-green canaries, though these only squeal sharply – and greenfinches, forever busy washing themselves warbling their humble, mellow "tway" – and there were twittering sand martins, prevented from burrowing into their favourite clay banks like little engineers; just as the larks were prevented from ascending, the wagtails from migrating, the chiff-chaffs from weaving their oven-nests. Still, who's to say that these birds were less fortunate than their wild kin? Even if frustrated; even if the insect-eaters amongst them probably had a diet of fish-bait?

"How," I hear you ask, "do you know so much about the aviary of your Grandad several times removed?"

"Ah," I reply, "that's because I've heard his birds. I'm an ear-witness to them."

"You're a . . . what?"

"Wait . . . and be amazed."

Mr Park obtained all his birds from the Papageno of North Shields, Joney Aird, who trapped them with nets and limed twigs and whatever – ranging over the whole locality from the ponds on the Town Moor to the woods of Jesmond Dene and Holywell Dene, from the corn fields to the sand dunes. Joney Aird sold his feathery captives from a stall on the fish quay. Some skippers liked to take a bird to sea, to remind them of the softness of the land, to distract from the harsh screaming of the gulls. Joney, who was on something resembling friendly terms with Mr Park, frequently called at the paint shop in Clive Street.

The bird catcher kept his things in a dilapidated attic above Brown's Flour Mill. He was a twittery creature of nature himself. Behold his patched-up raggy jacket, often torn by crawling through briars till it seemed like a sort of plumage worn by a man who was half bird himself. And could he whistle! Not Mozart, not popular airs, not hymns – but a kind of dawn chorus all of his own, which seemed to bring woodland and pondside to the fish quay. Joney lured birds by this means, and was very knowledgeable about their habits. A fey, strange fellow.

"Do you mean he was soft in the head?"

"I do not. He was always canny with his coppers, though he

never accumulated too many. I refer to the Irish in him, the leprechaun strain."

"So why, in the Winter of 1828," you may well ask, "should Mr Park have decided that this same Joney Aird was in actuality William Hare, murderer and resurrection man?"

"I may well ask," you say.

"Ah," I respond, "you must understand the nature of public hysteria."

It was on the night between 21st and 22nd February 1823, almost six years before the revelations about the dreadful duo, that Dr Greenhow of Dockwray Square, North Shields, was called to the bedside of a Mrs Gaunt. The Gaunts only lived in Tyne Street a hundred yards away. After examining the lady and returning home, Dr Greenhow made up a suitable prescription and roused his apprentice out of bed to deliver it. Half asleep, and knowing that it was no distance at all he had to go, the apprentice – young John Margetts – merely dragged on trousers and coat, ignored hat or stockings, and ran out.

He never returned. Enquiries next day revealed that Margetts had delivered the medicine, only halting briefly at the Gaunts' Had he then run away to sea, on impulse in the middle of the night? Unlikely! When John Margetts quit Dr Greenhow's house he might have looked slipshod, yet in other respects he was diligent. He was almost ending the term of his apprenticeship He had never shown the slightest interest in a mariner' life.

A mason called Mr Profit, who lived at the end of Church Street, reported hearing a scuffle in adjacent Tyne Street at that hour of the night, and a voice crying out, "What are you doing with me?" Furthermore, a watchman stationed at Chapman' Bank in Howard Street had witnessed two men leading another down Union Street. He supposed that the man they led was drunk, not an uncommon sight, so he took no more notice.

Had agents of the Honourable East India Company kidnapped Margetts for service abroad, the way that they had kidnapped other victims? Had they fastened him under hatches in a ship in the Tyne till the hue and cry could die away?

If so, it failed to die away. During the succeeding weeks and months and even years the whole of Shields remained in a feverish froth over the lad's disappearance. For years the offices of the Hon. East India Company in London's Leadenhall Street were bombarded with passionate letters and pleas and suggestions from the citizens of Shields. Deny as they might that anyone called Margetts was on their books, they weren't believed. When news came that Afghan rebels had captured an army surgeon with a name that resembled Margetts, hysteria broke out afresh on Tyneside. Then a soldier came forward to declare that he had known Margetts in India. Now an army surgeon, Margetts had described his kidnapping. A public meeting was held to hear the soldier's tale. But later the same soldier wrote to the newspapers confessing that the Gaunt family had bribed him with £100 and the offer of their prettiest daughter in marriage – to clear *them* of suspicion.

For yes, the Hon. East India Company were not the only targets of calumny. When the news of Burke and Hare finally broke, a fellow swore that he had seen John Margetts enter the Gaunts' house that night and *never come out again*. Rumours soon spread to the effect that the Gaunts' little son – who must have been rather young six years earlier – had blurted out in school that "they had soon done for Margetts, and put him in a box". Before long the distressed Gaunts were having to issue writs for defamation. They won damages, but no matter; in danger of their lives from a half-crazed public they had to flee the town. New tenants moved into their house in Tyne Street, and presently a sizable skeleton was dug up from the back garden. This proved to be that of a Newfoundland dog, beloved pet of the previous occupants. But no matter; no one quite believed it. The house was branded as haunted.

Any stranger visiting the neighbourhood became an instant suspect. One fellow who moved in, accompanied by long boxes –

which actually contained machinery for spinning worsted cloth –
was nearly lynched. He did escape with his life after the boxes
were jemmied open at his insistence; though he wasn't any too
welcome to pursue further business in Shields. The boxes *might*
have contained bodies; and might do so again.

Oh I heard it all. The rumours, the whispers, the howls of the
mob crying "Burke him! Burke him!" at the unlucky owner of
those boxes.

As for the family of the missing lad, at first they enjoyed the
warmest public sympathy, and derived much practical benefit
from this. A local bard gave tongue:

> "Good people, to my tale give ear,
> Sad, shocking news you soon shall hear,
> For I have lost my darling son.
> Alas! alas! I am undone.
> > I fear he is no more.
>
> Two ruffians stole my son away,
> 'Twas on the twenty-second day,
> At five o'clock on Thursday morn.
> My heart! my heart! my son is gone,
> > And now he is no more.
>
> He with some medicine was sent,
> To cure the sick was his intent,
> When these two ruffians seiz'd their prey,
> They bound my son – took him away –
> > And never yet was found.
>
> Now, with a mother share a part,
> And judge the feelings of my heart
> As I am left for to deplore
> My dearest son I'll see no more –
> > I hope he's happy now."

I have omitted several verses.

However, the fickle populace of Shields began to take umbrage at the way the fortunes of the Margetts had improved thanks to that selfsame kindly populace. Could it be that the Margetts knew perfectly well what had become of their son – but weren't saying, in case the stream of charity dried up? Thus suspicion fell upon the Margetts household too. As a result, John's mother went insane. Every day she would make her way to a nearby ash-heap, and poke it for hours trying to find her son's slippers. Mr Margetts sank into imbecilic dotage. John's brother eventually became a lunatic pauper confined in the Tynemouth Workhouse. What mumblings, what ravings.

Let's call another witness. I summon Mrs Cornforth of the Whitby Arms in the Low Street near the New Quay. Mrs Cornforth declared that on the night in question she heard a cry of murder. Upon looking out, she saw two men dragging a third man along the Low Street. This trio never arrived at the New Quay, otherwise – "Next witness, please!" – the watchman posted outside the Northumberland Arms would have seen them.

Thus the three men must have cut down the lane towards Brown's Flour Mill.

By now Dr Greenhow's son, Mr Conrad Haverkam Greenhow, was pursuing his own enquiries assisted by the Reverend Mr Neal from South Shields, an Anglican precursor of Chesterton's Father Brown. Procuring a warrant, the amateur detectives searched the mill and found evidence of a struggle in Joney Aird's attic in the shape of a torn leather neck collar. True, the collar could have been ripped during an over-hasty exit from a briar patch clutching a frantic song thrush. But Joney Aird had also disappeared! The bird had flown the nest.

Aird, Hare.

Hare. Aird. Do you note a resemblance?

No? Well, Mr Greenhow and Mr Neal did. Struck by this, and by the puzzle of where Joney Aird had vanished to, the two gentlemen were electrified by the news from Edinburgh about Hare's arrest, and Burke's, and their terrible crimes; as was the whole country. Burke and Hare hysteria reinforced the local Margetts hysteria. Ignoring the conundrum of how Joney Aird could simultaneously have been trapping linnets on Tyneside and stifling down-and-outs in Auld Reekie – unless he metamorphosed into a bird of passage himself, and a fast one at that – Mr Greenhow prevailed on the bird-loving Mr Park to set out post-haste for Edinburgh to identify Hare as Aird; and pressed guineas on him for his fare.

Alas, winter's storms and snow drifts held up the coach, with the result that Mr Park arrived in Edinburgh only after Hare had been released (to vanish, like a bird on the wind), and Burke had been newly executed, though not yet buried in quicklime. Because Mr Park had travelled such a long way all for nothing, the warder in charge of Burke's corpse asked if the gentleman would care for a piece of the murderer as a memento.

"Wey aye, Aa'd thank ye!" said Mr Park, who must bring back something to Shields for his trouble, apart from a chill.

The warder promptly took out his clasp-knife and cut off Burke's right ear. He presented this to Mr Park, who hurried to an apothecary's shop to have the flap of flesh embalmed in a jar of formalin. Thus for many years on the mantelshelf in Grosvenor Place the last remaining earthly trace of Burke floated in its little preservative bath.

But maybe there exist situations beyond good and evil, when ordinary reality bends a little, into the shape of an ear, say?

During my childhood that ear was an accepted part of the furniture. Some visitors would glance at it askance and refrain from comment, perhaps imagining that it was a pickled cancer, souvenir of a successful operation, or even something gynaecological. Later in life I read how the poet Verlaine's mother – I think it was Verlaine – kept the preserved foetuses (assorted sizes) of all his miscarried would-be brothers and sisters in a line-up of jars on her mantelshelf.

But if someone asked my mother, she would explain matter-of-factly, "That's the ear of William Burke the murderer, who sold his victims' bodies to be cut up by anatomy students in Edinburgh." And she would add, "It's been in the family for generations."

This was what she said to Cousin Dick from Canada, when he visited England in 1947 or so. Though the war was over, rationing was still strict and our relations in Vancouver continued to send food parcels containing tins of red salmon, which my mother would serve up in a white sauce dabbled with vinegar poured over mashed potatoes.

Cousin Dick seemed to think we should show our gratitude by being healthier, cleaner in mind and body and household management than he found us. A pickled ear was hardly a wholesome antique.

"I guess the Red Indians used to take scalps," he remarked, looking baffled at the warped uncleanliness of the old country as my mother agitated the jar, bumping the ear from side to side. The mantelpiece – and by extension the house – would have lacked a certain character without it.

I was only five at the time, and I remember asking, "Did they punish the man by cutting him up? Was that the only way they could stop him?"

I imagined a story-book ogre whom the citizens of Edinburgh finally trapped in a pit they dug; they could only destroy his power by cutting him into little bits and sending the pieces all over the kingdom to be kept securely in separate locations, one of these being our front room. I gained the idea that we were, from father to son to grandson, Custodians of the Ear. An important, secret duty.

"Why, of course they didn't cut him into pieces, Jim. They hanged him."

"Did they hang him *by* his ear? Is that how it came off?"

One of the teachers at the school where I had just started used to twist the ears of older boys who annoyed him, till they howled.

197

Did it kill you if you had your ear torn off? Fear flooded me.

My mother chuckled. "Of course not. They cut it off afterwards, and gave it to us."

To us, us especially.

"Scalps, yeah," muttered Cousin Dick, knitting his brows. Here was some primitive dirty native ritual which his own modern, sanitised country had outgrown. After years of generosity, to save us from malnutrition, skin diseases, web eyes, or stunted growth, he had come all this way thousands of miles along the Canadian Pacific Railway and over the Atlantic Ocean to visit the old home country, and had discovered us roosting in this dingy room in a drab town with a pickled ear as our mascot, our totem.

"What's an Atomy?" I asked my mother. "Is that like bombs?"

"Anatomy is the body," she explained. "The parts of the body. How they join together inside you."

Cousin Dick looked increasingly offended, and in fact he made his excuses within quarter of an hour and departed to tour Scotland's glens and heathery moors where maybe other branches of our family were neater and less sordid. Cousin Dick made his living in the salmon-canning industry, but fish guts were one thing; a human ear in a jar was another. The ear had large lobes and little brown hairs sprouting from inside, with a blob of orange wax still attached. Ear-wax! It hadn't even been cleaned out. Yeah, that was the score – I imagine his mind ticking over – he had sent all those cans of good red fish flesh, and we showed him our own version, our own satire on his kindness: a preserved lug-hole. Food parcels ceased thereafter.

Before too long it was 1951, which was the year of the Festival of Britain. Down in London, in Battersea Park, the silver Skylon pointed up at the clouds just like a rocket-ship in the new comic *The Eagle* – and the Dome of Discovery was a larger version of the flying saucers in which the green Treens from Venus anded during a village cricket match in the far-off South of England.

I compared the coloured pictures in *The Eagle* with the photos of the Festival in the *New Chronicle* and dearly wished we could visit London. But my father hated the smoky smell of steam trains, which made him sick – he had chest trouble; and the bus journey down the Great North Road would be a ghastly, cramped twelve hours at least. Besides, the cost!

In a fit of frustrated hope, when no one was about, I sneaked into the front room – our ceremonial room, which was otherwise unused. Maybe if I held the ear, maybe if I rubbed it genie-in-bottle style, my dream of visiting the Festival would come true?

After all those years the lid was tight. I almost skidded the jar off the mantelpiece to shatter on the tiles of the fireplace.

Sticking in two fingers, I removed the dripping ear and dried it on my hanky then dabbed up the drops I'd spilt here and there. An ear's quite like a soft sea-shell, isn't it? You can listen to the sea in sea-shells, the hiss of the surf.

So I held Burke's ear to my own ear.

"Chivy-chavy!" cried a birdy voice. "Chivy-chavy!"

All at once a dozen birds were cheeping, twittering, and trilling. I was harkening to this same front room of ours a century and a quarter ago, when it had housed many of Mr Park's bird cages!

Of course I didn't realize that immediately. I wasn't yet aware of my ancestor's hobby. Mainly I thought that the ear was kept under liquid to drown the noise it would otherwise make.

Yet when I jerked the ear to arm's length I couldn't hear a thing.

So maybe the jar and the liquid were a device to deter people from picking the ear up idly from the mantelpiece, and hearing secret things? (I wasn't too much *au fait* with the chemistry of preservation.) What could be secret about bird-song, so much like the warblings of morse code on the short wave radio band?

We had a big walnut radio set through in the kitchen, the glass

panel marked with strange stations with names like Hilversum
. . . Aha, maybe the ear could play other tunes as well? Holding
it to my own ear again, I rotated it slowly, as I would turn the dial
to tune our radio set when my father let me.

Voices!

"Good people, to my tale give ear!" recited a prim young lady.

With the literalness of childhood, I decided that the ear I was
clutching must be the selfsame ear to which she referred. This
was the ear which had been given to her tale, of – it began to
unfold – a lad's mysterious disappearance . . .

Subsequently we took a holiday. Instead of going to London to
see the Festival of Britain we travelled a shorter distance in the
opposite direction, just over the border into Scotland. We stayed
by the seaside at St Abb's in Berwickshire, in a sort of semi-
religious hotel. Before tucking into meals, all the guests would
sing in chorus:

"Let us with a gladsome mind
Praise the Lord for he is kind!"

Since the weather was hot, a lot of salads were served; or
maybe it was cheaper to serve salads. I assumed that we were all
singing, "*Lettuce*, with a gladsome mind." Children are a literal
lot.

Again I twisted the ear.

"Burke him! Burke him!" a mob roared in the distance, voices
burring with hatred like many big pussy cats with sore throats.

Even as I put the ear back into its jar I was thinking in a very
practical way that, the next time I was able to extract it, I must
empty every last lurking drop out of the coil of the ear into the
container itself to keep the level of liquid from diminishing and
thus betraying me. Already I had become cunning, and suspected that maybe my parents might be innocent of the secret.

Might be. I wasn't sure.

As I say, our front room was a ceremonial room, seldom
entered unless there were visitors. I kept my eyes and ears open
for any hint that my father and mother might slink in there

surreptitiously. Often I climbed out of bed and tiptoed to the stairhead to peep. Or I lay awake and strained to decode noises in the house until my parents also turned in for the night. Within a year or two I was sure that they hadn't the slightest notion of the ear's unusual properties.

Not that *I* had many opportunities – initially – to use the ear without risk of discovery. Back in those early years, before I grew older and supervision loosened, I had to ration myself strictly, which was good discipline for the future. Instead I would play with the radio set in the kitchen. Noting my apparent interest, my father reminisced about the first radio sets when *he* was a lad, the crystal sets, and the excitement of sticking a "cat's whisker" inside a big china cooking bowl to amplify the tinny voice of "2LO". It occurred to me that those first radio sets, with their "cat's whiskers", no doubt plucked from the family cat, must have been semi-organic – something like *my* private radio set, of an ear in a jar of liquid. Perhaps science had missed out on a neat trick by going in for wires and electricity and glowing valves instead.

At school I learned that the name science gives to the external ear is the "auricle" – which naturally echoed the "oracles" of olden days who spoke about the future; though my oracle only voiced the past. I also learned the word "penance". Was William Burke's ghost inhabiting his last remaining earthly segment as an atonement for his misdeeds? If so, he never spoke to me directly.

Alternatively, was Margetts' ghost involved? Was I destined to solve the mystery of his disappearance and lay his spirit to rest, whether his bones lay mouldering in an Edinburgh charnel pit or at the bottom of the sea or up the Khyber Pass?

Was Joney Aird involved? Joney the fey bird-man, endowed perhaps with second sight (thus he fled from Brown's Flour Mill), or in this case, with second hearing. Oh no!

It was years before I realized that the magic wasn't inherent in the murderer's ear, but in myself. Many years before I *under-*

stood my unique talent, so fortuitously – so accidentally – awakened by our possession of an amputated sense organ. But for Burke's ear, I might never have discovered my true self, the quality which sets me apart like saint or artist from the rest of the world. I might have grown up to be like Cousin Dick the Canadian.

"So welcome, new friend, to my museum of resurrection in Grosvenor Place, North Shields! Definitely not open to the public – otherwise they would chorus, 'Burke him! Burke him! Burke him with a gladsome mind!'"

Nowadays a couple of dozen jars sit on the mantelpiece. Old friends, new friends. Please join them.

Do you find it gloomy here, with the curtains closed? Has the house degenerated since my father died (that chest trouble! – early heart attack) and since I moved my mother into a nursing home? Has our home grown fusty and dirty and ricketty?

We wouldn't want any cleaning woman to pop in, or any decorators, or workmen to repair things, would we?

Keep it all exactly the same. Keep the spirit of the place identical, just in case my talent breathes this air, and no other.

Same easy chairs, same drapery, same cracking plaster; same ancient radio set and cooker; same china sink, same cutlery, same family photos and large framed print of a sunset. Same pile of tattered old *Eagle* comics, which I still read and enjoy, featuring Harris Tweed the portly amateur detective, Sergeant Luck of the Foreign Legion, Dan Dare the pilot of the future, and cut-away centrefolds exposing the entrails of a luxury liner (creep, little finger, from cabin to cabin) or of an imaginary space rocket, like anatomy drawings not of cut-open animals but of huge machines. Really, all life is here inside this house. For I am the pilot of the past – which I resurrect.

Keep uninvited visitors away, too. Let them have their Canada, their fitted kitchens and TV sets and all mod. cons.

But let economics intrude, by all means. You're curious as to how I earn my keep?

"Do you have a job, Jim?"

"I was wondering when you'd ever ask. Actually, I'm away from Grosvenor Place a fair bit. So obviously I had to move my mother, now that she's ailing. I have a fine job for my purpose."

"Really?"

"Yes, I'm a publisher's representative for the North of England. Take proof copies and covers around the bookshop and library buyers; sing praises; solicit orders. I've an instinct for what'll appeal. Give me a cover, a quick flip through, the blurb in the catalogue – and I'll tell you the advance orders to within twenty-five. Don't need to study the books in depth; I've other more vivid things to "read". Don't make a fat income by any means – don't need one – but I get around in the old Cortina car. Lancs, Yorks, Cumbria, Borders. I get around.

"And I'm disciplined about collecting specimens for my jars. Discriminating, and disciplined. Never more than twice a year. Always at least fifty miles from where I've lately been doing business.

"Likelihood of being detected? Tracked down? Not high! The events don't make much sense, or form an obvious pattern, do they? Dead body in Liverpool lacking an eye. Corpse in Leeds, with the tongue cut out. Finger missing in Manchester. Miles, and ages, apart. What on earth for? BLACK MAGIC CULT OPERATING IN NORTH OF ENGLAND? Ha ha!

"Let me unscrew this jar and take out the tongue that floats within. Hold the tongue to my own tongue, turning it to tune through the waveband of the menu. Indian lady, Leeds. Spicy banquets.

"Now put it back.

"Next jar. Eye of former merchant sailor; years of travelling the globe. Rotate his eye against my eye to see foreign parts. Hong Kong, Singapore, Sydney.

"Take out a nose and smell such fragrances. Lilies, patchouli, bonfires, sweat.

203

"Take out a finger, and feel all manner of things.

"And you, my friend – I believe – were once a bit of a Casanova, eh? You had a way with the girls, and you had your way with them, didn't you? Whereas I, living the life that I have, a life that guards a secret, needed to avoid girlfriends or fiancées. While away from home, I have never been to a prostitute. Leaving aside the danger of disease, I'm sure it would have been unsatisfying. Thus: no sexual experience, on a mutual basis, for Jim.

"Now, at long last, you're here to remedy that, aren't you? When I hold your organ to my organ, we shall make up for lost time. We shall make the music of love.

"How sweet life has been since Burke's ear first twittered bird-song at me! If that Irish navvy was a king of resurrection men, I must be the king of kings, the emperor, the sultan. After a banquet, after a vision of Bangkok, after a dazing with musk, let me turn out the light. In the darkness let me discover my harem."

Good people, to my tale give ear. And eye, and tongue, and nose, and you know what.

JOAN'S WORLD

On my fourteenth birthday my parents gave me the planet Earth as a present. They couldn't afford a regular gift.

Who could, in our neighbourhood? Paying for essentials was hard enough. How sad to see some mothers and fathers scraping together a little spare cash only to waste it on trash which wouldn't last, from the camp market. I sympathized, and had told Mum and Dad well in advance that I wanted nothing but their love.

They told me that, on the contrary, they would give me everything; and they kept their word.

It happened this way. We lived in a mobile home on the edge of a camp of a thousand such, stuck in the middle of the country-side. None of the homes, in truth, would be moving anywhere. All had seen better days twenty, thirty years earlier. The air had leaked out of tyres, the rubber had rotted down to the bare axles. A twice-weekly bus service linked us with a town ten miles away, where you could only wander around feeling sad; hardly anybody used the bus. The landscape around the camp was a patchwork of pasture, woodland, and river meadow where you could snare a few rabbits and catch a few fish to supplement your rations. During seven months of the year I'm sure the vicinity of the camp, if not the camp itself, was pleasanter than some moribund town. Throughout the winter a fence may as well have enclosed us. Inside, we had all our basic needs: school, clinic, library, church hall, welfare office open every Monday – five corrugated iron buildings of assorted sizes. A small canvas-covered market was held every other day in the open air. School, clinic, welfare, and market were run by outsiders who drove in from town, foreigners commuting from another country, though they too had their sorrows. We in the camp were simply a special case of a more general condition. Power was laid on to all homes with reasonable reliability. In a fair proportion of the caravans old TV sets were switched on from breakfast through to bedtime.

Once, so I heard, there'd been fights and drunkenness as signs of frustration. No longer; frustration itself had worn out. One section of our camp – "the monastery", we called it – had turned religious. Make a virtue of your poverty and limited horizons; hitch your wagon to a prayer. Some young people were cultivating different inner resources by meditating, staring at the sky, chanting to themselves, trying to open the third eye. Others read romances or day-dreamed or played endless games. Babies were born, but not many. I'd been born in the camp myself and basically had known nowhere else, though thanks to TV you might say I had also known everywhere. Yet this was an out-of-date everywhere, an everywhere from the past before life turned grey, before new things quit happening, or seemed to quit. The aliens in orbit saw to that, we were sure.

Those unseen aliens who had dimmed the life of the world, who had turned down the lights of existence for us! Every few weeks we could spy their artificial world crossing the night sky, a brighter Venus, as it wove its complex orbit around us, taking it over every portion of the Earth at some time or other.

"It's a spider wrapping up a fly in silk till the fly can't move a muscle," I'd said to my teacher from town, Miss Perry. She was skinny, with freckles and hair like rusty wires. I thought of her as rusting away along with the schoolhouse walls, yet still with some spring inside her, some bounce. She did her best to make us think.

"Maybe there aren't any aliens *living* up there, Joan," she said to me. "Maybe it's just a huge machine, all automatic."

"When we're thoroughly paralysed, they'll arrive from the stars?"

206

"What do the rest of you think?" she asked the class at large. Most faces remained blank. We kids never played truant, though. Coming to school was something to do. Leaving school at sixteen was a threat – of emptiness and inactivity.

"Miss, I still don't understand what they're doing to us," fat Peter Dimble said stubbornly. What they were doing to Peter was making him fat and sluggish. That was the result. "Are they shooting some sort of ray at us from space? Why didn't we ever shoot back? We could have. I've seen rockets and missiles on TV."

"In our universe we didn't shoot back. On our world-line we didn't."

"You mean we *did* shoot back in the other universe? I wish I lived there. How do I get there?"

Miss Perry sighed. "You can't. Maybe the other universes are all just ghosts, possibilities that vanish."

She had been explaining how each single event which could occur gave rise to two whole universes. In one universe the event happened. In another it failed to happen. The aliens forced our world to be the one where the event didn't happen. This was what the scientists believed.

Over and over in innumerable ways, large ways at first then lesser ones, the aliens made our world-line switch from non-event to non-event. Initiatives ran out of steam. Decisions had no consequences. Choices led to inaction. Plans were cancelled, unless they were of little importance in the first place. It had to be that star in the sky which was responsible, that new little moon. How else to account for our paralysis? Wars had long since ceased. Violence had tailed off. Try as we might, always the least dramatic choice was made, the choice to do less, or nothing. Things stopped being built, designed, discovered. The economy ticked by in low gear. I suppose it had to tick, otherwise something dramatic *would* have occurred: such as chaos and starvation. We had seen an end to disasters as well, to any terrible accidents, tragedies, calamities of the human or the

207

natural variety. All such wild events – good or bad, proud or bloody – only existed on TV, in old films, old newsreels from back when there was news.

"It's as if we're walking through an endlessly long building," Miss Perry told us. "We pass through a succession of rooms, where each room has two exits. Behind one door there might be anything at all – from a treasure chest to an exploding bomb. Behind the other door there's nothing except two more doors. Always, always we choose the door behind which there's nothing. Always, that empty room's waiting for us, not the one with something in it. The aliens empty the room the moment we grip the door knob. They switch the doors around. Or the rooms. The moment we decided to shoot our missiles at them, we were in a universe where we didn't."

"Can't we decide *not* to do something, so that it'll happen after all?" asked Jimmy Taylor, one of the black kids.

"It doesn't work that way, Jimmy."

No, it wouldn't. If we decided to do nothing that was fine by them in the sky. It was a very acceptable world-line. Had the aliens aimed to be kind to us by stopping war and strife and calamity, the heart-blood of those old films? I doubted it. They wanted to make us grey and slow, so that we would quit. That's all. It would take a long time for everything to run down calmly. We'd already had twenty years of it, starting before I'd been born. We might have another fifty or a hundred to go. The whole of my life, then some more. A life of less, and less.

"I'm born with three-score pennies in a purse. Each year a penny gets lost, next year another penny till finally I'm poor, utterly poor. By the time I'm old we shan't even understand those old films. They'll seem as absurd as cartoons, full of crazy impossibilities." That's what I wrote in an essay for Miss Perry.

On my birthday morning as soon as I opened the curtain along my bunk Mum and Dad were waiting with smiles on their faces, holding out between them . . . nothing. They acted as though that nothing was large and spherical and maybe breakable too.

"Here's a special present for a very special girl!" exclaimed Dad.

"It's the world," said Mum. "It's the planet Earth. We're giving it to you. No one gave their daughter the whole world before, did they? Never ever. Because no one ever did, *we can*."

I believed them. Mum and Dad weren't mocking me. This wasn't any bitter joke. It was a true expression of their love and kindness. Their gift counted for more than any other gift could possibly have done, for in that electrifying moment what they were giving me was vision. They handed me nothing, therefore I *saw*. I was overwhelmed by a sense of everything, and whole-someness. I felt replenished, filled with strength. You need strength to hold a world, don't you?

So I took it into my hands, careful at first. I was about to lay it down upon my bedding like some egg in a soft nest – an ostrich egg, the egg of a Roc! – when Mum protested.

"Don't hide it away. Take it out with you. Take it everywhere! No need to be shy, not now that it's yours. It had to accept *you* as well, you know? Well, now it has. So it'll go anywhere with you. You can balance it on your head if you like. It won't fall. If it does fall, it won't break so long as you always believe in it."

"Oh I shall, Mum. I shall."

"It won't become a different world, somebody else's," Dad assured me. "It can't, because it's your own, your very own."

"So long as *I* don't change, you mean?"

"So long as you don't lose it. Though to do so, you'd have to lose yourself."

That we had all lost our selves was my immediate thought. The aliens had taken our selves away from us and substituted changeling selves who were weaker, ineffective, hamstrung.

They wouldn't do that to me! My talisman was nothing they could steal, nothing they could alter, nothing they would notice. I had walked through one of those two doorways Miss Perry described, and absolutely nothing was waiting for me in the room beyond – yet at the same time I had received, secretly, everything that mattered.

Arriving at school, I placed the world carefully on my desk so that it wouldn't roll off. The other kids watched me curiously yet no one rushed over mischievously to shove or snatch. We weren't like that nowadays. Even so, they couldn't have harmed my world or taken it unless I let them.

Miss Perry eyed me. "What was that about, Joan?"

I smiled. "Today's my birthday, Miss. My Mum and Dad have given me the world. Here it is." I lifted it, and set it down again. Only a few of my classmates tittered.

"Honest?" asked Jimmy Taylor. "Can I hold it for a mo?" Before Miss Perry could react Jimmy had left his desk. He placed his hands where mine had been.

"Hey, it is too! I feel it. Like a balloon, in' it?" He tried to lift it, but couldn't, and frowned.

Miss Perry descended upon us. Jimmy skipped back to his seat. She faltered; her hands fluttered like birds caught in a net. "May I?"

When I nodded, Miss Perry spread her hands wide as the desk itself. At first her palms came together ever so slowly as if she was apprehensive that she might touch . . . either something, or alternatively nothing. Next, she seemed about to clap a mosquito between those two hands of hers as if her hands were a spring trap which might fly together, triggered by a tickle, exploding my birthday present, popping it with a smack of flesh on flesh. She might *imagine* she was assessing whether to burst my dream for my sake, or whether to let me keep it, also for my sake. Oh she might imagine this, but I saw deeper: all the way inside her to her fearful desire for Jimmy to have been serious, not spoofing, to her yearning for this truly to be the world, and her fear that it wasn't, and her twin fear: *that it was*. Her hands stalled just where I knew the surface of the world to be.

"It's," she murmured. "Yes it is, it is." At that moment she too

210

had opened a door in herself and had discovered, within, a nothing which possessed more substance than she could have thought possible five minutes earlier. All my other classmates came and touched the world, with cautious wonder. I suspected one or two of pretending so as not to seem empty inside. Once everyone had returned to their seats, and Miss Perry to the front, I lifted my world fussily to reposition it. Before, I had hardly noticed the slightest weight, if any. Now my world seemed a bit heavy.

At mid-morning break we spilled out into the market-place, bathed in cool April sunshine, me with my world. Word about it spread quickly through the school population. Soon a stream of kids were coming up to me. "Joan, Joan, may we?" Seniors proved shier than juniors – afraid, as Miss Perry had been afraid at first.

Those older kids who missed their chance seized it at lunch time. That day, the school canteen was dishing up bowls of thick pea and ham soup with wedges of wholemeal bread. I had to balance the world on my head to carry the meal back to the classroom, stooping when I stepped through a doorway. I was stopped by so many seniors wanting to reach above my head that my soup was luke-warm by the time I got down to it.

When school ended, colour was fast fading from the sky and some rainy-looking clouds were arriving to wash the afternoon away. The market had already packed up. Would a world balanced upon my head act as an umbrella? Probably not, on account of the shape. Rain would run around in little seas and soak my crown. Raindrops might simply pass straight through like radiation because they couldn't notice the world in their way.

During a shower you mightn't notice rain slicking the world, but how about when the year rolled round to winter and snow fell? Would the flakes cling? Would I wear a great cold snowball on my head, the world in a new ice age?

Jimmy offered to carry the world back home for me but of

course I couldn't let him. With all the kids touching it, the weight had grown noticeably. Yet I wasn't struggling. The world wasn't a pail, empty to start with and now half full of water. I felt no physical strain, just a sense of increase. As if to compensate, my hands were buoyed up.

Earlier in the day, when I was new to having a world, perhaps I could have let Jimmy take it. Not now, no longer. I should have loathed for the skin to be torn from his hands, and burned, for his foot to be crushed by the fall of the world. He walked with me, chatting about how fine it must be to have such a Mum and Dad.

"If only mine would give me . . ." he began. "I guess they can't. Yours is the only one."

"How was it at school today?" Dad had been watching some film about Romans and gladiators which he now switched off. His tone was light yet I heard the underlying anxious note. Mum waited too, either to wreathe her face in smiles, or be sad.

I lowered the world gently on to my bunk, where it didn't make a hollow in the bedding, though that didn't matter. The blanket couldn't feel the weight of the world the way I could.

"It was so wonderful!" I told them. "Everyone touched my world. Miss Perry, everybody."

My parents' faces swelled with joy, each like some toddler's crayon drawing of a radiant, beaming sun. We hugged, all three of us.

By the end of the following day most of the adults in the camp appeared to have heard the news. During break, at least fifty grown-ups asked to touch. Though no traders were present that day, the market place was packed with people after school. It took me ages to get home. Families and stray individuals kept knocking at our caravan for a couple of hours more. I had to lift the world dozens of times and carry it to the door. My world seemed as heavy as a horse by now, though somehow it continued to be no burden.

Most people's reaction was one of calm delight. A few shed tears, which was embarrassing. One or two grumbled. Maybe those were the grumbling sort – and they'd come to me, hadn't they? Nobody asked stupid questions, or made wishes on the world, or tried to hog it longer than others. They touched, and went away satisfied.

Our final callers were the vicar, Reverend Mumfats, and the mayor of our camp, Joe Wibbits. Since it was pitch-dark by now, Dad invited these special visitors inside, even though we would be cramped. I brought the world from my bunk yet again, and both the vicar and the mayor rested their palms against it, so I could tell that they weren't intending to act in a heavy-handed style.

Reverend Mumfats sniffed; he had a cold. "Where did you get it from, Joan?"

"From Mum and Dad, as a birthday gift."

"Ah, but where did they get it from? Where, Mr Archer, Mrs Archer, where? And how? Was it from God?"

Mum didn't believe in Mumfats' God yet she didn't wish to offend, so she chose her words.

"It came into our minds to give it to Joan. So we did. At the time we gave it, you'd hardly have known it was there."

"Now it is," growled Mr Wibbits. "Oh yes. I felt it, same as you did, Vicar. Joan, we really called here to ask . . . not about your plans, oh no." He barked a laugh. "Wouldn't wish to use that word, would we? What I'm saying –"

"A moment," interrupted Mumfats. "Does it . . . *progress*, would you say, from day to day? Similar to, um, a pregnancy? An egg underneath a hen?"

I nodded. "The more people who touch it, the heavier it grows. Yes, it gets heavier all the time."

"Oh dear." Mum looked concerned. This was the first time I'd mentioned the weight.

I explained. "It isn't your usual heaviness like a big bag of carrots being heavier than a little bag. I *know* it's heavier, you

213

see, but I can still hold it easily so long as I feel right about holding it. Feeling right is . . . well, it's as if something's flowing through me to support it. The heavier it gets, the more flows through me."

"More power of the spirit?" suggested Mumfats.

"Energy, that's what!" said Dad.

"What *I'm* saying," resumed Mr Wibbits, "is there's a bus service into town on Saturdays, if you take my meaning."

Personally I suspected that my world might be immune to the "empty room" effect. Mr Wibbits wasn't taking chances by making dramatic pronouncements, nevertheless the Saturday morning bus was over half full, to the surprise of the driver. Mr Wibbits himself was on board, and the vicar, and my Mum and Dad, and Jimmy and his Dad, and oh, a good thirty others. I sat by Dad with the world in my lap as the bus lurched along the potholed road past fields grazed by sheep, rooted by pigs, or gone to wilderness. We picked up a few extra passengers from villages en route. Of course I had to let them touch the world.

For once, town wasn't depressing and colourless, even when the day grew overcast and a chilly wind blew from the north. Miss Perry had turned out with friends to greet us. Myself, Mum and Dad, and half a dozen others established ourselves at the bus station where there was ample open space, a sheltered arcade, and a coffee stall. The others dispersed through the streets to spread the word. By the time our bus departed at the end of the day hundreds and hundreds more people had laid their hands on the world.

I felt it was a start.

How did it feel to sleep with the world every night, to bunk up with it? I could have stowed it on the floor but I preferred to stay in contact. Sometimes I kept the world down at the bottom of my bed, with my blanketed feet splayed on either side. Sometimes I curled myself around it, knees-up-fashion. Mostly I had it up by my pillow and rested my cheek against it. When I lay in this position I thought I could hear the faintest humming sound. Not that my world was any spinning top! Even if it had been revolving at the same rate as Planet Earth, turning on its axis only once a day, I'm sure I should still have felt its slow slide against my face. Maybe the murmur was inside my own ears. I wasn't aware of my world having a temperature other than my own. Certainly it wasn't hot around the equator and cold at the poles.

Did a moon the size of an apple orbit my world invisibly and intangibly fifty feet away, swinging slowly around our caravan in the night? No, the moon was stone dead. The aliens didn't affect the moon, where nothing happened anyway.

Miss Perry suggested that I skip school on Wednesday and go into town again on the bus; which I did, accompanied by Mum and Dad, Mr Wibbits, and others. More and more townsfolk touched the world.

Again on Saturday. By the Monday a restless new feeling was stirring in me because fresh people *weren't* constantly touching the world every single day. At our camp everyone had already done so. My parents and I held a confab with Miss Perry, the upshot of which was that Miss Perry invited me to come and stay with her in town in the house which she was sharing with three other teachers. Every morning she would drive me to school. I could lunch with Mum and Dad, so as to see them. Afterwards she would return me to town. Longer evenings were approaching. I'd be able to put in several hours of world-showing at the bus station, which was proving such a popular venue.

Within a week of this new schedule commencing, most of the town must have turned up and numbers were tailing off from thousands into hundreds. Queues still stretched around the parking apron, yet what would once have seemed an overwhelming demand was beginning to frustrate me just a tad. My world continued to grow in weight, but I could always hold it without any bother. Invitations were arriving from other towns and cities, spurred by travellers who had touched my world before departing and who witnessed what was happening.

A party of four scientists, from the remnants of the university twenty miles south, turned up at Miss Perry's house in a minibus packed with equipment to test my world and me; and I imagine that if TV stations had any longer transmitted news, or if newspapers still flourished, I might have been besieged by reporters as in those old movies.

Their measuring devices told them next to nothing about my world, or myself, yet they couldn't easily argue with its existence. Giles Collyweston, the team's leader, grew downright excited. He was in his sixties, with snowy hair, and his colleagues weren't much younger. Doris Dobey, a stout woman, was determined to play devil's advocate.

"This is an alien artefact," she suggested. She wore a tweed suit belted about her waist, and scuffed old brogues on her feet. I imagined her striding across a moor trying to shoot pheasants. We were in the shared lounge of the house, where the peeling purple and gold-striped wallpaper suggested a spectrum of heathers, while the easy chairs were soft brown boulders. Dr Dobey's thatch of grey hair might have been self-trimmed, using a pudding-basin as a guide.

"At last they have sent something down to Earth – an enigma to raise false hopes and make fools of us. Or worse! When people touch this thing, it registers them. It stores their imprint. Many more people will touch it. One day it will reach out and *touch* *them* and, I don't know, control them, suck their personality and free will away. It's an alien weapon."

"It isn't," I told her. The pendant lamp, glass cups branching from brass arms, flickered, and shone more dimly from then on.

"How can you be sure, Joan?"

"Because it's mine."

"Has a voice been whispering in your dreams?"

216

"No, Mum and Dad told me. First our vicar asks if God has anything to do with it. Now you're wanting to know if aliens have been talking to me."

"It's a fair question," allowed Collyweston.

I shook my head. "I hear no voices in my head. I have my world, and I know how to hold it and believe in it. I want everyone to touch it." This was when I finally understood the sheer extent, the enormity of what I might need to do.

"Soon, we shan't be able to stop her, shall we?" asked John Imbow. A tubby effervescent fellow, he didn't seem to mind this prospect too much, though his phrasing worried me.

Doris Dobey certainly minded. "Exactly, John! Soon there'll be too much popular momentum behind her, because this seems the only hope. It's deadly dangerous."

Who would they report back to? What could they do to stop me?

"You daren't believe any longer," I accused Dobey. "That's why you're scared. It's better for you if life just fades away."

I was afraid too. A few weeks ago would I have argued – really argued – with a grown-up? Now if necessary I had to withstand grown-ups, however important they might be. I was also afraid because I guessed that if I didn't continue to carry my world to people an anguish would well up inside me, a trickle of pain at first, then an unbearable torrent. I didn't dare let myself be too aware of this, otherwise I might have wavered. I might have asked myself, "Could my world really be a trap?" and lost my trust in it so that suddenly it would weigh as much as I sensed that it weighed, and it would crash through my hands, through carpet, through floorboards, burying itself deep in the foundations of the teachers' house, impossible ever to lift again. Because . . . I had let it down.

The fourth member of the team, Iris Ackroyd, hadn't committed herself to an opinion. Middle-aged and scrawny, her eyes held a certain predatory gleam; yet she refrained from comment. Since the others didn't press her, perhaps this was her usual manner: to spend a long time hovering like a hawk, spying every last detail, before swooping down.

Luckily Giles Collyweston disagreed strongly with the devil voice.

"Life," he said, "creates order; whilst the universe proceeds towards disorder. These aliens are forcing entropy upon us. I believe they're exploiting our world as a power source, a battery which will end up flat. They're drawing negentropy from the battery of human life."

"Personally I think entropy's over-rated," remarked John Imbow mildly. "The universe is creative. Order evolves out of chaos. Organization emerges."

"We've heard this kind of thing from you before, Giles," Dobey said. "What are they *doing* with this stolen energy, eh?"

"I don't know. Accumulating it in their mini-moon? Building up the potential for a stargate, a tunnel through superspace by which they can come here in person? To take our world away from us confused enfeebled monkeys? Maybe their probes go out slowly to promising star systems, taking hundreds of years, and where they find life they leach the life-force of that planet by switching its world-line so that nothing energetic ever happens."

"Doesn't that activity require power, Giles? Doesn't it demand an almost Godlike power on their part to start with?"

"They may draw that power from the sun, or from the fabric of space-time itself. Yet to create a tunnel which can be travelled by conscious beings might demand – what they are doing to us. Perhaps it's a necessary sacrifice on our part, for which they'll apologize when they finally arrive here. Perhaps they'll compensate us. Maybe their coming will boost us all back again into a greater cosmic history. I misdoubt this. Oh I do. We're being drained, as Africa was of its slaves, as the third world was of its raw materials and its sweated labour. Now the whole Earth's a third world, weak and poor and helpless. Yet at last the flow is reversing! Energy starts to stream back into our system through you, Joan, and your world. How, I don't know. There's a science at work here that's a thousand years beyond ours –"

"And this invisible mini-world of Joan's is a product of it," stated Dobey.

"No! I trust it. We must trust. A power, a counterforce has arisen from the human spirit."

The tweeded woman shook her head. "You're no longer a scientist, Giles. You're a dupe. You're a silly fish rising to a bright fly with a hook hidden in it. What shape is the hook? That's all I wonder."

How I wished I could provide some wonder to convince this woman, something more than my world. Yet what could be more?

Miss Perry had been sitting in on the investigation. Now my teacher erupted from one of those enveloping, camouflaging chairs like a red fox breaking cover when challenged by a hound. She rushed to the cold fireplace, whirled, and faced my interrogators.

"Joan can't stay here much longer. She needs to travel – to let everyone touch her world! Will *you* take her back to the city with you, Professor Collyweston? Will you lodge her for a while?"

"Over my dead body," said Dobey.

"Good way to keep an eye on her," suggested John Imbow. "Else, we'll miss the real start of her snowball."

"Melt it, while there's time. Put a flame to it." Did Dobey mean that literally? The dead body in question might be *mine*? Unbelievable.

"I'll explain to her parents," promised Miss Perry. I darted a look to accuse her of treachery, of delivering me into the hands of an enemy. When she frowned at me, lips pursed, I realized that betrayal was far from her intention. Supposing I set out by bus around any and every old town, accepting the touch of grateful multitudes, I might presently turn into a prig who thought she was a saint. By going initially with these scientists I would have a

219

check on me. My "innocence" would be tested – the better to confirm it. I nodded.

So did Collyweston. "I don't imagine she'll be with us long. She'll need to move on. City's a useful place to start. Yes, I see that. I'd feel privileged."

"You'd lend the weight of your authority?"

"For what it's worth, Doris – compared with her own."

"A child!"

"The bearer of the world. The masthead of humanity, bringing back the fire that's been stolen from us."

How confusing this image was of myself as a sort of blazing boat. My hair wasn't even red, it was fawn. I couldn't help but giggle. Dobey was right on target in that respect: I was still a young girl. Collyweston darted a quizzical glance at me, as if perhaps he had been fooled. I smiled at him, and held my world high.

"I'll need to mix with all sorts of people, won't I? Takes all sorts to remake a world. Eventually I might need to mix with everyone alive."

At last Iris Ackroyd revealed some of what she'd been thinking. "I should like to accompany you on your travels for a while, Joan – to observe and record, so that there's a true chronicle."

"Me too!" offered Imbow. "We could be a kind of uncle and aunt to you – look after your welfare, make arrangements without interfering with your own decisions."

Iris Ackroyd shrugged. She didn't view me as a substitute niece nor necessarily a saviour either. She would be my watchdog, whilst back at the university Collyweston enthused about me, and Dobey tried to stonewall him and denounce me as a fraud or worse.

What with all the equipment they had brought in vain, plus my world and myself as extra cargo and passenger, we were crowded in that minibus as we bounced towards the city through the darkness with "Uncle" Imbow at the wheel, our headlights often picking up potholes too late to avoid them. The alien moon was due to fly over our part of the land at ten, so we stopped in the car park of a country pub to stretch our legs, refresh ourselves – letting the other customers touch the world – and wait on the weed-cracked tarmac to watch the transit. Our own ancient moon, three-quarters full, spilled dull milk across fields, pubs, trees beyond. Sky was cloudless, night breathless; likely there'd be a late frost.

Duly at ten, the gleaming white moonlet climbed up across the black, star-studded sky; and a spark leapt from it, arcing away before hanging and brightening. As Earth's camber cut off the sunlight reflecting from space, the sparkle vanished. I could still see a faint glow in the same position, like an afterimage. But it lingered: a reddish spot. That was no afterimage. Nor did it move – which meant that whatever-it-was must be falling directly towards us!

"It's noticed," muttered Collyweston, as though we shouldn't raise our voices.

"Dear God," exclaimed Imbow. "Let's take cover."

"If it intends to destroy her, what cover could we possibly take, man?"

"If it *wants* to harm her," Dobey said. "Maybe she's doing its work very nicely, thank you. Maybe it's after the doubters: me and Iris."

"Me?" asked Ackroyd archly.

Dobey headed towards the pub door, then hitched her shoulders and paused to watch.

The object wasn't larger yet seemed more substantial, as if a giant balloon was sinking rapidly, approaching closer but also shrinking as denser air pressed upon it.

"Rubbish, Doris," called Collyweston. "It wants to nip her in the bud, that's what."

Now the thing was like a ruddy, angry boil on somebody's neck. Was it a flake off the alien moon? A ship? A bomb? I held my world defiantly above my head, towards it, willing my world to protect us and shelter us somehow. The oven-glow swelled to eclipse a pool of stars, and hung above us.

Of a sudden the pub was a heap of tumbled stones. Broken bones of rafters jutted amidst stumps of walls.

Almost immediately the building was intact again, as before. The red disc pulsed, lighting the car park eerily – a car park no more, but only a shrubby heath with no sign of a building in sight. Car park and pub returned. Forest crowded about us – for moments. A waste of water hemmed us in, where we stood on a weedy hummock of mud. A towering shape crashed through ferns which were the size of trees, screeching, teeth biting at the stars. Battle erupted: mounted soldiers wearing weird plumed helmets wielding curved swords. How fiercely I clutched my world overhead as a shield – in that car park outside that pub. The boil in the sky vanished; the shining white alien moon dipped below the horizon.

As we drove on towards the city, Collyweston rejoiced.

"It tried to force you on to another world-line, Joan. It tried to expel you, but it couldn't! Not even this early in the game. So we've won, already we've won. Just provided –" He hesitated.

"Provided," said Imbow, "that she spends the rest of her life carrying her world to everywhere on Earth, this country, every country, till sufficient millions of people have touched it, till it weighs as much to her as the real planet. Are you up to it, Joan? Summer and winter, well or sick?"

"If I don't," I mumbled, "it'll hurt me."

He misunderstood. "I don't think they can harm you now. They might try other tricks, but surely they played their best card first. Let's just take care when their moon's in the sky."

"You fools," cried Dobey. "Can't you see what a mock attack this was? What a feeble, deliberate failure? Oh yes: to convince the natives that their last hope is the true one, so that they'll tamely lay tens of millions of hands on this world of hers, instead of burying it in a deep pit! Surely there were more devastating ways of attacking?"

"How could there be?" Collyweston asked her. "Missiles: is

that what you mean? If they used missiles, why, so could we – against them. You know why *we* can't. Therefore neither can they. They could only try to jerk the world-line, Joan's world-line and ours to unravel it from the rest. To pull it loose and tie it to a different universe."

"You're wrong!" I shouted at Dobey. "You are, you are! I know my world."

"It won't let you stop, will it?"

"*I* shan't let myself stop. If it takes me all my years." Penny piece after penny piece, till all were spent, the price to pay for our freedom.

"At least you'll get to see the real wide world," she sneered, "even if none of us ever sees *yours* until it's too late. Until it shows its true colours at last, with all our millions of selves mirrored in it, captured in it."

The spires of the city rose black against the stars as John Imbow steered us into the dim suburbs.

Next morning when the frost had melted I went with John and Iris to the city bus station to hold my world out to everyone who passed, and soon to everybody who came intentionally.

Joy lit my heart as if the sun in the sky was shining through me. Energy coursed through the muscles of my arms, my wrists, my fingers as if I was being nourished by the sunlight. I felt that Mum and Dad must surely sense my happiness from twenty miles away, and must be grinning too, for how could they have lost me now? They too had touched my world, indeed had been the first. Whilst I held my world, I held Mum and Dad in my embrace, and everybody I'd grown up with in our camp, likewise thousands of others; and eventually I would hug tens of millions of people, and they me, all by a simple trustful touch. We would all have joined hands, to strike the sky. Our reach would be enormous, and gentle, and strong.

223